Broken

Borderlands-Whitehall

Carissa Marks

Published by Crazy Town Publishing, 2022.

BROKEN

First edition. May 11, 2022.

Copyright © 2022 Carissa Marks.

ISBN: 978-1393245155

Written by Carissa Marks.

Also by Carissa Marks

Borderlands-Whitehall
Hellfire,Brimstone & Whiskey
Broken

Heroes N Hearts
Love Is A Battlefield
Love In Their Stars
Love By Design
Assigned To Love
Ambushed By Love
Tides Of Love

Standalone
Broken
The Gold Standard
A Little Christmas Magic in Cedar Springs

In memory of my brother, Sua Sponte...Rangers lead the way. My teacher, my friend, my cohort in mischief and mayhem. Missed daily,loved much.

1

Sophie came out of the barn, between the rainstorm coming in and the season; late afternoon was already dark as midnight. She checked her phone; there was a new text from her sister, Charlie. *Mom is on a kick, don't be surprised if she calls. Back to you should come home to go to school.* Grumbling as her fingers skated over the keys, Sophie sent one back, *she needs to stay in her lane. She didn't have her stuff together to earn a say in my life.* "One, two, three, I definitely don't look great in orange, four." Her words were followed by a deep breath and long exhale as she fired up the engine. One last stop at a local indie book store for the hard to find final book in a series for another sister and then it was on to her apartment. "This would be easier if I was a duck," she muttered as she ran to her car. Tucking a stray strand of raven's wing black hair behind her ear as she turned the corner, Sophie sang along with Carrie Underwood on the radio. Fat raindrops thumped on the hood of her car, a strong wind sent stray yellow-green spring leaves and a plastic bag skittering down the road. Her phone made a rude sounding noise; she chucked the device into her purse without even looking to verify the caller. No need, the noise was her mom's ring tone. Cramming her foot on the brake pedal made the rear end of her car slide. "Jeezus effing...who the hell lets a doggoe out in this crap-ass weather?" Her door creaked open, sort of like a haunted house with an amplifier. Using a slight falsetto and sing-song tone as she tried to lure the soggy dog, "Here baby, come here. Poor puppy." Her tail wagged, "Man, she's even got a toy. How do I not rescue this one?" One look around as thunder rumbled, and rain fell harder made the dog decide to trust her. "Good baby, in ya go." Climbing back in and shutting the door gave her two seconds to realize she broke her own rule about strays. Neon lights reflected in the water drops on the hood of her beat-up Cavalier. Sophie glanced at the pooch, noticing the tag on a bright red collar. "So did you make a run for it? You better not bite, the week I had...I may bite back." One side read "I'm lost, my name is Madge" The other listed a vet and a phone number. "Madge? Really?" Her head tilted, her paw went to Sophie's shoulder. "Yeah, I gotta call girl." Her thumb was lightning fast as she dialed the number. "Hi, I found a dog with the doctor's name and number on the tag." She eased back out into traffic. "Yes, this number is fine for a return call, her name is Madge and there is a pound sign or hashtag symbol and the number twenty-three under the name. Thank you."

Two blocks more and she pulled over to answer the call. "Hello."

"You called about Madge."

"Yep, she was running wild on Taylor."

"She must have escaped from a pet sitter, her owner left instructions, I can text his number to you."

"Cool. That works." Her phone vibrated with the message. "Have a goodnight." She dialed as she pulled back onto the street.

"Hello. You have reached Liam Boone leave your name and number and I'll get back to you."

She rolled her eyes. His voice held a bit of the low-country. "Yo dude, I found your dog, soggy and carrying a toy on a busy ass street in the rain. Call me and be ready to identify the canine." She made two right turns before hitting the interstate heading for her apartment complex. The location worked for her, a mile or two from the barn, a mile or so from her school. There were days she could do cartwheels she was so happy her old university arranged for an early transfer for her. "I bet Chase had a hand in that one," she mumbled. One thing she hadn't planned on was falling in love with the area. People seemed nicer, the area was beautiful and there was a beach not far away. Her first weekend in town, she stopped at a small eatery with Charlie. She asked what the favorite meal of the day was.

A lady sitting next to them leaned over and said, "Oh honey, it's Friday. You gotta do the fried catfish." She was right. Moultrie State University was the perfect place for her. Small enough to not get lost, not so small one couldn't receive a decent education. She found a bar where she could go tip back a few beers in Junction City. The Keg-n-Cube was great, delicious food, cheap prices and was far better than any place in the Hall.

Turn signal ticking for her exit, country music on low, Madge stared out the window, watching where the pretty dark-haired lady was taking her. "Okay doggie, the rules are, no peeing on the floors, no chewing of the furniture, and both you and lovey-dove are getting a bath." Sophie's hand swatted at the back seat a half dozen times before landing on the lead rope she knew was back there. Mojo's lead could do double duty and be a leash for the time being. Sophie grabbed her purple and gold backpack, her purse and the lead rope which she clipped to the dog collar. "Come on girl." The dog led the way, her once lime green bird hanging out of her mouth. Sophie was adamant; the green thing was getting a bath. Madge gave up the toy, but whined as the pillow case went into the washer, and continued to whine through her bath and towel drying. Her ears perked up when the pink and white striped pillowcase came out, but the lady tossed the case into another box and made the bag go round and round. She stared at the dryer as Sophie cut up two chicken breasts, sautéing them, before adding half into a pan of water, followed by rice. She pulled a couple of paper plates down and put a spoonful in the middle to cool.

"Pizza bites, yeah sounds like a plan." She up-ended a box on to her own paper plate and stuffed her dinner into the microwave. A second spoonful went on top of the meal prepared for Madge. "Here ya go baby." She figured in front of the sink was probably the safest place to feed the dog. Sophie grabbed her plate and a soda and headed for the love seat. Secretly, she was hoping the guy never called back. Madge seemed like such a sweet pooch. Her coloring was unique and beautiful. She was a bit of blue merle, black, white and some odd bits of fawn here and there, and the palest caramel-colored eyes. "Why do these things either come out cold as ice or hot as the face of the bloody sun?" Blowing on her dinner to cool it off gave her another minute to contemplate the dog still watching the dryer go around. The timer made Sophie move, speaking to Madge as she did. "Hold on poochie-poo. I'll fetch your lovey-dove for you." Madge's tail twitched as the dryer opened and the pink striped pillowcase came out. Doggy toenails ticked against the tile as she tried so hard to sit and wait. Sophie felt the bird making sure the toy was dry. "Okay girl, here's your baby." Madge took the bird gently and then spun in circles doing her imitation of a whirling dervish, which made the human laugh until her sides ached. Sophie wiped her eyes, trying to not smudge her eyeliner as she went back to her seat.

Madge leaned against her leg as she watched TV with her benefactor. Three pizza bites in, her phone rang. "Oh, your guy is calling." Her thumb shot across the screen, "Hello"

"Hi, I got a message from this number, about my dog." His voice held a tone, as if he was questioning how that could be.

"Describe the dog."

"What? You called me..." he waited for a second, "Okay, she's a mix of colors, red collar, gold bone tag with her vet's number. Her name is Madge." He waited, holding his breath.

"Say something." Sophie flicked the device to speaker.

"Like what?" Madge jumped up and started to wag.

"Okay, she responded to your voice. Now how the hell did she end up at Fourth and Taylor in the rain?" Liam was about to send up a mushroom cloud he was so angry.

"Good question. My, friend was supposed to go take her out a couple of times a day and feed her. When I find him, the boy is going to need a dentist."

"So, where are you?"

"Georgia, finishing up a job. I'll be home early Saturday morning. I can call Dr. Brent and see if he can board her."

"Why don't I keep her here? My Friday class was canceled."

Liam processed her speech pattern, definitely not a southern girl. "You wouldn't mind? She needs special food. The brand is a bit pricey, I can PayPal you if you need money. Only place that carries it is Jones Feed and Seed."

"I gave her chicken and rice tonight. I need to go buy horse treats anyway, you can pay me when you get here." She took a picture and sent it on in a message.

"Hey, hey, my girl. I've had her since she was a couple of weeks old. You sure you don't mind?" He despised trusting a stranger with his baby and had every intention of pounding Jared when he got home.

"Naw, I'll be writing a paper after I leave the barn. She'll be awesome company." Chit chat filled what seemed like a couple more minutes, in reality, it was closer to an hour. When she hung up, Sophie had the oddest feeling, as if she knew his voice or something. She shook off the notion and settled in to binge recordings of her favorite show until eleven. "Come on girl, potty break for you and then I'm going to crash. I am beat."

She hooked the lead rope to Madge's collar; she tore down the stairs and waited for Sophie. Back upstairs with the door bolted and alarm set, she headed for the kitchen. "Be nice if you had water." She found a thrift store score, a huge bowl and filled it halfway with water. "There ya go baby." Sophie just climbed into bed when she saw Madge and her toy silhouetted in the doorway. "Okay, come on." She patted the bed. Madge curled in right behind her knees. It was the first decent night of sleep she had in several months. Thinking she was being silly, but the jerk responsible for her leaving school in New York made enough threats to be booted from classes for the rest of her last semester. Having a dog there, made her feel safer.

Morning brought sunshine and a light breeze, Sophie threw a load of wash in the machine, a load of dishes in the dishwasher and grabbed the bag of trash, from her door made an easy toss into the dumpster. Madge eyed the bag sailing and crashing into the crayon blue box of smelly stuff before trotting off to do her thing. "Come on girl." Sophie opened the door, Madge hopped up into the passenger side seat.

Jones' feed store was about five minutes away. With her new canine friend in tow, she headed inside. In a way, the store reminded her of home. The walls were bright white with a farm feel to the rest of the décor. It felt, welcoming. "Goodmorning Ted."

His head immediately tipped sideways. "Uhm, she looks like..." He stopped as Madge ran to the biscuit bin. "It is, that's Madge!"

"Yeah, she was in town, soaking wet, muddy, and carrying a toy. Her owner will be back in the morning. I need a bag of food for her."

"Yep-yep, she eats the Blue Ribbon one," Sophie selected a plastic container of horse treats. "It's a bit pricey," he hit the key and thirty dollars popped up. For a small bag.

"Holy Jeeze-oh-petes. Yeah, he warned me." Her hand ran through her hair, holding a good bit of her mane on top of her head. "He's paying me back."

Ted shook his head, "Who'd he leave in charge of her?" Sophie shrugged, "Boonie will beat them silly. He dotes on her."

She gave the man a fifty, pocketed her change and rolled her eyes at Madge. "Yes girl, I'm getting you a cookie." Ted reached in and snagged a couple, dropping one in the bag with the horse treats. "For later."

"Thanks, Ted." She gathered her purchases and walked toward the door, "Come on girl." While Madge had been quite well behaved at the feed store, the closer they got to the barn, the antsier the dog became. She was ready to climb right up into Sophie's lap. Unwillingly at first, Madge exited the car, a bit slower than usual and stuck next to Sophie like she had been glued to the human's hip.

"Oh my gosh, you got a dog!" Lara Moore strolled in; one of the few friends Sophie had in South Carolina. "Just gorgeous."

"Yeah, her owner left her with someone who didn't take care of her. He sounded a hair perturbed with them."

"What's his name?"

"Liam Boone."

Lara furiously tapped away at her phone screen. Her head jerked up, "Whoa Nelly, he's a stud."

"I don't have time for a man."

Lara shrugged, "Riding today?"

"Naw, Brooks assigned a major paper, due date is Tuesday."

"Have fun with that." She strolled on down the row of horses, petting some and talking to other riders.

Mojo was always a bit nosy, his shiny, black, head dropped over the stall side, so he could investigate the newcomer. Madge moved to where she was peeking from between Sophie's knees. "Oh, come on, you ran away from home and now you're afraid of a horse?" Madge wasn't about to be shamed into coming out from behind the safety of a person. Hooves were picked, while Madge sat statue-still at the door. She brushed the huge horse down, filled his water bucket, and hay rack before stepping out—having to weasel around the dog to not step on her. "Honestly, you are such a fraidy cat it ain't even funny."

She made a stop for a five-dollar pizza and hit the highway for the trip back to her apartment. Winds picked up over the course of the day, bringing rain before two in the afternoon. Sophie barely noticed, her head pivoted from a book or article to her laptop as she cited the passages needed and wrote what she hoped was a coherent paper. Madge's whine at the door got her attention. "What baby? You gotta go out?" Shrugging into her jacket she hooked up the make do leash and ran down the steps. "Brrr. This crap needs to go. It is supposed to be spring." Madge threw grass with her right paw and spun towards the stairs. Once inside, Sophie put down food for the pooch and re-heated another slice of pizza. Later that night, curled under a blanket on her love seat with her temporary dog next to her, Sophie had to admit, she could get used to having a pet around all the time.

BOONIE HUNG UP, FIGHTING the urge to drive home and pulverize Jared. Stewing on something was never good, he ended up ten times as mad as he would usually be. At noon the next day he was on the road back. He pulled his big Dodge dually into a spot across from The Flaming Frog. Most of the clientele were bikers with no affiliation to any club, some locals, and the odd student. He slammed the truck door, tall, muscled, with a two-day growth of beard, he resembled a pirate. Smitty, the bartender, popped a cap on a bottle of beer as Boonie came in. He tipped the bottle toward the barrel-chested man. "Catch you at the end of the night." He prowled the room searching for Jared. The pool tables proved to be pay dirt. "If you were a probie, your ass would be in the dirt out back lickin boots."

Jared froze in place, slowly standing up straight when he realized being bent over a pool table was probably not the safest position for him. He refused to make eye contact with Liam. "Now why would that be?" He could only hope Liam wouldn't pulverize him, he doted on Madge.

Boonie slapped the backside of Jared's head hard enough to make the others go quiet. "Tell me how long she's been missing, better yet; tell me what you did to make her run." It was like the Red Sea parting. He grabbed the younger man, hauling him to the back door. Liam set his bottle on the brick ledge as they exited the building. Flinching and face making followed as they observed the payback. I paid you to feed, and care for my dog. Imagine my surprise when I got a call saying she's been picked up." His fist met Jared's jaw with a resounding thud.

"I'm sorry dude, I was on the phone with this hottie and I guess I didn't close the door..."

"Guess?" He gut-punched the twerp and then planted his boot into the tailbone of the offending one. As Jared writhed on the ground, Liam yanked the boy's wallet out—he wouldn't call him a man at that stage and pulled out a hundred dollars before throwing it back at him. "Get on your feet and outta my sight before I break you in half." Liam strode back inside, finishing off his beer as he went.

Ted Jones wandered in close to nine p.m. "I saw Madge today."

Boonie's head whipped Ted's direction. "She's fine, if she was going to pick a person to get saved by, she couldn't have found a better one. The young lady is part of the equestrian team at the college."

"So, you know her?" She had a slightly sultry quality to her voice. He hadn't really thought much about the woman in question, other than the fact his dog had been rescued by a responsible person.

"A bit, she's polite when she comes in. Takes care of her horse, doesn't take crap from the bunch of yahoos that like to hang out instead of working. If looks could kill—they'd all be in the emergency room." They both got a chuckle out of the idea.

Boonie's phone vibrated in his pocket, he slid the device out to see Sophie's number, "*yo man, I forgot, I have a show at ten, can you meet me a Fraser Stable? I'll be the one attached to Madge.* He laughed outright at the message. *"I can pick her up now, I'm home."*

"We're two hours out and plan on crashing. Sorry."

"No problem. How early will u b there?"

"8-ish

"Okay, that works."

Liam had always despised alarm clocks. His alarm rattled him long before he wanted to see sunshine. If it hadn't been on his phone, he would have thrown it at the wall. With his head pounding, and his knuckles throbbing, he rolled over until he needed to either put a foot down or fall out of bed. He found his jeans on the floor and did a hop dance to slide into them as he muttered, "They didn't walk away, so they're wearable." On the way, he found a drive-thru and ordered coffee and a large juice. One hand fished around in the console until he found something to dull the bang in his head. Without thinking, he pried the lid off the cup, grousing as he did, "When you want them to come off, ya need dynamite."

His truck blended into the mix of expensive vehicles to haul pampered horses and their equally spoiled riders. One sip of coffee had him swinging his head around as he tried to drain the last drop from the orange juice container to dampen the heat. "Holy hell! It's as hot as the sun."

Ted's laughter from behind him did nothing to improve Boonie's mood. "That's why the menu says "hot" coffee." His chuckling hadn't ceased.

"He-he-he-he yourself, old man." Boone nearly took another sip before he caught himself, saving the last few taste buds from becoming sacrificial nubs. "What are you doing here so early?"

"Wife is a judge. Your girl is down at the end of the row there." Mojo stood two hands taller than most, it was hard to miss him.

"Easy boy. Easy." She brushed his leg with her hand, "Still sore?" Mojo threw his head around. "You're being a snot." He shook his head again. Madge sat in the trunk of the car, tied to Sophie's belt, but not about to leave the safety of her cubby hole. Her tail wagged, crashing into everything when she spied Liam. "Whoa baby, you're knocking crap all over."

"She's happy to see me." Sophie wasn't sure what she'd see when she turned, but six feet of jeans and leather topped with an unruly curl that kept falling across his forehead had not come to mind. Sunglasses hid his eyes, he needed a shave, but Madge was happy to see her guy. He sat on the edge of her trunk, so the dog could crawl up into his lap, complete with the now clean toy in her mouth. He stuck a hand out, I'm Liam Boone, Boonie to most.

"Sophie O'Hara." She shook his hand; surprised to find the callouses of someone who actually worked not sat around a video game. "Can you sit here for a minute while I go change?" She untied the lead rope, tossing it into the car.

"Yeah, no problem." He'd sit there all day. She was quite fetching, as his grandfather used to phrase it. His head tipped as he watched her walk away. "Yowza" he rubbed Madge's ear. "Good girl, very good girl." Five minutes and she was back, black boots, stark white riding pants, crisp white shirt, carrying a deep green jacket and her helmet.

"Thanks, oh, and you were right. Her food is expensive. Holy moly."

"Ah yeah, can I Pay-Pal that to you?"

"Uhm, yeah. I really hate using the app but..." she gave him her email as she brushed out her gleaming black hair. He fought to keep his eyes on the screen as she flipped her mane up and twisted the mass into a bun, anchored with several dozen bobby pins and a few small shiny black barrettes before she tucked it into a hairnet. Liam watched as a severe-looking blond walked up, clipboard in hand.

"O'Hara, okay, you're ready. Thank you." She rubbed a spot at the bridge of her nose. "Due to several riders from one of the Virginia schools being or rather, were friends or related to a soldier killed in action, we are all entering the arena, doing a moment of silence, and then we'll file down, them on one side and us on the other. We'll go rider for rider exiting the arena."

"Sure Coach." Whatever, she didn't care.

"Oh, the next call for horses, you're exempt. Everyone is afraid of Mojo." With that, she was off to the next student.

"Excellent, none of them are competent enough to ride him anyways."

Her comment brought a snort from Liam. "That was a bit harsh."

"Truth hurts then maybe they need a new sandbox and softer toys." She shrugged into her jacket, kissed Madge and over her shoulder said, "Close the trunk when you leave." Sophie led Mojo over to a mounting block by the barn. Liam's gaze followed her as she walked by on her horse, ramrod straight in the saddle as she pulled gloves on. She filed in as instructed; at the far end was the team from Valley Ridge. Sophie had a feeling that every 'mean girl' meme ever created was about that batch. A new face caught her attention. Not truly new, it looked like both had moved on to southern schools.

Margot Bridges. Her dad owned a string of Cadillac dealerships and a couple of hotels. Too bad daddy's money didn't equal out to brains and ability of the daughter. Coach kept the pace up and soon enough they were filing out. Most of the girls were finding a place in or under created shade. Dressage riders turned to get their numbers and wait. Valley Ridge led, it wasn't long before Margot was claiming her horse was injured. She practically had a meltdown until her coach arranged for her to borrow Mojo.

"Your major should have been theater Maggot." Washed out blond, bright pink lipstick and 70s baby blue eye shadow stood out like a neon light in the dark against her pale skin, her nose in the air as Margot responded,

"From the scholarship kid, isn't that rich. Oh, yeah, you wouldn't know what rich is."

"Pfft, rich won't buy one the first drop of ability." Her eyes narrowed, "Don't even think about using that thing on my horse or I'll use it on you." She flicked the end of the show bat as Margot mounted Mojo. Liam watched from the bleachers, Madge at his side. He noticed the stranger flinch, the head shake, trying to watch the blond and Sophie about made him seasick until moments later, he couldn't believe his eyes when he saw the crop rise and come down with an echoing crack.

Mojo reared and spun. Sophie bolted into the arena. Mojo screamed as he counter-spun. The crop hit the ground, followed by Margot. Sophie's pinkies were in her mouth, the whistle made Madge cringe. Mojo turned in mid-reel and went head-on for her. His sides heaving as he slid to a stop. Liam stood, thinking he was going to see Sophie become a welcome mat for the big beast. "Shh, I got ya, baby. Mama's got ya." His nose rested against her forehead. She gathered the reins and handed them to the official. When she spun, Boone understood one thing. The blond was in deep and getting ready to be deeper in a world of dark and smelly. "What the hell did I tell you Bridges? Do Not. Two simple words." She picked the crop off the ground and used it on the woman still on the dirt before she snapped the shaft in half. "You got bounced from one team for abusing your horse. I heard all about your bullshit." Sophie had her by the collar, snarling more than talking. "I may be the scholarship kid, but you'll never be daddy's main bitch...not with the model he's dating." Sophie let go of her like a drop the mic movement. Liam watched as she jogged for the tent with the vet and farrier trucks parked by it.

From the floor, Margot went into full meltdown mode, she screamed "bitch" and a few other terms of something nowhere near endearment. Her coach nearly dragged Margot out of the arena.

Another team was given the go, a move not lost on Liam. "Come on Madge, let's check on your rescuer." She led the way to Sophie. "Hey, how is he?" nodding toward the horse.

"He has a huge welt. Split the skin, she got off lucky. I'll probably get bounced for smacking her. I told her not to use the damn thing on him. He freaks."

The vet piped up, "It's most likely the equine equivalent of post-traumatic stress, with his past." Liam's brows wrinkled.

"I got him from a family friend, they breed them. Their barn went up in flames—a trucker, afraid of horses went in to get them out. He grabbed a crop and swatted all of them. Mojo was a baby; he nearly killed himself trying to run back inside. He had welts all over, busted the skin in a few places. We took him, mama, and one of the geldings to our farm. I nursed him back. They said he was too big for dressage...I'm proving them wrong."

Ted walked up, "Your coach said to eat, you're riding." Several food trucks had found parking spaces across the main road. Sophie looked that way and groaned before stalking off to her car to search for a granola bar or a half-eaten bag of something.

"Here, hold Madge. Is there anything you won't eat?" "No fake meat, I'm a carnivore. But," he was off and half-way running toward the trucks. In a few minutes, he was back, cup carrier in one hand, tote bag in the other.

"Okay, something called a lemon spritzer, more like a red berry lemonade with fizz to me. Your choice is a taco box or a chicken teriyaki crunchy salad."

"From which truck?"

"Chicka-Boom."

Her face lit up. "Salad, thank you. I'll pay you back." She wolfed down half of the bowl without slowing down, the rest went into a shiny silver cooler bag. In her head, she was going over their routine. She spent enough time with Mojo, if she never gave him a cue, he could still do the required moves. Sophie led her horse out, "How're your legs?"

"Okay, I guess."

"Great, bend this one," she tapped the leg closest to her mount, "Grab the back of my heel and hold on." Her foot landed on his knee as she hoisted herself into the saddle. The move also gave him a clue as to how muscled she was. "Thanks."

Liam followed, finding a seat by Ted. "This is always fun to watch, it looks like the horses are dancing." Liam's brow inched up, questioning the man's perception. The first rider entered and he had to agree with the assessment. Sizing up the competition was going mainly on gut instincts and watching Ted. When Sophie entered the ring, Ted sat up a bit straighter. Liam focused in on Madge's rescuer. Sophie entered the ring and addressed the judges before turning Mojo and setting him to his paces.

"How does she make a giant-sized animal do that?"

"Hours of training and practice."

"Who's in the ring with the clipboard?"

"Her caller, not like she needs one. I can guarantee, every square inch of this arena has been memorized and that horse and rider team could do this if both were blindfolded."

Sophie couldn't worry about what the judges would dock her for nailing Margot, all she could do, was run a flawless program. She knew Mojo had it down. Each step, each move, they went as one.

Liam was spellbound. "She's better than most of the others." Ted chuckled and nodded. He sat, mouth open—not enough to toss food in, but when Madge stood up fast, he got a mouthful of dog tail.

Ted filled in what he didn't know. "Walk is a four-beat gait, the trot is a two-beat gait with a second of suspension between each step, meaning two legs are always off the ground, diagonally." Liam watched intently, mystified at how the large horse managed to look elegant. Ted kept up the explanation and commentary. "The canter is a three-beat gait, the diagonal feet need to hit the ground at the same time. There is a time where all the feet are in the air before the beginning of the next stride. But, an ideal canter has a clear beat and shows balance. Now, a horse naturally leads with one leg, which means one front leg extends out further than the other."

Liam had at first thought of her as a bit of fluff, but, as Sophie went to a corner, it became clear, she was very much in charge. Mojo's pirouettes were dead on, watching him as he skipped along and then high stepped into a cross-over step that frankly scared Liam. Amazing, she is just amazing. At the end, she again addressed the judges, Sophie fought to control the "I got this grin," instead she gracefully acknowledged her accolades and exited the arena.

Ted leaned his way. "That should put her at the top of the heap if they do not take her reaction to the horse being injured into account. She had excellent scores at last week's Eventing meet also."

Outside, Sophie found a familiar face, someone from the same area of the country she was from. They had competed in high school and had a mutual respect club going. "Sophie!"

"Cherie! Hey, did you hear? My sister is marrying Chase...finally." They were off into family gossip, commiserating about classes and waiting for the final runs.

Liam was still there at the end of the competition when they rode in for the awards ceremony. He fought the urge to ask her out that night, in a steady stream of chatter with Madge he offered options. "Well, I have her phone number and email...I could send her a second payment and come up with an excuse to meet her to get it back. Nah, she's too smart for that one. Okay, plan B. I didn't actually think of one...how old do you think she is? I mean, she's something to look at, but that doesn't tell me her age. I know I'm older than her. Hmm, well, maybe I could resort to a classic and send her flowers as a thank you for taking care of you, what do ya think Madgey? Sound like a plan to you?" Madge huffed three or four times, around the ugly green toy. "Yes, good. That's what I was thinking too. Wonder if I can find her address? If not, I know someone who can."

MISTY FOG HUNG OVER the field, snuggling next to buildings and fence posts, crawling along the ground, weaving through the dandelions and tall grass. Soon the sun would climb high enough to burn it off, but for the moment, everything was shrouded by the mist. Sophie's trunk sat open, she vanished into the fog around the front of the barn and then was out—ducking the doorframe as she headed for the track. He watched as she faded into the gray only to reappear on the other side in a few minutes. Liam contemplated sending her a message. That would only give away he was doing the same thing as the guy in the fancy sports car with New York plates. Three days in a row was no longer a coincidence. Instead, he called in a suspicious vehicle and waited until the local cop rolled in behind the car. "Maybe you should call daddy's attorney." The cop had the driver out, slapping handcuffs on him. "I should call her, a pizza, pitcher of beer, nothing major." Sipping coffee as he contemplated the possibility, he sat up when the second patrol car pulled in behind the first, spoke with the original officer and eased down the driveway. The barn manager pointed to the track. Shaking his head, he strode off that way, hanging over a gate—waiting. "Hmm, waiting isn't progress. I think it's time to man up and go ask the woman out." He let his truck roll back to the flat spot in the medical center parking lot before starting it and left by the side road. Humming along to the radio, he pulled in next to her car and checked it for keys before deciding not to close it. Another rider came out, "Hey, is Sophie on the track?"

"Yeah, the vet should be here anytime now, so she'll be back soon."

The cop's ears perked up, "You know Sophie O'Hara?" He gave Liam the once over.

"Sort of, she rescued my dog."

The cop held eye contact long enough that thoughts of silly commercials ran through Liam's mind, it took everything he had to not be a smart aleck. From the look of things, the car was more of a problem than he knew.

The clopping of horse feet on the ground got both of their attention. "Little drastic isn't it, I rescued Madge, I didn't steal her."

Liam grabbed the reins as she slid out of the saddle. "Not me, I just stopped by to see if you got that payment okay." It seemed like a plausible cover story.

"I did, and the flowers. Thank you."

The officer stepped up, clearing his throat. "Miss O'Hara?"

"Yeah." She felt cold. From the inside out kind of cold. The kind that said nothing good was going to come of him being there.

"I'm Officer Cooper, we arrested Bennet Ashby, he was at the gate."

Liam stepped closer to her. The news rocked Sophie, she paled and swayed before regaining her balance. "How? How did he find me? I got a restraining order, a cease and desist thing...I changed freaking schools for god's sake." Panic was clearly evident in her wavering voice

"Whoa," Liam touched her arm, "You're shaking. Who the hell is this guy?"

"I was going to school in New York, this jerk asked me out, I wasn't at all interested. In the offseason, I carry one hella class load." She glanced at the cop, "Twenty-seven, twenty-eight hours unless I had a lab science, then I cut back to twenty-two. He didn't like being turned down. So after two weeks of hearing we had sex," she shivered in revulsion. "I told the next jackass who said it—Yeah, sure we did and it blew chunks. Most boring five minutes of my life. There had to be a special trip to the drugstore to find the smallest size condoms available, plus he had to wear a neon purple, fuzzy knit hat with a silver lame' unicorn horn and mane, old lady furry slippers and he wanted me to spank him first. The whole time he was yelling "Beat me, mommy," he was done before I even got warmed up and I swear to Christ, I've seen bigger thumbs."

Officer Cooper's eyes watered from trying to hold in the laughter, Liam didn't even attempt to hide his mirth. He was bent in half, holding his ribs. "So, he started making threats because the only way he could deny it, was to admit he lied. Things got so bad, my sister talked to a zillion people, or her fiancé did, and the school agreed to let me test out and move. They booted him for a semester, but his daddy got him back in. No one knows where I am."

Liam's brows meshed, "Didn't you say that chica went to school with you, the one who hurt your horse?"

Sophie's deep green eyes sparkled with unshed tears and anger. In a breath, she went from shaken and scared to vengeance in riding boots. "Thank you officer, do you have a card by chance?" he fumbled in pockets until he found one. She took it and strode off to the barn with Mojo.

Boone and the cop sized each other up, the cop spoke first. "I think she's ready to put a boot in someone's butt." Liam was already nodding in agreement. Seeing her in fear did something to him, it made him want to find this character and send him back home in a box. A shoebox. A kid-sized shoebox. Sophie came back out of the barn, with a full head of steam going as she flipped the blanket off the lockbox in the trunk and spun the dial on a combination lock. Her phone in hand, she reached for a thermos. "Hey Charlie, guess who was arrested at the barn gates?" She used her teeth to pull the lid off a Styrofoam cup, she threw the leftover soda across the grass, shook it, and poured coffee into the cup. Liam chewed his lip to keep from saying anything. While she may have the looks of a beauty queen, there was nothing prissy about her. "Nope, Bennet Ashby. I think one Miss Margot Bridges may have dropped a line to him. She also injured Mojo."

Liam leaned against his truck, watching as she dug a toaster pastry out of her bag and tore into the wrapper. "She pulled off some crap and was put on him, she used a crop on him...and I used it on her." Her eyes rolled, "No, I still placed. Hey, let me call ya back."

Liam turned to hide the smirk, "Placed, yeah, you took a top spot. Way to understate the facts." A tow truck came for the car. Trying to pull a U-turn on the narrow road was not happening, the driver turned down the drive to the barn. Sophie whistled and waved at the driver. Things flew around the back of her car until she came up with a glass marker. "Hey," The driver had a start of a very early five o'clock shadow, a jelly stain on his shirt and powdered sugar on his arm. "Hi, hey, the car belongs to a Yankee stalker, I want to leave him a message, you can say it was already there."

Liam was trying to figure out where she dragged a southern drawl out from. Sophie leaned over the back of the car as she wrote "Fuck Off Maggot" in bright white on a tinted window. "Thanks, 'preciate it." They followed the driver's progress as he pulled out.

"You seemed pretty sure he'd let you do that."

Her smirk made his brows rise. "He owns Turtle's towing, Turtle is a nickname from his high school football days, anyway, a year ago his sister was attacked by a stalker, she crammed a pen in his eye. Needless to say; he lost the eye, and he sued her. She countersued. He went after her a second time. If the neighbor hadn't shot him—he was going to cut out her tongue. He escaped on the way into court, tried a third time. Turtle beat the dog snot out of that ol' boy. Stalker's now doing forty years. I'm betting the car gets more than one ding on the way to the yards."

"And you know this because...?"

"I'm nosy."

He let the response go. "Okay Miss Nosy, how about dinner? Pizza and beer."

Her lips twisted off to the side as she pulled her hair back in a ponytail. "I have two weeks before I can legally drink."

"Why do I have this crazy suspicion there should be an addendum to that, like maybe, not like that has ever stopped you?"

"Well, maybe." She laughed at his expression. "Tell you what, you grab a pizza, meet me at the park off Central at...?"

"Seven?"

"Okay, I'll take care of the libation part." Sophie shut her trunk and climbed into the driver's seat. One tap on her phone screen. "Call Molly."

"Calling Maw-lee" Sophie rolled her eyes at the pronunciation. "Hey Girlie."

"Holy cow, sit down. You ain't even gonna believe this."

2

Whitehall:

Logan Cole stood with the deputy he was grooming to take his place. "Is it just me, or does it seem like the younger folks are the smarter ones? They're all home practicing that baby-making motion and the older ones are out here acting like horses asses." Tag nodded along.

Glass from the front window shattered and sprayed across Moby's parking lot, followed by someone's ranch hand. A couple more from Juniper Springs joined in. "Might as well load the bike, I imagine it won't be long before Noah bounces out." Two more men hired to work the season for some rancher either crawled through or were thrown through the opening.

Pushing his hair back out of his face, Noah Driscoll stumbled to the hole in the wall. Drunk was an understatement. If anyone lit a match near him, he would resemble a roman candle. Slurring his words, he greeted the pair. "Sherf. Tag," He fell against the frame, cutting his hand on a stray, broken bit still stuck in place. Yanking his back with a couple of expletives aimed at the shard got the attention of a couple of officers.

Deputy Ridge lifted a piece of glass from his hand before leading him out to her squad car. "Watch your head, Noah. I don't want to do a report because you dented my vehicle with your noggin."

He grinned and knocked on his head. In the morning Logan opened the door and kicked the cot. Noah rolled over, grimacing at the daylight. "Breakfast will be here soon, roll out." Halfway through the meal he noticed his knuckles were raw and one hand sported a serious bandage.

" Did I dump my bike?"

"Nope, threw some guy through the window at Moby's" Noah's head dropped to his chest, a string of expletives followed. Logan started to lecture him, realizing that was a waste of energy, he let it go. "Luke is coming home soon. Still has some more rehab to do, but home is better." Logan watched to gauge if the news of his brother's return would effect their old buddy.

"Is he able to walk?"

"Short distances, he'll improve." Noah stared out the window as he chewed. Logan needed to try, "Look, it isn't my business, but the VA has people..."

"Yeah and the backlog at the Veteran's Administration is stupid long. I'll be okay." Logan sat back, hands clasped behind his head. Since Noah came home from Afghanistan, he ping-ponged from working himself into the ground to being drunk as one could be and stay alive—for days on end. So far he had been lucky, no major accidents, nothing an antiseptic and a Band-Aid wouldn't fix. They both knew his luck wouldn't last. Everyone tried to talk sense into him. With luck he'd stay alive long enough for Luke to try to talk to him. Logan was more than ready for his twin to come back. Noah swept the office and mopped the floors, his form of payback for them taking care of him...again. The phone ringing didn't phase him. "Hey, how're things?" Noah stared out the window, lost in thought. "I'll tell him," Logan leaned over his desk. "Hey Noah, Cullum needs a body, they're branding."

"He called here, to find me?" His head shook. This needed to stop. "I'll be there in twenty." Logan relayed the message, thankful he would have something to occupy his mind for a while. All Luke would say about Noah's record could be summed up as ugly stuff and he didn't want to talk about what he found. Left to use his imagination coupled with Noah's behavior led him to believe the demons haunting him were bigger and meaner than he could deal with. Maybe Cort would be able to come up with some ideas or Billy Wilmott.

Sundown painted trails of pink and purple across the sky. Noah sat on the fence rail; he felt a need to be busy, to make something if nothing else. He considered the idea, when branding season finished, he'd go clean and clear the lot he bought way back when, when he still had dreams and ideas and hope. Now all he had was guilt and not enough liquor to numb the pain. He felt a calling and couldn't identify what exactly called his soul.

One good thing, Cullum was a teetotaler and ran a booze-free ranch. Noah popped open a tent and set up for the night, the old man brought him out a plate of food. Mrs. Cullum was a good cook, meatloaf and gravy, mashed potatoes, green beans and an ear of corn with a couple of biscuits. Things were looking up, at least until dawn.

SOPHIE WAS LEAVING the barn when her phone rang. "Hi, Boonie."

"Hi, uhm Madge asked me to call."

"Oh she did, did she?" her lips rolled in trying to not laugh.

"Yeah, she said she thinks it would be an excellent idea to meet at the Flaming Frog and have some food, maybe a beer or two."

"Does Madge know she's underage?"

"Nah man, she's like...what's four in dog years? Twenty-eight?"

"Medium size, closer to thirty-two but I don't think bars do dog versus human years."

"Damn." He snickered, "So, are we on?"

"Has to be early, I have homework."

"So now is ok?" Hearing her laugh made his insides feel like jelly.

"Okay. Leaving the barn now."

"Madge is happy."

"Yeah, okay."

Boonie patted his leg, Madge sat up, paws on his leg. "She's coming to see us." He got a low woof in return. Twenty minutes later Sophie parallel parked her car outside of the Frog.

Madge barked as soon as she saw her rescuer. "Hey, baby." Liam smiled until she kissed the dog. "Such a good girl."

"I see how you are. You only came because of Madge." There it was again, her magical sounding giggle. He was enthralled. "What's your weekend look like?"

"Competition in Ocala and I need to cram a paper in there." She picked up a menu and nosed through the offerings.

"You know, if I drove...you could do your paper on the way down."

"What about the job?"

"I hired Craig for a reason. He's a good second in command. Ten years and he'll be good to take over and I can retire."

"Damn, you are old." Smitty heard her as he came out with their drinks. His boisterous laugh drew attention to the couple. "We need to be on the road early, and will your pretty truck pull the trailer?"

Boonie looked slightly offended she would question his truck. "With luck, the ass hasn't pulled my address yet. I'm liable to come home to a trashed apartment." "Yes, my truck will pull the trailer. And don't worry, I know some people." By nine a.m. Friday

they were on the road and an armed security officer sat parked in Sophie's spot.

Two months later:

Either Sophie fell asleep or fearless should be her middle name, Boonie wasn't sure, but several of the hairpin turns would have made him hold on tighter. He was used to rolling out of bed at an obscene hour on Saturday mornings now. Sunday afternoon used to be fishing or watching football with Madge, now he was usually at the barn with her. The fact they managed to align schedules for this escape, surprised him most of all. Hearing what Sophie's week consisted of boggled his mind. He remembered the sparkle in her eyes as she laid it out. "I have two years in and two to go, my week is insane. Monday, Wednesday, and Friday I have weight training, I'm in the gym for forty minutes every day except the weekend, I ride Mojo every day unless it's raining buffaloes and hippogators. If he's been uppity he gets lunged for thirty minutes. Because of the crazy season I'm only running twelve credit hours. But, homework never ends and somewhere in there I'm supposed to do laundry and eat. And the whole I can sleep when I die is about the size of it. So, if you think you can hang..."

He was up for a challenge. The thought brought a smile to his lips.

Spring fired up a roaming battle of the bands, usually with a mile of food trucks. They sidled in next to the closest thing he had to a best friend, "Roadrash," Tom Rashman and his live-in girlfriend, La-la. "Yo, Boonie-man, hey there Sophie," Large and in charge fit Tom. La-la was more like someone crossed a coonhound, squirrel, and a Maltese. Slow and leggy, until she opened her mouth and then it sounded like she had been sucking helium. They found a place to park at the end of a line of bikes of all sizes and makes.

"Man, I gotta pee like a racehorse, go with me?" La-la looked at Sophie. She shrugged, ran a hand up Liam's chest and smiled.

"Tease." It came out as a whisper on a long breath.

She winked at him. He was convinced; she had no clue as to how aroused she kept him. "Yeah, come on." Sophie spun, her hair in a long thick braid, her black jeans fit like a second skin, her boots were as black as her hair and matched the tight, mid rib length crop top. They headed off toward the double rows of porta-johns. "Thank you, I swear I have like a big neon thing over my head, 'give me a hard time, come on to me, don't take no for an answer' or something."

"You need to develop a look that is menacing and lose the super high baby voice when you are mad. If I growl at someone, they usually back off." They were next in line. Sophie made a wide sweeping bow letting La-la in first. Her gaze slid over the crowd, she could usually spot who was going to be trouble and avoid them.

"Wow, deluxe models, they have sinks, so you can wash your hands." La-la came out wiping hers on a brown paper towel.

"Cross the street, stay tight to my hip, if I smack you with my purse, take it and run like your ass is on fire and find Liam." Their speed hadn't changed. La-la looked like a scared rabbit. "Son of a bitch is out of jail already."

Behind them, they could hear him calling out. "Sophie, stop. Bitch I said wait!"

Her shoulder bag smacked La-la in the chest. "Go!" She spun and swung. Her foot went out, tripping the jerk with Bennet Ashby. Her key chain was a built-in weapon. Molly sent it to her. Like brass knuckles, she could fit three fingers into the holes; the design was one resembling a cat head. The pointy ears were sharp and would cut down as far as she punched or to the top of the cat head. She came back with a bloody hand. Like her instructor taught her, she kept punching, and turning to put him closest to his friend. Liam and Road Rash burst into the area behind the not so bright rich boy. One boot planted to the side of the friend's head dropped him to the sidewalk. He got wedged into a trash can, to the delight of many walking by. Bennet Ashby didn't fare so well. Liam planted a fist to the boy's head hard enough to make his ears ring. Then, he was dragged to a cop. The last they saw of him, he was handcuffed to a gurney and screaming threats at her.

"Okay, I'm hungry." Liam stared at her. "Are you kidding me? You were just attacked and all you can say is you're hungry?"

"Technically, I did the attacking, but he did call me a bitch so...and FYI, the reason girls head to the bathroom in packs is due to guys like him. And yes, I'm starving." She took him by the arm, steering him toward the food trucks. They headed back with shrimp tacos, bar-b-que, and teriyaki beef skewers with a couple of side orders of bacon mac and cheese and loaded tater tots. La-la shook her head as she bit into a chili dog. While they ate, the first bands set up and got things rolling. Eventually, they made their way to the stage area. A local band took the stage. Liam stayed at Sophie's back, watching for more trouble until she stepped back into him, her head tipped back to see him better. "Relax will ya."

They hung out later than they planned on, watching far off in the distance and seeing tiny lines of lightning made them move toward the bike. "Okay, you need to teach me how to drive a bike. If you ever drink too much, I don't want to be calling a cab for a fifty-mile jaunt." His brow inched up. "Long story, but I won't ride with someone who has had more two drinks. You know that."

"Why?" his finger traced her jawline. "There's a reason. I can tell."

Her thumbs hooked into his belt loops as she stared back at him. "Yeah, there is a reason. Leave it there."

Liam wasn't sure what had flashed across her features. Pain? Anger? Both? He could wait. Whatever bad weather was out there, hadn't followed too close. Their ride back was a repeat, Liam decided she was simply fearless. They pulled into Liam's driveway to find a rusted, heavily dented old cream-colored Buick with two women in the yard. One of which was at a window with Madge was raising all sorts of hell, howling and crying. Liam tossed his keys to Sophie. "Go check my dog, she has pepper spray." He already dialed nine-one-one and dispatch was asking what his emergency was. Sophie ran to the door; swearing profusely as she hunted for the key.

Once inside she raced to the small three-season porch. A younger woman had her hair caught in the screening where she tried to break in and stopped her. Sophie ripped the container out of the woman's hand, the words she used would have made her sister blush and her brothers too. Sophie sprayed the offending wench, then scooped up Madge and ran for the bathroom, kicking off her boots as she went. "Come on, come on, there it is." She hit the icon with a German Shepherd. "I'm sorry to call so late, I need your help" she had to scream to be heard.

"Sophie? My Gawd hon is that a dog?"

"Yes, she's been pepper-sprayed."

"Rinse her face, for as long as she'll let you."

Sophie's phone hit the back of the toilet as she fought the dog and the shower attachment. "Ouch! Madge." At the sharp tone, she sat, then cried as she tried to wipe her face on Sophie's leg.

She hit the speaker button. "How long Rayna? Will it really hurt her?"

"Chemicals are going to burn for sure. Don't try milk. It's the oil, and while it will calm the burn, the oil is the real culprit." She could hear the desperation in the dog subsiding. "What kind of dog did you get?"

"She's not mine, it's a friend's doggie, a good girl, yes you are. Some idiot tried to break in and sprayed her, so I returned the favor. I would like to feed the wench the container."

"Well, you answered my next question—how?"

"She's a border collie mix, and so sweet."

"If she's still crying or doesn't seem any better soon, take her to the vet. It can take an hour to clear though."

Liam crashed into the doorframe, "Blood. Holy hell. Is she bleeding?"

"No, she nailed me."

"Sophie, you need to have a doctor see that." Rayna was chewing a knuckle as she paced.

"I will Rayna, thank you. I so, so appreciate your advice, you're the best."

"Okay, let me know what happens." She hung up before she realized the other voice was male. She knew Charlie well enough, there was little doubt, she'd have a cat when she found out.

"Rayna's my friend from home, she trains dogs and puts them with servicemen and women in need of a PTSD or battle buddy type animal. If anyone knew what to do, she's the one."

"Madge bit you." He was shocked. She never even truly growled at someone.

"She didn't mean to, did you baby?" Madge tried to face her but couldn't keep her eyes open. "Aw, the poor baby. Liam, call your vet."

His phone in hand as he walked away, scowling as the tow truck towed his mother's car to the impound lot. It was the third time he had to have his mom and sister arrested. "Okay, thanks doc." He went back to the bathroom, "Do you want to hold her, or drive my truck and how bad did she bite you?"

"I'll drive, she needs daddy, and grab her green thing. I'm not sure how bad the damage is, it's just starting to hurt."

He yanked a beach towel from the back of the door to wrap Madge in, then carried her to the truck. Sophie left her wet socks hanging over the tub. She grabbed the duck, locked the house and made a stop to grab her flip flops from her car. Liam was impressed; she handled his truck like a pro. Once they got Madge taken care of, he fussed about the blood trail Sophie left until she agreed to go to the ER.

He made a call on the way, "Hey, yeah man, it's late. I need to go to County Gen. Madge bit someone and I'm insisting they seek medical attention." He glared at Sophie and got a "pfft" in return. "No dude, she got maced, long story, but guess who is back in jail." He stroked Madge's head, "Poor girl. Naw man, I need you to come sit with her while I make sure this is done right...thanks bro."

Sophie was checked in when he got inside. He walked into the middle of her discussion with the doctor. "The poor baby had been sprayed in the face at least twice trying to defend her home, she was screaming in pain and in full defense mode. If she hadn't bit me I would be more surprised. She's up to date on her shots and is a very sweet dog. Nothing is going to happen to her. She was just seen by her Vet, she has a cream we have to put in her eyes so, she was really not at fault."

Watching her stare down a uniformed officer as a doctor examined her arm was priceless. "Ya know, I'm betting you have a buck seventy-five on her and she'd take you."

"Hey, Boonie, what's shaking?" Sophie's adversary shook hands with Liam.

"Not much. Just checking to see what sort of damage Madge did to my lady friend."

His eyes grew large as his head swung back and forth between them. "Madge? No way. What the hell?" "She got sprayed in the face, that pepper-mace crap. Soph was trying to help her and well...you heard the lady."

"Dang, she's gonna be okay, yeah?" Liam nodded.

"You know state law says you have to cover the lady's medical bills."

"I would anyway, my dog." Sophie only half-listened to their conversation, she had been more involved with the doctor and hearing "cauterize" in connection with her arm. Without ever turning, her right arm swung out, her hand smacked into the middle of Liam's chest and tightened around a handful of his shirt as she tugged. Her face buried in his shoulder, his thumbs tucked into her belt loops. Crackling sounds with a sweet, metallic odor filled their cubicle.

The cop seemed a bit queasy as he ducked out. With Sophie put back together, bandaged up, and a prescription for antibiotics in hand, they headed for the Nurses station to be sure his address was on the paperwork for billing. Madge came close to wagging her tail off when she spotted them. Sophie was in the driver's seat, waiting on Liam. It took him a minute to fill in his friend, satisfied all was well, he fired up his bike and left. A smidge over halfway, she pulled over. "The hot sign is on, I want a donut and we need to do the fire drill thing. I can't. Pain killer." He figured he'd have to carry her as groggy as she was. Madge curled up between them, her head on Sophie's lap. Donuts bought, Liam in the driver's seat, his brow lifted as she ate with her eyes closed and was accurate as she reached for a second one. He chalked it up to being an odd talent, like touching your nose with your tongue. "So, who was the idiot broad I sprayed and smacked in the face?"

"Long story."

"Seems we both have those." She licked a finger. "I did notice a definite resemblance before I emptied the canister in her face." Liam grimaced, she nailed that one. He made the last turn into his drive.

"Okay miss, you are not getting back on the road tonight, it looks as if the crummy weather has caught up with us."

Sophie's mind was in a fog, all she knew for sure was moving any faster was not in her game plan. "No."

"Too bad." He had Madge moving toward the door. Once she was in, he went back for Sophie. "Come on Miss Space Cadet."

"Am not."

"Are right now." His chuckle gave her goosebumps.

"My brain is in over-drive, my eyes said see ya tomorrow." She was light as a feather compared to construction equipment he hauled around and manhandled on a daily basis. He flopped back onto his leather sofa.

"I've had days like that. Does your arm hurt?"

"Some, the numb it stuff is wearing off." Her head rested against his shoulder. "Who is she? A sister?"

His head dropped back, "Yeah, and my mother. They're both way into both drug and alcohol addiction and want me to fund their bad habits."

"Insanity. Don't feel bad, my family put the cray in crazy." She sat up fast, throwing out an arm to steady herself. She grabbed her phone and scrolled through saved sites. "There we go."

"Someone's birthday?" he saw the flower bouquet she ordered.

"My sister, Tammy. It would be her birthday." She wiped a tear, and then a second, and a third. "Damn it. I said I wasn't going to cry anymore."

"What happened?" His lips hovered over her shoulder. "She..." her head shook.

"There was some big-time crap that went down; my mom was absolutely no help. Tammy started drinking, she came home way too drunk to be on her own and either passed out or tripped and landed in my pool. She died. So not fair."

He pulled her into his lap, his arms wrapped around her, "No baby, it isn't. Not in the least. I'm sorry about your sister, thank you for sharing." Leaning back, he waited as Sophie rearranged herself. "You have goosebumps"

"I'm cold, I have been in the south so long I acclimated."

Liam stood, turned and deposited her in his place and scooted down a short hallway, grabbed a blanket and unfolded it on the way back. He held a pillow edge between his teeth. "Okay, let's put this here." The over-filled pillow went to the arm of the sofa, "get comfy" Sophie rotated and eased back. He grabbed a squishy pillow out of a chair behind him, "for your arm." Liam covered her up, slid the coffee table out of the way and moved a chair up closer to her. His hand stroked her head. "I have a cardinal rule, no seducing any woman who is loaded on booze or drugs even if they are legit, so relax. And I owe you a thank you."

"For what?" her voice was a bit thick, he still thought it was sexy. "Rushing in to save Madge...again."

"Pfft."

Hearing her name, she stepped around the corner, carrying her toy. Her head rested on the seat. "Come on girl." Madge hopped up behind Sophie, resting her head on her savior's hip.

Night sounds from outside filled the empty space from their lack of conversation. A wall clock ticked every third sweep of the second hand, an owl hooted, a whip-or-will called its name into the darkness. Peepers called the rain as only a frog can. Sophie was in that place where she wasn't awake, but not fully asleep. Her thoughts wandered all over. She needed to call Charlie. And Molly. Did the equine encephalitis medicine come in? Did she have enough hoof black? He's really handsome and older. Did I finish that worksheet? Liam's breathing evened out as he drifted off to sleep. Could he be my fairy tale? My happily ever after? Maybe I should let him close enough to find out. Thunder rumbled, the breeze picked up and Sophie settled in.

Sometime later her phone alarm jarred her awake as thunder boomed overhead. She checked the messages, "Show canceled due to weather." That was as far as she got. Sophie dropped the phone back on the table and went back to sleep. It was close to noon when Madge scrambled back over top of her legs. Bacon cooking and the aroma of freshly brewed coffee whittled away at her resolve to not move. Faint, leftover pepper spray clung to her shirt, making her nose wrinkle in distaste.

"Hey sleepy, how do you like your eggs?"

"Cooked."

"Coffee is this way." Sophie untangled herself from the blanket, grimacing when she forgot for a second and tried to use her arm. She stumbled toward the kitchen, missing the horified expression on Boonie's face.

"Holy crap. Do you always bruise like that?" Purple, three shades of it, peeked from under the bandage.

"Wow. I did bruise." She pulled a stool out, sitting at the breakfast bar to savor her cup of life's elixir—coffee. Liam slid a plate with grits, hash browns, bacon and eggs in front of her along with a short glass of juice. "Not bad." She speared a potato chunk as she spoke.

"Thanks...I think." She scooped some grits with a slice of bacon and devoured it. Madge brought her toys, one at a time, placing them on the floor around Sophie's feet. Her last trip was with her favorite green duck. Both humans quietly ignored her actions until she sank to the floor.

"Silly goose. What are you doing?" Madge's ears twitched. Sophie slid off the seat and went to the floor. "What's the matter baby? Are you apologizing? I know you were scared and it hurt. Nasty old bat." She gave Madge a belly rub, making her one happy pooch. "Come on, let's put your toys up. Sophie handed her a big red and white striped chewy bone. Madge grabbed it and ran for the box. All the while, Liam watched as she made sure his fur baby understood there was no animosity over a stress-induced bite.

They dated for a couple of months, his bad-boy reputation led many women his way, each hell-bent on taming the rebel soul he had. Usually, he had a one and done policy. Once they found their way into his bed the first time—it became the last time, they never came back and if they did, Liam escorted them to the end of the driveway. He contemplated that one. Maybe that was it. He tossed a couple tried and true lines her way and had been told she had two speeds. One was, "I'll let you know", and the other was "Try it again and you'll wake up with my shoe up your backside, wedged in sideways." Sophie wasn't like any other woman that crossed his path. Deep inside, he'd bet she hid as many secrets as he did. That could prove to be interesting.

"Okay sweet Sophie, what's on the schedule today now the rain has quit?"

"I need to swing by the barn. Feed the beast, see how wet the field is. May have to lunge him some, get some of the contrariness out of his system." Prying herself off the floor took a minute. "Why?"

"Some friends are having a bar-b-que pool party thing." One look at her expression was all he needed. "What? And don't say "nothing," I know what I just saw."

Tears pooled, ready to escape down her cheeks, "Is this about your sister?" Sophie nodded. It was an effort to draw in a deep breath. Liam grabbed their coffee cups and refilled them, "Come on babe." He walked on through to the deck overlooking the marshlands. "As soon as I said pool, it was a flash of terror. What happened?"

"It's a long story." He sat on an Adirondack style lounge chair, eyebrow arched in question. "Okay, try to keep up, at one time, there were ten of us kids. I was next to the last and close to three or four, maybe. Sadie was less than a month old. Two of my brothers were playing baseball, Joel and Dillon. Mom and dad were loading us up to go watch and I was having a day. Nothing made me happy. So grandma took me. Charlie and Tammy were in the middle seat of the station wagon. Faith and Robbie were in between them. In the back were the bigger kids, Sutton, Hope, and Johnny. Hope was nearly killed, she's spent years in rehab learning how to eat, talk, and walk again. Her skull was fractured in so many places she wasn't even allowed to brush her hair for six weeks." He watched as her eyes went from something dark to somewhat happy. Hopie got married a couple of months ago. Johnny was killed, along with Sadie, Faith, and Robbie. Our mother went off the deep end. She blamed Charlie for the wreck, she was nowhere close to being the reason. Daddy rolled that land yacht six times from what witnesses said. Tammy eventually started drinking to numb it all." Liam set his cup down and held her shaking hands. "Charlie was upstairs painting, the dogs started to raise hell. She went to go see why they wouldn't shut up, screamed bloody murder and did CPR until the dogs finally woke up dad. She was gone, but Charlie kept on until the ambulance showed up. An hour. She tried to save our sister for an hour. Charlie dislocated her wrist and an elbow but, she didn't quit. I have not been in a pool since then. Of any kind. Charlie hid in her artwork, Sutton and Joel left and never came back. I didn't know if they were dead or alive. Then I get this phone call, Chase's plane is coming for me, pack a bag and go to the airport. They brought me in for Sutton's wedding, he came home to save Charlie from some jerk who wanted to kill her. Still no clue as to what happened to Joel...I miss her, Tammy, she used to play princess with me." A sad half-smile from Sophie made his heart lurch. "She made me a camo princess dress, blue camo to be exact. She'd read me stories and do voices for all the characters. It shattered our family. Dillon, Charlie and I went to live with grandma, mom went somewhere, and dad was lost in his own grief. Dillon is in the military, he gets out in December." She let out a long sigh. "I'll swim in the ocean, lake...okay, not these lakes but, where there are no snakes or alligators, yeah. Rivers, again, where there are no angry water beasts. But, a pool..." her head shook. "Sounds crazy huh?"

"Nope, I get it. I was thirteen and got in trouble at school. They called my old man, he pulled up out front and gave me the look of doom as we were leaving. He took me home and got out to unlock the door, took a leak and headed back to the car, I stepped out the door to call him to the phone. This black sedan pulled up at the end of the driveway. Two guys shot him like twenty times. I remember holding him, listening to his last raspy breath as he said he loved me, that I was a perfect son. We were all over the news." Sophie curled up in his lap, her head on his shoulder. He stroked her hair as he went on. "Three days after his funeral, I was mowing the yard. This car pulls up. Man in a suit comes over and introduces himself. His men botched a hit, got the wrong man. "They were dead, it would be on the news, and here, take this. I'm sorry about your dad. He was a good man from the sounds of it." He handed me an envelope crammed full of money —a big one. Then he turned and walked off. I grabbed a dog turd and threw it at him as I told him to go to hell. He stopped, sort of laughed, and got in the car." For a few minutes, it was quiet. "I know all about crazy hon, you don't have the market cornered."

"Well, aren't we a pair of wonder kids."

"Yeah, okay, so how about we hit the barn and then you get all dolled up and let's go someplace all fancy-schmancy for dinner?"

"Define fancy."

"Dress to impress."

"Alrighty then."

Five o'clock and running out of time, Sophie stood in front of her closet. "Dress to impress, is that long or short? Classic or slutty? Crap. I should have asked more questions. Okay, let's go short-ish and classic." She decided on an off the shoulder forest green not quite knee-length dress and black strappy heels. Pulling her hair up into a rhinestone clip and putting the finishing touches on her makeup gave her a couple of minutes to transfer mandatory items to a clutch. A light spritz of perfume and she was ready. Her doorbell rang right on cue. "Man is punctual." She tucked her keys in her bag and opened the door after checking through the peephole.

Liam's hand slapped over his chest, "Be still my racing heart. Wow. You look amazing." Her slow smile sent a heatwave through him, if he closed his eyes he could imagine waking up with her, having kids with her, growing old with her. It's crazy, I just met her a second ago.

"You look like you slid off a page from GQ." Her bandage was artfully hidden behind a green and blue watercolor scarf. He led her to a car she hadn't seen before. One glance and she knew it was far from cheap. Valet parking at The Sword and Rose on the Waterfront made her queasy. "My stomach is going to think it's dreaming, it's gotten used to canned spaghetti sauce, blue box mac and cheese, and pizza."

Liam laughed as he handed her out of the vehicle. The front was an old plantation style with an expansive porch and columns. Inside, tucked back in a corner, a piano player kept the low-key entertainment going. "Good evening Mr. Boone, welcome back."

"Thank you." They were led to a table with a view of the water feature in the enclosed garden.

Sophie flipped open the menu, spying one of her favorites right off. "May I suggest a wonderful red wine?"

She smiled, answering in her best southern lady voice, minus the accent. "Actually, I prefer whites and I see you have a Schloss Johannisberg Riesling Eiswein." Nodding as he spoke, "Excellent choice Miss." He took Liam's order before leaving.

"I saw your eyes light up, what did you find?"

"Bison, haven't had it since I left home." They dined on Diver scallops in a frothy champagne foam with pearls of tabasco and pear, Bison strip loin in a smoky blueberry bar-b-que sauce and a trifecta of chocolate dishes for dessert. She wasn't exactly sure who thought using a vegetable puree was an idea, but the mush stayed on the plate. Sophie held her breath when the check came. Her allowance was there, Charlie always bumped it a bit during show season, she was sure there would be enough if he couldn't cover it. His gold card landed on the tray. She tried to breathe normally as the receipt came back for his signature. As they walked through the dining room on their way out, Liam was aware of heads turning to ogle Sophie. His blood pressure rose enough to make his pulse throb at his temple. "So, you're okay with babysitting Mojo while I'm home for the week?" He wondered if she knew how the light played off her eyes and the sparkle they held or how enticing she looked in the firelight of the torches outside. Liam would bet she didn't.

"I'm sure; everything will be fine while you go get your sister married off." They were at his favorite hangout when the call came in. She raced for the door, he caught up to her outside. Laughing, crying, jumping up and down—all at once. It took him five tries to get an answer out of her that came close to making sense. The memory made him smile. A valet stepped out of his car, his eyes stayed on Sophie a little longer than Liam thought was necessary. He stepped on the boy's foot as he ushered his date into the car. *Damn man, you've never been the jealous type before, what the hell? Get a grip. Okay, so she is smoking hot. She has obviously been treated to the finer things...like the wine. Was that her sister's doing? There's something magical about her. Madge, you should get a steak for this one. Should I tell her I have an armed guard lined up to keep her horse safe? Or that the jerk was out of jail again? No, not yet.* "You're quiet tonight. Did you enjoy dinner?" Liam had a thing about quiet women.

Sophie stifled a snort. "I was thinking how nice it was to be taken out by someone who didn't need a "loan" to cover dinner."

"You deserve better." Over the last few weeks, he witnessed her step up when a little girl lost her pony to old age. Sophie cried with her, posted all over social media and started a page to raise money to replace the much-loved animal. She enlisted the vet to help out and do a check when a couple of prospects had shown up. He never said anything about the anonymous donation coming from him. One fifty-dollar offering made her tear up. Knowing they had enough to buy another pony and cover stall rent for a few months had her almost as excited as she had been at her sister's wedding announcement. Watching the joy she got from the child's response cracked the hard exterior of his. Then seeing her put a handicapped teen on the big beast she referred to as 'baby' and walk with him...seeing others grimace and her smile as she spoke to the kid and the parents, cemented his belief. She may have crawled through hell, but she was every inch a lady of grace with a style all her own. They, his exes, her school mates may have come from money, but all daddy's resources couldn't instill heart or humility in them. Empathy couldn't be bought. Liam was certain one more kiss would get him inside for the night, however, he wasn't sure she was truly ready in her heart to commit and he knew that's what she needed to do. He did do a check to make sure no one was hiding and waiting. He didn't trust the Ashby boy any further than a monkey could spit.

A week later he drove her to the airfield. "You have everything in a carry-on?" One bright teal metal-sided carry-on with wheels. His brow rose in skepticism.

"Yep, I can fit three weeks of clothes in here if I'm going to a warm-weather place or two if it's cold. That includes shoes, makeup etcetera...I'll call when we land." One more thing to like about the woman. Boonie couldn't believe his luck, or that he felt strangely empty thinking of her leaving. She leaned up, the first kiss she initiated. "Take care." Sophie went up the stairs calling out a greeting to a crew member. His guards noticed a car matching the description of Ashby's vehicle cruising the area. He wanted an easy five minutes with that meathead. Just five. Sophie would never have to worry again.

JARED EYED THE BLACK, dinged up car in the alleyway. He had the drop on the city boy before he knew what was up. "So, why are you watching the Frog?"

"I'm looking for a girl."

"Try online dating."

"No, she owes me, in more than one way." He spilled his sad story.

Jared heard all manner of "Sophie for queen of the world", which cemented his place behind the eight ball. "I've got a score to settle too. I think we could be of mutual aid to each other. They met at a dingy hole in the wall bar on the other side of town to hash out the deal.

3

Whitehall:

"Hey, look who the cat dragged in." Noah couldn't believe his eyes. Molly's best friend had gone from leggy and pigtails to someone who made your heartbeat your chest black and blue.

"Noah! Oh my gosh." She hugged him, "I didn't know you were home." Chit chat had filled a few minutes until his sister stole her bestie and left him there in a daze. One thing he had to give the O'Hara women, even Wanda, they were definitely head turners. His head tipped as he recalled a conversation she had with Molly. She had said if she could have anything, other than her siblings to have never died, it would be a treehouse. That's what he could build. He had agreed, he felt gypped as a kid. Their end of the state wasn't heavy in the trees needed for a treehouse; they weren't even light in them, more like non-existent. That should keep him out of trouble for a while

Liam paced the area where he dropped Sophie ten days before. Her absence cemented one thing in his mind. She was the one for him. It didn't matter what the topic was, if she didn't agree, there was no demure acquiescence to his point of view. A boxing match could ensue, but he liked that aspect. She was fire with an icy side. One look from her could either cut you to the core or warm your soul. Sophie made him smile, made him think, made him want more than a nine to five job, a big screen TV and his dog. Lights on the building side began to spin, warning a plane was coming in. It was her, Madge barked from the front seat. Chase's jet rolled to a stop. Liam stayed back as the stairs rolled out. Trying to maintain his cool factor, he strolled her way; hands in his pockets, his muscles pushing against the short sleeves of his t-shirt with his company logo on the upper left side. Liam's resolve held to the halfway point before he gave in and ran to her. Her laughter as he spun her around was music to his soul. His head shaking as he grabbed her suitcase. "Not sure how you do it." He pulled her close enough to kiss the top of her head. "How about checking on Mojo, and going on a quick vacay with me. A week of sun and surf, being pampered and spoiled." After more than a week around her parents, she could use a break. "But, who would take care of Madge and Mojo?" "Ted will stop and check daily at the barn, I hired an armed guard and Ted is also going to Madge sit. They need to termite treat their house, so they're bringing their pug and cat to my place." "Well...okay then." Four days later they were on their way to the Caribbean. A puka hut over the water, way out away from the others, a freshwater pool, fully stocked kitchen with the option of gourmet meals delivered to them. Fresh fruits and juices were left at their doorstep every morning. Sophie had the devil's own time keeping her jaw in place when they disembarked from the boat. It didn't take long for her to find a bikini and water. Liam had to make more than one adjustment to his nether region as Sophie took advantage of the bay. "The netting is weighted at the bottom."

"Shark nets, twice a year they're thick through here."

"Well then. Tell me this isn't one of those times."

His hand ran through his hair, "from what the guide said, they'll be here soon." At least they had a couple of days to enjoy the salt air and crystal clear water. Dinner came out by boat, they ate by the poolside, watching shooting stars and sharing parts of their time apart. "Life is so strange, I walk through grandma's door and it's like I'm a small child and I can walk back out and friends are getting married and having babies...like Beau, Charlie's brother-in-law. Only he didn't even bother to invite the family." Laughter bubbled forth, "He's also the baby of his family. I think you'd like him." The more she told him about people back home, the more determined he became to take her back there.

Liam lifted her hand to his lips, "So how would you introduce me? Your personal, one-man entourage, or fetcher of pizza on show days, fixer of dead cars... a man who wants to do this stuff forever?" He kissed her fingertips again.

"Maybe I'll tell them you are my, hmm, I'd say sex slave but as much as you would love that, I couldn't sell the slave part. Probably, just as my guy."

Liam's lips skimmed her hand again. "I suppose I am too old to be a boyfriend."

"You are definitely not a boy."

"I can live with being your anything."

Her lips curled into a smile. "Good."

Twenty minutes later, he had to move. Sophie watched as Liam tried to stretch the kink out of an old football injury aggravated a year before when he dropped his bike to keep from getting smashed by a fool who ran a stop sign. "Stubborn man, we have a hot tub here. Plunk yourself in it."

"I put in some long days so my schedule was clean when you got back. Think I may have overdone things a hair."

"Suit yourself, I'm going to grab a drink. You want something?" She was on her feet and turned into him.

"You." His gaze locked with hers, he pulled her closer. Kissing her was like holidays, fireworks and magic in one green-eyed package. When she kissed him back, his heartbeat so fast he thought he might pass out. Feeling her thumbs slide between his skin and the waistband of his board shorts only doubled it.

"Prove it." Her words were more of a purr at his ear. His brain yelled no, his body had other ideas. Divesting her of the tiny bikini and placing his lips where it had been, was a dream come true for Liam. Her brow arched when he reached into his suitcase and pulled out a metal case with a skull and crossbones on the top. The latch popped open to reveal a stash of condoms. Round shiny blue packages, he managed to pull one out and not dump the contents. His hands shook as he opened the round packet and slid the condom on. Slowly sliding into his goddess gave him chill bumps. Somewhere between a kiss and his slow whispered name, Liam broke his own rule. "Damn, I love you woman."

Sophie's cat eyes went to slits, "Say it again."

"I love you." No more talking, he was all action as he took her to a new level of ecstasy. Gulping for air and resting on his forearms, They were no sooner back then Sophie was nosing through her school catalog. "Okay, sexy. Explain this to me." His hand waved over her equestrian notes and print outs on upcoming events. "Most of the schools are part of the NCEA," she looked up to see she had lost him, "National Collegiate Equestrian, they have a set of four events where they do what's called hunt seat equitation over fences. It's where the rider guides her horse through an obstacle course of jumps. You've seen me do that." He nodded, "Then there's a series of what they call flat moves, but no jumps and two western categories. Their season is also off from ours, done totally different. I do something a tad bit different and under a different founding organization; NCEDA. We're one of eight schools focusing on Eventing and Dressage. Eventing is best described as an equestrian triathlon, so theirs is a different version and the host school provides the mounts. One aspect I don't like. Too many riders do not put the time in with their horse as I do."

"Then how do they get decent results?" Liam was confused. "

Some have skill, some are lucky and some don't." She was rummaging through all the papers on the table. "Hells Bells."

"What babe?"

"I must have left my show calendar in my car." Liam grabbed the keys and kissed her forehead. "I'll go get it, you start plotting."

Liam had ulterior motives. Sophie's car always looked as if an office exploded in it. He found the folder in question and her phone bill. Quickly, he took a picture of it. All four pages. One of the Wyoming numbers had to be the elusive big brother. He spotted the black car out of the corner of his eye. Whistling as he went, he took the stairs two at a time and bolted the door as soon as he was in. "Call nine-one-one. The jerk is back."

Sophie threw a pen and dialed, muttering under her breath. Local cops rolled in within a few seconds. Followed by a tow truck. In ten minutes they were beating on her door. She signed the paperwork and was assured the fool wouldn't be out overnight.

"This makes what? Four times now we've carted him off, boy has a steep learning curve." Boonie shook from sheer anger. He wanted to pulverize the creep. With Sophie wrapped around him, he calmed down enough to think a bit.

"I've got a buddy, has a place in upstate New York. How about we load the beast and Madge and go up there for the holiday?"

"Okay." She spent an hour gathering Mojo's records so he could travel. Pulling a trailer with a horse wasn't totally out of Liam's realm. He preferred it to the heavy equipment he usually dragged all over. Madge sprawled across the backseat, content that her people had it down. They made excellent time leaving before the traffic jams hit. Sophie wasn't sure what to make of Liam's friend. Gordon Dumont was a head taller than Liam, tattoos up his neck and across the back of his hands led her to believe there were more. They greeted each other like a long lost brother.

She stepped around the back of the trailer, Dumont stopped dead, stared at Boonie, slugged his shoulder and then wiped his hands off on his pant legs before he stepped up to meet her. Leading out Mojo, she watched the man's eyebrows rise as he glanced at Boonie. She walked the fenced paddock and decided it would work. She had him saddled and making circles in the pen and ran him through his paces before sliding off his back. He followed her back to the fence, nudging her in search of a treat. "Don't get pushy. Brat." He looked behind him, she couldn't be talking about him. "Don't even play innocent with me mister." His big head swung around. Liam handed her the jar of peppermint candies, she dug one out and waited. Mojo walked up close and lowered his head to her forehead. She kissed his nose and gave him his treat.

Something was different with Liam, she whispered it to her best buddy, her horse. He threw his head up and down as if to agree. "He seems...lighter? Not like," she ran a brush over his side. "Like he's always in a good mood, he took pictures on the way here and posted them to social media. He's never done that before. He's up to something."

Liam leaned against the trailer, one foot resting on a tire. "Well?"

"Lord son, that little woman leaves a trail of fire behind her."

"I told you she's a special sort of woman."

"How special?" Dumont cut him a side glance. Special was not Liam's usual choice of words when it came to women.

"I'm going to convince her to move in when we get back."

"And? I know that look."

"I might man up and call her brother, see if there is an objection to a proposal." Dumont missed the corner of the trailer with his knee, the funny side step threw him off balance. He lay sprawled out in the grass. "The hell you say!" He laughed heartily. "Nice to see one is ready to take your jaded ass down. Take it this is all on the QT?"

"Yup." Sophie sauntered across the yard and into Liam's open arms. Her shirt rode up, Dumont tried to read the tattoo. "She lived, loved, laughed and left with a heart missing a piece. Memorial for one of my sisters."

"Oh, I'm sorry for your loss." He felt like a heel, Boonie could tell by the expression and head dip.

"Thank you." Madge held her bowl in her mouth. "I agree baby, it's time to find some food."

Two days in, the Dumont clan was in love with Sophie. Boonie was at the grill, Gordon and Mary, his wife, were in the midst of hauling out food. When the oldest son, Matt, went racing through with a friend. Like a slow-motion replay, she saw the grill get bumped, Madge dodge getting stepped on, and the pool coming up to get her. She splashed in, fighting to not do so. She was in a war with an unseen demon.

Gordon yelled at Matt as the water splattered on the patio. Boonie could see the panic on her face, the wide-open eyes as she clawed her way to the side, mouth open, the silent scream refused to find vocal cords. She grabbed his hand, nearly pulling him with her. Both men lit into Matt. He wasn't sure what he had done and ran through the house and out the front door.

Sophie was hot on his heels, she tackled him to slow the boy down. Still wild-eyed, sucking air and fighting panic, she held an iron grip on Matt's arm. He saw something in her expression that kept him in place. "Sit down" Violent shaking took over.

"I'm sorry. I thought you could swim." His head held up by his hands, he sat cross-legged in front of her.

"I can." She stuttered. "I've had a fear of pools since my sister drowned in my kiddie pool." His head jerked up, so many emotions ran through, each one accompanied by a change of expression, she couldn't begin to count them. "I'll swim anywhere except a pool. I know it's crazy but watching one sister doing CPR on another leaves a scar on your soul. My mom said it was my fault because I had to have the damn pool." She swiped at the tears with wet hands.

"Oh man. I'm a dumb ass."

"Naw, you're just a boy having fun with a friend and you were in a bad place. I'm not mad at you Matthew."

Her voice was soft and calm, it was what brought tears to pool in his eyes. A breeze blew over them making her shiver. "I'm really sorry Sophie, I am."

"Hush, help me up. I've gone southern from time spent there and I'm freezing." Matt went to his feet in one fast move, he held a hand out to her. Walking back she looped a foot around his and pulled nearly tripping him like she had done with her brothers before they left.

"Hey!" They were laughing when they made it back to the door. Both men stood there, arms crossed, heads shaking.

"I need a towel." They moved so she could get in. Sophie ran to their room and changed into something dry and warm and put her hair up in a towel. Back downstairs both parents tried to apologize for their son. "He's a boy, they're like puppies, all ears and paws and everywhere at once. It's okay." She missed the look between Gordon and Liam. By the end of dinner, the mood was restored and plans were made for the next day.

They were heading to the County Fair. She wore a pair of cutoff shorts and a t-shirt with the Equestrian Team logo on the left shoulder and across the back. The guys went for food, Sophie migrated to the horse arena. The buzz kicked in, like a hive of bees. Mary glanced at her toes as she spoke. "There is a lot of interest in you."

Sophie looked over the program, "Oh, they're going to do Trails. This is pretty cool to watch."

The guys came back with beer flats loaded with food options. Liam looked over the arena. "They know you're here." Gordon's brow rose. "She does this stuff, quite well I might add."

She waved him off the accolades, grabbed a corn dog and bit into it. One of the coaches made her way across the arena and stepped through the gap in the wooden fence rails. "Miss O'Hara?"

"Guilty." She stuck a hand out, "Hi coach, what's up?"

"We have some kids who would love to meet you if you wouldn't mind." She took another bite of corndog before she re-wrapped it in its tinfoil bag. Standing, she wiped her hands on her backside and kissed Boonie, "Be right back."

"It's not every day they can meet someone so high up in the rankings, I can't think you enough."

"Pshht. There are some riders who need to get over themselves." They were at the gaggle of pony clubbers. "Hi girls," she stopped and pointed, "You have boys too. Amazing. Y'all are so lucky. Boys are rare in the clubs." Both boys went pink-cheeked and ducked their heads. She answered questions, all the while watching one pie-eyed pony. "Who is riding the one with the blue blanket?" A girl of maybe eleven raised her hand. "Your pony needs the near front hoof looked at."

"I just picked her before we came out." Her small eyes rolled up in a display of agitation. Sophie walked over and lifted the hoof.

"Need a pick." One of the boys handed her one. She dug under the stone and popped it out, and then properly cleaned the hoof. "Thank you," She gave the tool back. "Then you need to do a better job." She dropped the stone into the girl's hand. "More importantly, you should have been able to see that. If you can't tell something is off by watching your mount, you are not spending enough time with them." She answered more questions and then made her way out.

One pigtail wearing little girl followed her. "Wait. Please." She hadn't said anything during the time Sophie was with them. "Please, please, please, can we take a picture together?" Her little hand shook as she offered her phone. Liam stepped down to do the honors. "Oh my gosh!" she hopped about "and sign my program?" Sophie giggled as she signed it to Amy Lynn and her scrawled signature under it.

In the stands, Mary asked what the deal was. Why was there such a fuss? Little Amy spun on a small booted heel. "Are you kidding?

Sophie O'Hara is fifth in the nation and has a chance at the Olympics." She ran back to join the others.

Sophie stepped between the boards, "she's a tad bit excitable." She polished off whatever food Boonie stuck in front of her as she did a horse by horse assessment of their skills. "I rode for a University up here before I had problems with a moron boy." Mary looked her way, "One of the Ashby's."

"Oof, they are a lot of trouble. On a good day." She slurped the last of her iced tea. "I heard daddy wasn't happy with one of them. He's getting ready to run for something and his kid can't stay out of jail."

They headed for the midway, rode some rides, played some games. Gordon and Liam both had to grab the sledgehammer and ring the bell, they smoked the cigars they won to keep mosquitoes away as fireworks lit the sky.

CHARLIE TAPPED HER computer with a fingernail. "Who is this man with my baby sister?"

Jesse leaned over her shoulder and checked out the mini-album. "Says," he pointed, "his name is Liam Boone. He looks happy as a clam too."

"Well, why have we never heard of him? And of course he's happy; could her bikini get any smaller?"

The Monroe brothers laughed outright. "She's over twenty-one now, she doesn't have to tell you who she is dating."

Charlie was oblivious to their teasing. "And where in the hell are they? Background looks tropical."

Jesse plugged the name into a database on his phone. "Nothing nefarious there. He owns a construction company and two houses.

With a net worth that says keeping the horse in oats wouldn't be a problem."

Charlie rolled her eyes at her old friend and brother-in-law. "She seems happy. I don't think I've seen true joy in her since Tammy died." Her chin sat in her palm. "He's not a bum?"

He was still digging, Jesse's back was to her as he read off what he found, "haven't found anything bad about him. No tickets, wants, warrants, no bankruptcies. Clean as a whistle."

"I wonder if he's the friend who was watching Mojo?" she ate a chip loaded with bean dip. "It's so hard to not think of her as a baby."

"From his smile, I'll wager it won't be long before you know all about him."

MONDAY NIGHT THEY WERE back home, Sophie had her beast in the arena exercising him. Liam pointed to the phone and outside. She nodded. He dialed the number he had determined to be the oldest brother. It rang twice, "Hello"

"Hi, is this Sutton O'Hara?"

"It is."

"Good, I'm Liam Boone. I've been dating your sister for a while now."

"Really? We haven't heard anything." Sutton lounged against a haystack. "

Yeah, that is probably going to change. She's liable to come bouncing out of the barn anytime now. I was wondering, the only opinion she seems to worry about is yours. Would there be a problem if I asked her to marry me?"

Sutton stood straight up. A hundred things ran through his mind at once. He heard all about this guy from Charlie. It also killed the age argument. He couldn't be a hypocrite with the difference in ages between Gilly and him. "She can be a handful."

Liam chuckled, "I could have used that info last spring."

"I have one request."

"Shoot."

"Be honest with her." Sutton had a million things to say and couldn't think fast enough.

"That's easy. And she will finish school."

"Well, welcome to the looney bin. Hey, what do you know about that fella doggin her?" Sutton wanted to call in someone to go pound the dude into a pancake.

"That he's an ass on a good day and daddy keeps bailing him out."

"Sounds like, he needs an attitude adjustment." Sutton paced a circle around Gilly's garden

"I've thought about that—hard." Sutton was starting to like the man.

They pulled up to Sophie's apartment, her nemesis was screaming from the back of a patrol car. Spray painted insults were all over the door and wall, a broken booze bottle lay scattered across the landing. Boonie couldn't have planned it better. "Soph, I can't stand this. I worry about your safety all the time. Move-in with me."

"But..."

"But what?"

"I'm worried that we'll get on each other's nerves and I have an apartment full of furniture."

"Sex was invented to cure the nerves part and I can have a moving truck here in the morning."

She held her bottom lip with her teeth as she warred with herself. He pressed on, "You may get sick of seeing me naked..."

"Never happen." She let out a long sigh, "Okay."

He opened his mouth to add to his argument, realized she agreed and kissed her instead. One long, slow, kiss in the moonlight as Ashby kicked and yelled until he was hoarse. As Liam left, he stopped to listen to the night noises. His grandmother's voice came to him, "When the whippoorwill sings and the owl responds, its death it brings." He shook his head muttering about what a crazy old woman she had been. Liam made a pit stop at the Flaming Frog. Smitty had more side gigs than anyone Boonie knew.

"Hey man, I need a moving truck for tomorrow, can ya hook me up?"

"You moving?"

"Moving the lovely Sophie in with me."

The older man's brow rose, it gave him a slightly sinister countenance . "So this is serious."

"It is extremely serious. Plus she has a stalker."

"Oh?"

"Some dude from her New York school. Bennet Ashby the turd, I mean third."

Smitty chuckled, "His daddy is running for Senate or something like that. The sitting bozo got caught with his hand in the wrong cookie jar. Been all over the news."

"I stay away from that anymore."

"Yeah, I got a truck for ya. See ya 'bout eight?"

"Fantastic. Thanks bud." Boonie was out and heading home. On the way he thought back to when he first met Sophie, he was certain she had bewitched him in some way. She was good in the dirt and grime of his work world, and when she wanted to dress up, she could easily hold her own in any Hampton drawing rooms. She had style and grace and on occasion, the mouth of a drunken sailor. She was fearless, unless it was a pool, and made his day better. "Yeah, this is the right thing." Madge went along in the morning. Stacks of boxes confused her, as did the truck. Liam backed right up to the stairs, the tailgate dropped onto a step making it easier to cart out furniture. "I thought college students were supposed to have junky stuff that one could leave at a dumpster."

"Tell that to my sister. Charlie furnished it, I had minor bits of input and that was it. The artwork is all hers, that's the coolest part." A couple of nights later they wandered through a local museum, one of Charlie's pieces was on display. They snapped a quick selfie with it. Liam was set for either buying the huge thing or trouble when the docent came their way scowling. "We have asked that no photography...what's this?"

Sophie turned her phone around so the man could see the half-finished piece. "She's my sister. Promise you, she won't mind. Want me to call her?"

The docent looked as if he swallowed a goldfish. "No, quite alright, enjoy your evening."

Over Sophie's head, Liam watched the skinny man sashay away, and then speak to a woman he knew to be the curator. "I don't understand the thought process." She stood in front of a huge canvas. "What does five blue ombre ovals on a three-foot square symbolize other than he didn't even square it up?"

Liam's fingers brushed her bare shoulders. "Honestly, I'm more interested in watching you. New dress?"

"Just one I never had a chance to wear." Black lace over a pearl aquamarine silk, off the shoulder, a bit short and paired with black lace heels. More than one head turned as they strolled by.

His lips brushed her temple. "Here comes the curator."

Sophie had her sized up before she ever opened her overly done coral-colored lips. Her accent was fake. Surprise shown in her expression when Sophie responded in German, Liam loved the showdown.

"Maybe we should speak English?" The curator's hand sat at her throat as she shifted her weight from foot to foot.

"Seeing as how your accent is as fake as..." she stopped there, "Yes, maybe we should."

"You look so much like Charlotte. It boggles the mind."

"I'm certain you didn't skitter over here to remark on my resemblance to Charlie."

"No, I wanted to apologize for our docent, he's new and"

"New? Really? His name tag had a six-year pin. When does he lose the new docent smell?" Liam had to bite the inside of his cheek to keep from laughing at her. "Cut your losses and toddle on." She leaned into Liam as they strolled away

"Too bad that was not videoed." Minor chit chat filled their walkthrough, with a share of other patrons they moved on to the next venue.

"Charlie has a couple of things here too. There should be a small structure with part of the Eiffel Tower and one that is a three-D before, during, and after the airport bombing that nearly killed her."

That brought Liam up short. "What?"

"Yep, she was in the airport when it went off. She has some nasty scars from it. This was cathartic in a way." They stopped in front of the display. "The outline of shoe prints is where she was at when it detonated. The bloody, broken heart was a couple in front of her on the stairs. The woman was killed."

"And that?" he pointed to a half grotesque twisted animal, half Corbin Benson. "The bomber. He had bought a couple of Charlie's paintings and a sculpture." She pointed to another outline with a phone next to it. "She helped a boy call his mom, he was trying to hold his face on. And the spot over there is where some soldiers managed to catch up to her and get her to a hospital." That was when she noticed more than just Liam had been following her tale. "But she survived, married the man of her dreams and now is expecting baby number two. So, life goes on." They strolled on through. "I love the current project. It is inspired by a dam in Amsterdam. The thing is also bloody huge and will be a water feature. It has water, light, movement, and flowers."

"Sounds magnificent, much like you." She twirled in front of him, stopping with her hands resting on his shoulders.

"I am starving." He led the way to the meal stop. It was in the city center with tables set up on the red brick square. Strings of lights crisscrossed overhead. A voice interrupted their tete-a-tete.

"Aha, look what the cat dragged out in public. Our very own Mr. Liam Boone, and who is this divine creature?" He bowed low and held a hand out. One finely chiseled eyebrow inched upward as her glance traveled over him. She never let go of Boonie's arm.

"Landon Rowley. I thought you had hopped a flight to another universe, far, far away."

He tipped his head back and laughed heartily. "Seriously. The talk of the town is you two." His gaze went from one to the other. Sophie wasn't sure what to make of the dandified being in front of her. His suit had an odd sheen with a near-microscopic print that ran in stripes, his hair was dyed neon white and spiked close to his scalp.

"Then, they need a better hobby." Sophie caught the waiter's attention. "Mojito please." He looked to Liam, Sophie spoke for him. "Sunset Bay Pale Ale." When the waiter left, she shrugged. "My brother- in- law owns the company. It's good stuff."

He slid around the backside of the table so Landon could join them. Off and on during their date, his phone buzzed. Liam ignored it, but once they were in the car, Sophie wasn't going to let it drop. "You really need to answer your pocket."

Liam reached for her hand, squeezing it as he totally ignored her suggestion. "You were a hit, Landon is enamored." He checked the rearview a bit more closely. "Is your seatbelt tight?"

"Yeah." He romped on the gas and shot onto the highway. Past their exit, and the next three, he put the Lexus into a turn that came straight from a movie or video game. Across the median used for emergency vehicles and to the blacktop back toward their exit. Sophie saw it, the battered black car of Bennett Ashby. A South Carolina State Trooper with lights and siren followed close behind him.

"Do you think he saw us turn?"

"Us, no. The dust cloud, quite probably." Not doing the speed limit, but not exceeding it as most do, they made their exit and home safely but rattled. Yet another police report was filed.

"So, man of my dreams...who is calling? If it's an ex" she left it hanging there.

"My sister." Right on cue, his phone buzzed. Arms crossed, her stance was one that showed how ready to battle it out she actually was. Liam gave in and answered. "What do you want?" Her wailing and carrying on instantly annoyed him. "Crystal. Stop it and tell me what the hell you want." "Mom got into some bad stuff, they think she had a stroke." "And? Do you have a point to make?" "She's your mother too Liam."

"No, my mother died when you got her addicted to meth."

"They said she's gonna need long term care."

"Apply for welfare, neither of you will get a dime from me." He hung up, scratched his head and grabbed a beer from the mini-fridge in the bar.

Sophie snaked her arm through his. "That had to be rough."

He kissed her forehead, "It was. I tried to save them both from that crap but, the pull was greater. I know it's a disease, it doesn't change the fact that I have to let them figure it out."

"I know. Finish that. I need help getting out of this dress." She reached up to kiss his cheek.

When she sauntered off toward the bedroom, he smiled. "Oh great doggy gods, thank you for putting Madge in her path." He left the beer on the bar, his jacket on the back of a chair, his tie managed to land on the doorknob. Leaving kisses up her neck and back down as he unzipped her dress succeeded in making him rock solid. Her dress landed in a puddle at her feet, his breath left in a rush. "Dayum woman."

Practically naked, she worked at his shirt buttons, once divested of that, she tangled her fingers in his hair, kissing him greedily, she felt his slacks brush her toes. "Were you this close to naked all night?"

"Uh-huh" her tongue darted over his bottom lip. "Just in case." He swallowed, hard. Between thinking of having Sophie in a public place and her hands, he was ready.

She took a little hop and wrapped her legs around him. "I specialize in making you forget your troubles." He had to shuffle to their bed and then fight his shoes so he could shed his pants, all the while Sophie was making sure the task was difficult at best. "Grrrr." He rubbed his stubble over her shoulder as he mock-growled under her ear just to hear her little squeal. Sinking into her was ecstasy, losing himself in her magical eyes was heaven, hearing his name on her lips as she arched into him was glorious. "I am a lucky man."

4

Going to court was becoming a joke. Until Ashby didn't realize the car in Sophie's old parking spot may have been the same make but not the same color. Ashby trashed it before he became a true menace. Yelling "I am so over you bitch, you will die for this," as he bashed in the windshield. He beat on the door with an ax, screaming the ways he intended to use it to kill her. Arrested, cuffed, and stuffed in the back of the cruiser and he still yelled. Right up to where the new occupant came out with police. Daddy's fixer arrived bright and early to pay for the car and provide a new one. Bennett Ashby II hauled his son up by his shirt front as he threatened his heir with everything known to parenthood. A vein throbbed in his neck as through clenched teeth he snarled, "I will cut you off, not a thin damn dime if you continue. You're damaging my chances at the Senate seat." He threw his offspring back into the chair. "...inherited this from your mother's side of the family." The elder Ashby tugged at the bottom of his suitcoat and righted his cuffs.

SOPHIE SAT ON THE BACK of her car, legs crossed, tatalking to her sister. "So who is the dude in all these pictures all over your social media?" Preceded by a dramatic sigh, Sophie tried to keep her voice light, "Liam Boone."

"Is he older."

"He is, a bit."

"And? It's not like you to be so quiet when it comes to a guy."

"Charlie, he's really a nice guy. Lighten up. This is why I didn't say anything. You go all mother hen and then the fixer squad comes in and nothing needs fixing." Sophie rolled her eyes, knowing there would be more questions.

"How did you meet him?" Charlie tapped a pencil off her note pad, Sophie rolled her eyes at the sound.

"I rescued his doggoe, she's the sweetest thing. Her name is Madge and she's a big love bug. She was out wandering in the rain with her favorite toy."

"Aww, poor baby. How long have you been dating?"

"Since early last spring. He is who I trusted to horse sit Mojo"

"Really. So, when can we meet him?"

"I'm not sure. We'll have to see what we can do."

"Well, at least you're honest. How's school?"

"Pretty good, the season is going smooth, classes are the usual. The only nagging pain in my ass is Ashby. We've had him busted like eight times and like the proverbial bad penny...he comes right back."

"You sound worried."

"He's a maniac. More than a few fries short of a happy meal; far from the brightest crayon in the box."

"I can send a security team there, just say the word."

"Thanks sis, we got this. I needed to squawk about the bullshit for a bit is all. And I need to take the lunkhead out and exercise him. Liam was going to meet me here. He hates it when I take Mojo out alone. Traffic must suck. Love ya." Charlie never had a chance to answer her or try to talk her sister into waiting. Sophie was up and moving toward the barn. Mojo needed the exercise. Part of the new equestrian team filled the barn with good-natured banter. They were all saddled up and moving out together. Being part of a group settled her nerves. Conversations floated through a dozen topics.

BOONIE TOOK THE PAPERWORK from the state cop. "Witnesses back your story, at least you were able to slow enough to keep from getting t-boned." "Yeah, my fiancée has a stalker and I know she's at the barn, this seems a bit contrived."

"Want me to ask a local unit to roll through and check on things?"

"Yes, please." He gave them the address and her name. The cop was on the radio as Boonie pulled out into traffic. If he didn't looked over to see if her riding jacket was in the back seat he would have missed the car running out of the field and almost into his side. Instead, the other driver kissed a bumper. Boonie was convinced it was the same jerk from the concert.

Lead footing the rest of the drive to the barn made him want to thrash the twerp Ashby. Making the turn on River Road he hugged the road edge so a pair of ambulances running hard could pass him, they turned toward the barn. Liam got chills. Two more went screaming by with three police cars in hot pursuit. He dialed Sophie's number. It went to voicemail. Repeatedly. Liam made the turn down the driveway the hay trucks used, putting him at the small barn next to where Mojo lived. Screaming from the indoor arena drew Liam, he beat on the door yelling to open it. "It's Liam. Where's Sophie?"

The door slid, tears left streaks on dirty cheeks. "We can't catch him."

Liam walked out, hand open. "Moj, come on buddy. Mojo. Come on. He walked slowly up to the animal. Reaching out to rub his neck and trying to imitate Sophie, "Come on buddy," He grabbed the reins and took him to his stall before going back to the indoor arena. "What happened."

He got three definite words. Gunshots. Trampled. Crushed. Liam spun and raced for the doors. EMTs waited at the gates for the all-clear. A cop finally waved them in. The arena resembled a battle re-enactment. Everywhere they looked, bloody horses, some running in an attempt to find safety, some on the ground. Bloody bodies, girls splattered with the life essence of their friends, screaming in terror or pain.

"Sophie." He repeated her name as he moved through the maze of mayhem. "Sophie!" Her hoodie was tucked under another rider's head. Splattered blood covered both women. She tried to wipe some away while holding her teammate's hand, as sobs wracked her broken body. Over the cacophony of chaos, one voice stood out, hers. His head swiveled trying to figure out what the hell happened and exactly where she was in the chaos. "Help is here, you'll be okay Rachel, just hold my hand, they're here. They're here." First responders zipped in, loaded her friend and got out of there. She jumped up to go check on another teammate. She thought she heard Liam and turned. He was there, leading her away from the girl she rode with.

Her car was bullet-riddled. "Ashby." Sophie stopped moving, looking around her at the gory scene, she screamed "no" as loud as she could until she was out of air. Parents tried to shove past the cops at the gate, it was getting louder. "My keys. They're in my hoodie." She ran back for them, a policeman stepped up next to her telling her to leave their crime scene when a final shot rang out. Liam jumped at the shriek and turned in time to see the officer go to the ground while Sophie screamed "Stop fucking shooting. For the love of all things holy just fucking stop." A barrage of return fire cleared the way. Other law enforcement ran to the officer's aid. EMTs raced out to load the rest of the injured riders as handlers grabbed reins to keep the frightened horses from trampling the downed riders or their rescuers.

"What the hell happened?" A young-looking local cop asked the same question at the same time as Boonie.

"We were riding and, Rachel was in front of me and Sara. Sara wanted me to follow her, she thought she was off gait, I turned Mojo and there was a loud crack and a scream. The horses panicked and more shots. More screams and then Victory went over the fence and Mojo followed, I ran Vic down and took them to the indoor and came back out to help. I told the younger girls to grab any horse, take them inside, and stay there. And..." she stopped, "There's so much blood." She wiped her hands on her riding pants. "I gotta check on Mojo" she pushed her hair back, "I gotta call Liam"

He traded looks with the cop. "Babe?"

Sophie dropped to her knees. "My head hurts." Liam went cold. She tipped her head back, multiple bruises began coming up. He was ready to hurl when he realized it was shaped like part of a horseshoe.

TV crews loitered as close as they could. Vets were let in to check horses. Liam spotted parents of a pony club kid, he waved and held up a finger. He sent one of the handlers to find the girl. She walked out to the road, stoic, having witnessed hell on her little world. Ten yards to go, her arms went out, "Daddy," then the tears came. She had her rock, it was okay to let the emotions flow.

Sophie was still talking to the cop. Trying to point out who was where. Her words slurred, she began to shake. Someone yelled and a gurney stopped next to them. Liam took her keys, grabbed her purse and ran for his truck. The barn manager opened the gate, he drove through and followed the ambulance praying they didn't stop fast. They were unaware their little town was now national news. In the ER it was determined to be shock and a bruised cheekbone that went back to her ear. On their way home, he pulled his phone out and hit a picture of the art exhibit. "Is it Charlie or Charlotte?" He glanced at his love, "She's alive and rattled and needs her sister." He handed the phone over, catching the flash of surprise. It all spilled out, with sobs and slamming her hand against his dashboard. It carried through as they pulled into the driveway.

It looked quiet, Smitty and Tom walked out of the shadows, one with an aluminum baseball bat and one with a shotgun. "All clear." Smitty staggered when he saw Sophie. He composed himself and hugged her. An unmarked police car pulled in. Liam opened the door and let her in, walking back to the officer, his stomach rolled.

"Brass sent me out...to inform Miss O'Hara, Rachel Simms is in a medically induced coma, Danielle Jenson has been transferred, they think she's paralyzed and Sara Greene didn't make it. Three horses were euthanized." He looked at his feet, "Any ideas who?"

Liam's hand ran around his neck. "Yeah, Bennett Ashby the third." He walked inside, ran a bath for Sophie and listened to her sobs.

"I have to go back out to the barn." She expected him to argue.

"Okay." In an hour they were back, he knew Sophie wouldn't rest until she had hands on her horse. It was quiet except for the occasional sob of a rider who lost a horse, a friend, or both. One of the girls came out to hug Sophie.

"Magic and Luna had to be..." she took a ragged breath and shook her head, "They're gone and so is Frosty." They held each other and cried. "Have you heard anything about Dani?" Liam delivered the bad news.

His phone rang, he walked to the front doors. "Hey."

"It's Charlie, Is she out?"

"Nope, we're at the barn they lost a teammate and three horses. Six months ago I would have said it is just a horse...but seeing how bonded a lot of these girls are. I can't even think of how to right their world. I know one of the girls has a mom doing chemo, there is no way they can buy her another horse. Not that it would replace Luna, and I have rattled on like a loon."

"Thank you for trusting me enough to do so. That means a lot to me. Let that child know that someone has offered her a horse. She doesn't need to know who or where. We know people. Chase, my husband, is sending one of his attorneys to you. Top-notch. This will throw a wrinkle in daddy's plans. I gave him this number, hope you don't mind."

"Nope, not at all. I better get back, I think a damn reporter is sneaking in." It was, they were booted in a hurry. Next to the door, a stack of flowers and animals were piling up. Riders from other stables came to offer a shoulder, or sit quietly with the girls who lost their friend on hooves. Sophie's cheek had swollen to where her eye was partially closed. It took watching the security video for the fourth time before they figured out she had fallen and caught the hoof of another horse. At three a.m. he forced Sophie out the door. They stopped long enough for him to relay to the manager that there had been a horse promised to the one rider. It broke the manager. In the morning, the remaining team members voted to take the rest of the semester off.

Noah rummaged through the collection of flotsam and jetsam on his property. Six old shipping containers held all sorts of goodies. One ancient travel trailer circa 1950 restored a decade before gave him a place to live. No one said anything when the electric company came out and ran lines to poles, giving him juice to run the old trailer on and his power tools. His first job was to build a fence; he didn't need any jack-a-nape telling him his business. He snickered, hearing his grandpa's voice in the statement. He spent the better part of a week augering holes and putting in poles. Not any poles, but old railroad ties and telephone poles he acquired.

Once his privacy was taken care of, it was time to start building a tree. Three sets of blueprints later, he had something to work with. It took a little finagling to secure the equipment to set the beams. Six in total and cementing them in required two other sets of hands to get them in place. Logan and a brother came to help, anything that kept him out of jail was worth the effort. Borrowing heavy equipment and trucks from people he knew and hitting every demo site he could find in five hundred miles got him quite a bit in the way of supplies. Auctions helped in keeping the cost down, although it hurt his soul to buy a farm just to maraud pieces of barns before he resold them, sometimes back to the original owners.

Abandoned buildings became his hunting ground and a place the government left when they were done turned into a stealth mission to get what he wanted and get out. Noah half expected some green glowing, jelly bodied alien to show up. Cement mixers ran in tandem most of his day as he let his artistic side run amok. In six weeks he finished the base form of the tree. Noah acquired a welder's suntan from hours spent meshing pieces together. Late into the night, one could see sparks flying as he toiled away on what was becoming a passion project. That morning when he crawled out of bed, he heard a dog barking. It sounded close, he went to investigate and discovered someone dropped off a load of wood. "Well thank you supply fairy. Much appreciated." He dragged, stacked, and covered the offering before going in to make coffee and a sandwich.

His phone buzzed with a text from Logan. *"Yo bro, someone has a batch of electrical wire for you, they're stopping by in thirty to drop off. Micah said someone paid him to make sure it was all the right stuff and what you would need."*

His brows furrowed. *"He say who?"* He had money, almost eighteen months of military pay that he hadn't touched, plus Noah was more than aware of the fact that he had a portion of his grandparent's estate in a bank. *"No clue. Said they didn't look familiar."*

"Okay." His last bite of food was followed by a horn tooting at the gate. "Hang on" he called out. It was obvious someone had done some homework.

"This box is all switch boxes, ya got some dimmers, miles of line, breaker box, pretty much anything you would need." Micah ran a hand through his hair, which had thickened and grown since his cancer treatment.

"Who sent this? I mean, I know Beau gave you a chunk of change..."

"Mmm, not me. I got lil man to raise and JJ is due any day now, I may have to breakdown and build my own real size house."

"Well...who?" Noah had gone over the list of possible benefactors as he ate.

"Middle-aged guy, not afraid of a meal if ya get my drift, sandy brown hair, going a bit gray, not quite six feet tall."

"Don't even sound familiar."

"Don't know bud, but he knew you're a vet. Put the supplies to good use. I got a job site to get to. Take care." Micah backed out and headed east leaving Noah to ponder who his supply angel could be.

Around the bend, Micah looked at his phone in its dash holder. "Call Trent."

Three rings later, "Hello Micah."

"Hello, delivery made. Hopefully, he never goes on the website for the store. I used that dude when he asked for a description."

"My little brother needs to get over this and let someone help him. Stubborn ass man."

"I hear stubborness is a family trait." From the laughter, he figured Trent knew it was fact.

NOAH PEELED OFF HIS sweaty shirt and spread it out over the seat of his Harley. His morning list of what needed to be done had gone well. Deliveries of PVC pipe and windows had come in early and the driver with plywood had sent a text saying he was in Gypsy Falls and on his way. It was a good time to slap some peanut butter and jelly on some bread and catch the noon news. An eagle perching on the fence derailed that plan. He wasn't just battling the build, or a love-hate relationship with booze, the big one was the weather.

Winter would be there. They had an unusually warm spell, but he knew the weather wouldn't hold for long. Days ran into each other, he was up with the sun, cooler mornings re-enforced his theory. They were also got him moving to stay warm. Looking through some of Charlie's photos, he found his solution for his steel tree. Welder in place, rods where he could reach them and scaffolding anchored down, he started placing the limbs. Large ones were a no brainer. The smaller ones had been the missing parts and made for an anorexic looking tree. As they went in, he began to see the pine or cedar shape.

It revitalized him. Before he knew it, it was eight hours later. Yes sir. I may treat myself to something from Mrs. Peatree's and a diner burger special." Waving to folks in town threw some of them off.

Logan caught up to him at Mrs. Peatree's Poppables. "Hey bud, how's it going?"

"Good, real good." He pointed to a square popcorn treat, "Those'll kill ya but man are they worth the calories." He turned to the next display case. "Hey, what's this buzzing about Sophie?"

"Crazy person with a gun, killed one girl and three horses; another girl may be left in a wheelchair for life."

"Damn man, you wanna shoot someone, join the military. Government can't get us out of this one, they'll send ya."

"Exactly." They talked while Noah picked out a few treats and headed for the register

SUTTON O'HARA CAME over to help with the build, and to get feedback on his own project. As the job progressed, Noah began to heal also. "Ya know, I expected Charlie to have some PTSD issues after surviving the bombing." Noah leaned against the scaffolding as he drained half a bottle of water.

"Charlie has always processed stuff differently. Like the wreck. I was mad as hell at the old man for not paying attention, still mad at the ol' lady for blaming Charlie for everything. She always seemed to love the littles and the older ones were a pain. Pissed me off. Charlie would let her babble on until she had enough and blasted her back. She lets it out. Nothing is held in to stew and brew into a firestorm."

"Wonder how much comes out in her art?"

"Early days, she painted some strange shit and then boom there would be something you knew you could walk into. Some of it I get, some just makes me scratch my head." They covered everything from new football rules to the new diner menu items as they worked through the day. Gilly showed up late in the day with their kids and a picnic supper. Watching them gave Noah a twinge of jealousy. He wanted a love like Bogie and Bacall, his grandparents, those epic long term stories and knew that there wasn't a person in Whitehall that fit the bill.

After Sutton left for the day, Noah broke down and fired up the backhoe. Getting a hole dug to drop the pool in and a hot tub was next on his list. Granted, his water hole was supposed to be above ground, but a wooden 'box' would stave off the heave of frozen ground and a topper would make it easy to locate. Cold hadn't been a friend, it bothered his old injuries at least soaking in a hot spot would help. When he quit for the night, he felt satisfied. Something he had not been close to in eons.

BENNETT ASHBY II STOOD by as his son was led out in cuffs. His glare was directed at the attorney. "I said keep him out of jail. Which one of those words was confusing?"

Mr. Clement C. Lester Esquire fired back, hard and fast. "You want him out of jail? When he gets out this time get him some serious counseling. He's fixated in an unhealthy way and if the local cops can pin the stable shooting on him, he will go down. You have two strikes against you, money and you're a Yankee. Do something with him." He spun, grabbed his briefcase and left. Ashby stared after the man, at least some of the women were more accommodating, and he had a date with one such woman. He left by way of a side door, out to his shiny exotic car and out of the parking lot. He never noticed the Camry following at a safe distance or that it circled the block and parked where they could watch the honorable candidate from New York.

"Good girl Lucy, right to the window. Ahh, yes. You were worth that stack." He let the camera run with the feed from the woman's apartment. With any luck, he could parlay that thousand dollars into a cool million. "Silly man, you shouldn't have messed with my people

"I WANT HER DEAD."

"It won't come cheap."

"One million dollars. Crisp new bills and the receipt where they came from the bank."

"That's not easy to do. Feds usually crawl all over a withdrawal like that."

"I'm not most people."

"So I see." He took the bag full of one hundred dollar bills and latched it. Out of an abundance of caution, a check of the backseat was made before he got in the sports car and got out of there.

BULLETS KILLED SOPHIE'S old hand-me-down car, when she picked up the new Chevy she spotted the dashcam right off. Loading

her stuff from Clyde, the car into this one, which hadn't earned a handle yet, seemed strange. She grabbed a wooden shoeshine box she bought at a flea market; the perfect size for hoof care. Remembering that day made her smile, she made a smart remark about how it was still a shoe shine kit in a way.

"Shit." Sophie peeked into the hole and then opened the lid. "Damn it." She pulled the detective's card out of her wallet, shaking her head as she dialed. "Detective Rosario, this is Sophie O'Hara."

"Miss O'Hara, how can I help you?"

"I found another bullet. In a hoof kit box."

"Where are you? I'll have a patrol unit stop by to collect it." She gave him the dealership name and general location. She finished loading things from Liam's truck into her new ride as the officer pulled in. He took a couple of pictures and dropped it into an evidence bag. He radioed in, "10-5 for Rosario. Tell him it looks like a .223, he waited for dispatch to acknowledge and turned to Sophie, "anything else?" She shook her head. "Take care Miss." He was out in traffic and down the street in a flash.

Liam was across the street at his lawyer's office. She was fast approaching being over a whole lot of things, mostly Bennett Ashby. Hearing he only pulled a ninety-day sentence had her fuming most of the previous night. At least she had a few days to breathe before the skunk was back out and causing trouble. As if she conjured him, Boonie stepped out into the sunlight. He checked both ways twice before sprinting across the street. "Hello gorgeous." He pulled her close and kissed her, long, slow, and deep. "Come on, let's go get Madge and go down by the beach, kick back and relax." The drive took them by the barn, news crews were still out there four days later. Sophie refused to look that way. They dropped a blanket on the sand and sat down, Madge wriggled into her pop-up shade tent, content to watch her humans. Salt air has long been known a balm for the soul. It was one of the first places Sophie had gone to when she arrived; it was one of her favorites. Wind, salt spray, gulls crying out as they circled overhead. Her worries magically disappeared.

THEY SETTLED INTO A pattern, every couple of weeks Ashby found his way into jail, Sophie cried, Liam calmed her down and made her feel like a queen. He knew his was way around the horse world, around her horse, around her crazy schedule and what made her happy. He also understood, if she was arguing with Wanda, back out of the room. That had been a barn-burner of an argument. Liam came back when he saw Madge crawl behind a chair in the corner. "Look, woman, from the day of the accident you crawled your ass into a hole and didn't come back out unless you were pointing fingers at a child...do you hear me, mother? A. Child. Sitting in a back seat and incapable of moving the steering wheel from that seat. Shut up. You damn well will listen because if I have to stick my unhappy ass on a plane and fly home, you will be able to fit in a thimble when I am done with you and then you can take this to the bank. You will never be welcome in my home, my life, or ever see any kids I may have."

She took a deep breath before she launched in again. "You even blamed me for Tammy's death, you know something, maybe if you had put on your big girl panties and been an adult and a parent, she wouldn't have turned to booze to numb her pain. You never should have had any children. They should have hauled you to a spay-neuter clinic and had you fixed before you figured out what sex was. So, no mother dearest, please note the sarcasm. You do not get a say in my life, ever. E-v-e-r. Ever. I do not care how much you boo-hoo it up. I believe this is our final conversation. Good-bye." Sophie's hands shook as she blocked Wanda's phone number. Liam stood there, arms open waiting for her to come get a hug. That took all of a hot second. Before they knew it, a year had gone by, she had a great show season. They had settled into a life that made them both extremely happy. They had gone from Liam and that girl he's seeing to Liam and Sophie. A couple. One entity.

5

Sophie sat at a traffic light, she recognized the bike on the cross the street as Jared's. The last time she saw him, he lay spread over some decoration in the median. She argued with Liam over how fast the light changed and videoed the sequence to prove her point. Instead, she filmed a car running the red light and hitting Jared. Her video won the lawsuit according to the jury. Liam had not been happy about the results, but she needed to do the right thing. They weren't friends, but he stopped scowling when she went into the Flaming Frog with Liam.

The light turned and she headed off to pick up a present for Boonie. They decorated for the holidays and spent most of the time marveling in simple things. They Skyped with her family often during December, one by one they decided Liam was an okay guy and if he made baby sister happy, so were they. January brought the new semester and a new season in the ring.

They had a sunny, fairly warm day in the middle of the month. "Come on, this will be the last free weekend until the end of May. No one knows you've been learning to ride a bike. It'll be a big surprise." She really wanted to curl up on the couch and snuggle, just them and Madge. But, he seemed so excited she gave in.

They left from the Frog, Tom and La-la, Landon, and five of Liam's close friends. He planned everything out. Her brother and some friends were going to meet them at a park, he had the ring in his jacket pocket. They stopped at an overpass, Tom was having issues with something. Sophie stood by Liam when his phone rang, "Dude, lookout. Ashby is out, he said he is going to kill you both." Revving of an engine caught his attention. Liam shoved Sophie a heartbeat before Ashby slammed into them. She watched Boonie sail into the field.

Ashby laughed as he sped off. Sophie ran to Liam's side screaming for someone to get help. People began to pull over and try to administer aid. "Love you Soph. Inside pocket," he tried to make the zipper on his leather jacket move. She rummaged inside his jacket and found the box. "Going to propose, not sposed to die." The whipporwill and owl came back to him.

Her jaw dropped, shaking she opened the crinckled box and was stunned. She crammed the ring on her finger. "Don't you dare die on me Liam Boone, I'll never love again. You're my soul. My one and only." She leaned over to kiss him and tasted blood. Screaming for someone to get some damn help in one breath and professing her love in the next. She didn't give the EMTs a choice; she dove in the ambulance before they could say no.

Memories from their first meeting ran through her mind, the first date, when he burned dinner trying to impress her, the first time they made love. She listened to the chatter back and forth with the hospital. Sophie had his hand when they wheeled him in. Blood trails marked their path. "Don't let Madge forget me, love you babe, only one for me. Promise me you'll find happiness again."

"I will with you. Liam...Liam. No." her cry came out in one long word as Sutton burst through the doors. Sophie fought to stay close to her fiancé. A nurse ripped open his shirt, the amount of bruising was bad, she remembered learning it in a class. Blood bubbled out of his side, she watched his color drain. Sutton's heart skipped a beat. Seeing his baby sister bent in half, reaching for the man she loved, mouth open in a silent scream, broke his heart. Sutton grabbed her as her voice returned and she wailed "no" into the room.

She pulled away and went back to Liam, brushing his hair away from his face, she kissed him and pulled him close to her oblivious to the amount of blood she soaked up. Eventually, the other's came in.

Shock. Disbelief. Anger. Sadness. They all had at least one of those emotions. One of the nurses muttered, "She needs to get a grip."

Sutton strode her way, the glare was enough to shut most people up. His lip curled as he snarled out, "Shut the fuck up." He gave his sister an hour, mentally sixty minutes became his cut off point. As if she possessed an internal alarm clock, with a couple minutes to spare, she stood, emptied Liam's pockets into a snap top bag, kissed his forehead and walked out to her brother. He drove by GPS, she hadn't yet asked how or why he was there. The others went back to the Frog. Jared threw a chair through a window, yelling he tried to warn him and that he would personally kill Ashby. Sutton wasn't sure if Sophie slept. She sat in a wicker rocker on the back deck with Madge all night.

Once, he heard the dog call into the dark, reminding him of a lone wolf. Landon arrived at the house as soon as the sun came up. He looked like hell. Sutton opened the door and nodded to the back end of the room. "Has she said anything?"

"Not a word. She hasn't changed yet either."

Landon ran a hand over his face and around his nape. Walking through the house he knew so well gave him chills. He felt as if he was marching off to his own demise. "Sophie?" he moved to where she had to see him. "I had a long talk with Liam last week. I tried to talk him into telling you."

Sutton stood in the doorway, his skin prickled. "He got several death threats from someone, pretty sure they came from Ashby."

"Define several." Her voice totally devoid of any emotion, her face a blank stare, gave him the creeps

"Twenty at least." Waiting for her to scream or cry or something made him a little batty. "He changed his will, everything, business, houses, Madge, cars, and insurance policies are yours." He ran a hand through his hair, "He loved you, Sophie. I have known him since fourth grade and never remember him being happier."

He left Sutton with a phone number. Sophie sat there for another hour, then brought Madge in and headed for the shower. She threw her blood-stained sweater in a tub and upended a bottle of peroxide on the stains. With her hair twisted in a knot and pinned up, dressed in black, she took Madge along. Sutton knew it was bad when she handed over keys and set the maps app.

A tinny voice took them to the lawyer's office. "Sweet pea, you need an appointment."

"Screw that." Madge had been there, she knew which door to go to. Sutton followed along. A brass plate on an inner door read "Archer Keene" Sophie stopped at the desk. "

"Good morning, do you have an appointment." Good morning. What the hell was good about it? Only because the words came from an older southern woman did Sophie curb her tongue.

"Liam Boone is...dead."

The gasp was enough. She moved well for someone her age. From further inside the office, she heard the almighty question. "What? How? Are you sure?" he walked out, it was definitely Sophie. He was struck by her beauty when Liam showed him a couple pictures.

"Ashby ran him down. I'm going to need you to bail me out. I'm putting the truth in his obituary." He escorted her into his personal office. Sutton filled in gaps as Sophie played with her ring. A silly joke, Madge brought a plastic container from a gumball machine to them one day in the park. Inside was a ring with a pale blue stone. She said the ring needed some embellishment. Off and on for the last year, Liam would decorate the trinket and leave it where she could see his work. Her ring, the one he picked out held six carats of blue diamonds with a vine woven through the smaller stones. "Sophie, did you hear me?" she glanced up, "Liam made arrangements arrangements. You have some wiggle room." She nodded. He slid a copy of the directives her way. "There is a provision for his mother, Susan, and sister, Crystal." Her brow arched in question. "One dollar each." She blinked in acknowledgment. "He was a damn good man. If you need anything, any time of day or night, call me. He scribbled a number across the back of a card for each of them.

Her next stop was the funeral home he specified. No one questioned Madge being there. Liam's attorney already called. A rotund man in his seventies met them. Sophie didn't remember his name even though they were just introduced. An hour later she finished picking out a casket and an urn. "Only going to say this once. Memorial, open casket. Then you can cremate him," she shivered at the thought. "When he comes back half of his ashes go here" she handed the man an urn she thought the style was something Liam would like. "and the other half goes in the box. Secure the spot next to his dad by hook or crook" he started to speak, she raised a finger, "I don't care how, if you have to dig someone up and move their boney ass, so be it. Are we clear?"

"Yes, Miss O'Hara. Is there anything else?"

"His mother and sister do not come in under any circumstances. And I will need an hour for Madge to say goodbye." Tears ran down her cheeks as she walked out. Sophie set the GPS for the Frog. She walked in, erased the chalkboard and wrote the place of the memorial service with date and interment to be determined.

Sophie dusted off her hands and walked to the bar. "Double shot of Boone's bourbon." Smitty was not sure a double was a smart idea, but if booze helped in the moment, who was he to say otherwise. He set the glass on the bar, she downed the tawny liquor and tapped the rim of the glass. He refilled the glass, the second one she sipped.

Madge whined until Sophie picked her up. Across the TV a Breaking News banner popped up. "Man sought in death of local business owner Liam Boone arrested." Something about the tilt of her head, the set of her jaw, the lack of communication, worried

Sutton. He called the family last night, stunned and heartbroken were understatements. Behind her back, Sutton left his number with a dozen people close to them. He understood getting her out of the last place she shared with him was not going to happen any time soon. Forty-eight hours later Sophie took Madge to the funeral home.

She hit the hour and minute stage. I can do X more minutes to the hour without crying or screaming or whatever she was trying to not do. "Come on baby, time to say bye to daddy." Madge's head tipped as she slowly walked to the casket. Per her orders, a chair sat in place for the dog to sit and see in. Sutton had Gilly on the phone when Madge once again let a single low howl escape. She pawed at the human who took care of her forever, turning to see the lady who was as sad as she was. Madge whined a couple of times then leaned over and tried to get Liam to pet her. When they left, a dry eye could not be found in the place.

True to her word, she went to the paper and paid for the obituary to run in Ashby's hometown newspaper. Liam Andrew Boone, 31, died on January 20th after being run down and mortally wounded by Bennett Ashby III. Survived by his fiancée Sophie A. O'Hara, a fur child, Madge and a host of dear friends. In Lieu of flowers, please donate to your favorite wounded warrior charity. Service information followed. By morning several local stations picked up the story followed by the big three networks on the morning shows the next day. Sophie wasn't even sure when the family came in. Suddenly they were there and trying to make her do things she had zero intentions of doing.

Charlie and Chase, Evonay and Beau, Jesse, Molly and Shelly along with their mother and Noah, Joel and Dillon came with Grandma; Gordon and his family showed up, her barn family came in in one big mass of crying girls, it was nice but also annoying. It was gray and dreary and befitting a funeral. As they left the house, Madge seemed to comprehend what was happening. Her much loved green duck usually went with her. She went to her box and pulled out the candy-striped bone. During the service, Madge laid under the casket staring at Sophie. When everyone filed by, she stood next to the casket and whined. Landon brought her a chair. She climbed up and dropped the bone in, following it with one more howl. Everyone went back to the Frog, they had food and booze to go around.

Sophie went outside with Madge, just to breathe. Landon eased out the side door. "If you need anything Sophie, please feel free to call."

She tipped Boonie's flask to her blood-red lips, "Not unless you happen to be into torture and murder."

He turned, "You're speaking my language."

"I am going to make sure Ashby hurts as much as I do. I'm going to make him as crazy as I feel. I am going to wreck their world. The whole damn lot will burn because of me."

Landon turned away from the building. "Princess, whenever you are ready, you say the word and I'll get started."

She tipped the flask for another drink, capped it and slid it back into her pocket. "Word."

She walked back inside leaving Landon trying to hide a malicious smile. "Boonie man, you sure as hell picked a winner."

Sophie had to practically order them all to leave. She finally did the only thing which would make them think she was back to "normal", whatever in the world that was. She went to the barn and put Mojo through his paces. When she got back, she pulled Chase and Beau into Liam's home office. "What the hell am I supposed to do with the business, he signed contracts?"

They looked over the papers, Beau nudged his brother. "What about Jonathon? He said he was looking for something out of Miami Beach. He understands the business. He's trustworthy."

Chase sat, fingers tented at his chin as he considered it. "He would be my choice. Would you like me to call him Soph?" He flew in late that afternoon. If Chase said he was good, she knew he would make everything right if the man screwed up.

The next morning everyone except Sutton left. He looked confused as Sophie came out and grabbed a couple boxes of Ziploc bags, following her back to the bedroom was cause for concerned. "Sis, what are you doing?"

"Preserving his smell." She folded a dress shirt he had worn a day or two before `he died and tucked the dark blue button up into a bag which went inside another one. Sophie repeated the process until she was out of bags. Her fingers trailed over his other clothes, remembering when he wore a shirt or that he had bought the other one for vacation and which one was his favorite shirt, holes and all. "I can't believe he's gone." Her words were barely a whisper.

"If I could make this not be real babycakes, I would do so. Just to see you smile." Sutton pulled her close, holding her tight.

"I may never smile again." Madge sniffed her food and wandered away. Sophie understood perfectly. How many strings were pulled, she had no idea; not a week later the funeral home called. They were sending a runner out with Liam's ashes. She spent the next few hours writing notes to go with vials for some of his closest friends. Two days later, the crew from the Frog, Gordon, Landon, and Sutton accompanied Sophie and Madge to the cemetery. Per his wishes, he was buried next to his dad. Getting Madge to leave took some doing.

Landon managed a minute with Sutton, "She looks rough."

"Sophie or the dog?"

"Both. Are either of them eating?"

"The dog will, if Sophie spoon feeds her. Sis, a bite or two at best."

"I wish you could have seen them together. She was his world. Her and Madge. He was all in from the first time he laid eyes on Sophie." He chuckled, "First night I met her, I called her Sophia and she let me know in no uncertain terms her name was not Sophia...he laughed. Liam met his match and to be honest, I was a bit jealous. God, how I loved watching her twist the macho man around her little finger." He glanced back at Sutton and shrugged, "I'm a sick bitch though."

Landon wandered away, rubbing the silver vial of Liam's remains. Sutton tried the next morning before he left. "I can cancel the car, miss the flight, get a truck and move you home babycakes, just say the word."

She sniffled and hugged him again, "I have things I have to do. Maybe for the picnic. No promises."

Her brother was no sooner gone than the lawyer called. "Hello, Mr.Keene."

"Miss O'Hara, I have heard from Ashby's attorneys. They are demanding you retract the statement in the obituary."

"Really? They will love the next move. Tell them I do not take orders." She hung up and turned to Madge. "They wanted to destroy someone, let mama show 'em how it's done." She filled the silver flask with his dad's initials on the front. Boonie carried the keepsake until he almost lost it. Sophie slid it into her back pocket and walked out to the desk, spun the chair around and dropped onto the buttery leather . A business card sat there. Mad Tatters Ink Emporium, they planned on matching tattoos. She remembered something about the artist being a school chum of his. "Later. First things first. Time to release the beast." Sophie emailed The Daily, Ashby's hometown paper. "Enclosed is the video of Bennett Ashby III running down Mr. Liam Boone, the act led to his untimely demise. As his sole heir, I give you permission to use all or part of said video. It backs up my statement on Mr. Boone's obituary." She looked at her feet, Madge's head tilted. "Round one. Goes to me."

Her next call was to schedule her tattoo appointment with Dean at Mad Tatters, the third was to Landon. Sophie had no idea what he did for a living, but she would bet it was slightly shady. Everything she dug up on him led that way. At four pm Landon pulled in, his baby blue Lexus backed up her theory. He was a rich boy wannabe. "Get a drink, you may need one." As he meandered that way, she turned on the jammer Cherie brought her. "This will be your only chance to run and hide."

"Your plans won't scare me. I promise." Sweet Sophie", that's what Liam tagged her with, Landon couldn't see her being vicious."

"I want to drain his bank accounts, payoff a guard, scare the bejesus out of ABIII, ruin ABII until he either ends it all or I run him over, preferably with his son's car."

Landon was starting to wonder if he had been wrong in his assessment. "I love it."

"How do I know you can do this?"

"I do computer forensics. I know what the law would look for and how to really make it go away."

"Fair enough" She sipped from the flask, "Game on. Full court press." Sophie saw him out, locked the doors and turned on the TV. Her video was all over the news. They blurred an up-close view of Liam going into the ambulance, but it would never be blurred in her memories. It was clearly Bennett Ashby behind the wheel. As the reporter came on air, she said South Carolina issued a warrant for Candidate Ashby's phone records. Sophie's brow rose as she looked at Madge, "Hmm, I wonder why? Mom needs a drink." She downed six more before falling asleep on the sofa.

DAYS WERE EASIER, PLACES were open, she could distract herself. Life happened during the day. Nights were lonely and hard, noises seemed different. Liam started to install an alarm system, Sutton finished the job. It turned on at dusk and she turned it off in the morning. Her life was forever changed; she no longer found joy in anything. Sophie had days where she got by with a couple hits from the flask, and days where she crawled in the bottle and swam laps. Madge would drag her out several times a day, but other than Landon, no one was there for her.

Jonathan had two meetings with her, both times he was sure he smelled alcohol on her breath. Duty-bound, he called Chase to fill him in, who relayed the message to Sutton.

Landon sent a text to Sophie, "*Frog @ 6*" the reply was a thumbs up. She pulled up in Liam's truck, it would always be that to her. With Madge on her leash, she exited the cab, meeting her co-conspirator on the patio. "Hello Princess," a mojito waited on her. He spun a tablet around, it showed Ashby II's bank account balance. "I had to do it in three batches. First one went to Switzerland, second to the islands and the third is going to Thailand. They'll move through twenty or so financial institutions before reuniting in Iceland. There's an LLC connected to it. "What's next?"

"Check your email. There is a picture of a kid from someplace in South America, kid was brought into a clinic with burns. The camera shot is tight on the face, the rest is fuzzy, it has to look like the elder Ashby was doing the kid...and any others you can find. I need them to be bulletproof. Social media will fry him. And we need dummy accounts." "I'm on it, Princess." As he sauntered away, his tiny doubts turned into full-fledged worry that maybe she was more than he banked on.

Lara, a coach, met Sophie at Mad Tatters. Sophie called the best artist she knew...her sister. A rose with a compass peeking from under the petals, the stem on the rose turned into the last thing she saw; Liam's heartbeat on the monitor before it went flat with his name and dates. Dean looked at the drawing, "Damn, someone is fantastic."

"My sister, Charlotte O'Hara, aka Charlie-O in the art realm."

His head came up. "Wow. So don't fuck this up." Within the hour she was in the chair.

Dean told stories of when they were kids. "He had some major dental surgery done, his jaw had been broken. Well, they got him home and we were sitting out back and his head turns darn near upside down and he points and says "Mokie." Well, me and Landon both thought he was still high from the meds...nope. He was trying to say monkey. There was a monkey in the tree. It escaped from its owner and had been all over the news. So for years afterward we called him Mokie." He ducked his head, "Funny, I expected him to stroll in and threaten to kick my ass for telling you. I can't wrap my head around this whole thing."

By midnight they cried and laughed a dozen times. Dean made one change in the background of the tattoo, he added a world map. "You were his world." Lara dragged her over to the Frog, Smitty brought her out a favorite sandwich and a pile of fries in hopes she would eat. Instead, she picked and fed most of the fries to Madge. That proved to be a bad idea, she exited the vehicle and brought them back up with all the sound effects a dog could manage. Watching TV that night, Sophie had an idea. She made notes, there was no way she was calling Landon at that hour.

A message popped up on her phone at midnight. "Don't read the news." Deciding that was an invitation, she scrolled through several releases with her and Liam as hashtags. "The family of Bennett Ashby III has petitioned the court to release him on bond so he can attend the birth of his child. His fiancée, Ashley Roberts, is due in late March." Sophie dialed Landon's number, groggy, but with it enough to recognize her number, he answered. The not calling because it was late, did not matter at that exact moment. "Yes Princess."

"I want her dead, or the kid, or both"

"Her?" "Ashby had a fiancée."

"Isn't that has a fiancée?"

"Not when I'm done with her." Sophie hung up. "Cat's gonna make the mouse wish he was dead."

6

In the morning, she was in Landon's office, large black coffee in hand. "Good morning Princess. " Her brow rose in question. "Ashley Roberts, Corinth family, old money but the fam is not happy with her choice of bad boy. They set her up, she lives in a townhouse, end unit. She went out to get in her car this morning and was snatched." The edge of Sophie's lip curled up. "Sergeant John Michaels is deep in debt, sick kid. We had a talk yesterday as he was leaving the hospital. Two hundred fifty thousand reasons to help us, broken down into five payments. One upfront. Another quarter mill went to a broke-ass CIA goddess with a penchant for the ponies. She needed all she lost back in the bank and the house payments up to date before hubby comes back from deployment. She has some interesting techie things no one is supposed to know about." Landon dug in his desk, calmly he set a folder on the blotter and flipped it open. "Took half the night, but these are ready to go. Accounts for sending anything else is in my server where it is well hidden. They'll be out in time for the noon news in twenty-six major outlets."

In the folder she found rather disgusting photos of Ashby and several children. They made him look so bad, any denial would fall flat.

"And where is the bitch?"

"Safe." He wouldn't guarantee she would stay that way if Sophie got her.

"You have the audio files ready?"

"I do. Tonight they be entertained by a double blast."

Sophie rose, "Excellent. Don't blow it." She was off to the barn. Madge was content to lay on the couch in the barn office. Mojo wasn't a total lunkhead, he seemed to sense she was off. From there she made a run to the feed store. Ted came out to hug her. She ordered horse feed and treats, got Madge's food and headed out. Force of habit almost made her turn the wrong way which would have sent her back to her old apartment. The idea rattled her.

Madge knew where their next stop would be, every other day, they stopped at the cemetery. Liam's four-legged friend sniffed all over the plat, his smell dissipated. She laid on the tufts of new grass with her nose to his brass plate. In a week the stone would be delivered. That epitomized gut-wrenching. Going through memories and things she, put Liam and Madge on one side standing next to his Harley and her and Liam smiling at each other in the clouds.

LANDON RAN A FINGER down Claire's cheek, "Okay Goddess of all things tech, what did you bring me?" Her eyes closed, she took a deep breath and exhaled slowly to steady her nerves as she opened the gym bag.

One by one her tools of the trade came out. "This little gem will attach to a tie clip, I put one together last night. You need to hide the clip into the man's stash." She handed over a vial with something the size of a pinhead and a tie clip. "Now, this one will attach to the rearview mirror or the back-up camera on a car. It will throw an image making it seem as if the victim is standing there." She placed a small metal container on the desk. "A little more advanced, from the office across the street, this will beam a projected image into Ashby's office, which has been bugged already."

Landon smiled; his hands together like he might clap with glee. "I love techie toys."

"These go to Ashby's cell and your inside man. They have labels." She turned away from him. "We have a deal."

"We do." He moved to his desk and the computer waiting on him. Clicking away at the keys, he nodded as he worked to untangle the funds promised her. "There you go, house payments are up to date. And, here's half of what the ponies ran off with. You really need to give that up."

"You said all of it." Claire spun, looking distraught.

"Aww, Claire, baby. Don't worry. I have it and as soon as I know they work, more money will filter into the accounts." He was still tapping at the keyboard. His brows meshed. His tried again with the same result.

Claire looked behind him, in the glass she saw Landon trying to access Liam Boone's accounts. One by one, he was blocked. His screen went black and then a screaming clown came speeding to the forefront as if it was able to hold on to the screen and laughed at him. "Problem? Your brows look like a pug I had as a kid."

"No, no problems. I'll call you." Claire understood. She had been dismissed. More importantly, he got outsmarted. Landon Rowley was at the top of the game, she only knew a few who could outdo him and they were all part of the company...unless they acquired a new player. Claire hustled back to her domain, where she could try to piece together who made a monkey out of Landon.

"OKAY GIRLIE, HE TRIED and failed, right now he's running scared from the looks of his mug."

"Excellent. Thank you Ace." Sophie leaned back letting the sun sweat out yesterday's booze.

"Not a problem. I'll check in with you in a couple of days." A balloon popped on the screen as he pulled out of the conversation.

"Child you are in deep with him." Rubbing his chin, he contemplated the next move. "What the hell did he have on Claire? Not that I'd trust her." He listened to sound of his sister-in-law's tires crunch on the gravel of his driveway and shut everything down. When they came in the only thing on the computer screen was commodity prices.

Bennett Ashby lay on his cot in a six by six cell. His dad came to visit him earlier. There was a fondness for the woman he took up with after Sophie screwed up his year at College. It was the baby he most wanted. While he could lay all matter of lies at Sophie's feet, he didn't see her as a kidnapper. He didn't have money of his own, not until his father died so they couldn't expect him to pay a ransom.

"Ass baby" Bennett startled, looking around. He had only been called that once, and it was by Liam Boone. "Psst, ass baby, ya hear me, ass baby?" Ashby was out of his rack and looking all through his cell. "Aww, poor ass baby. He's going to rot in jail. See what happens? You get stuck in a tiny cell. Teeny, tiny, cell. Are the walls closing in?" Bennett threw his blankets off his bed as he ransacked the small cell. He flipped his mattress off the wall-mounted bed and tossed the chair, bouncing the plastic seat off the bars, Sgt. Michaels stepped up to the door. "Settle down Ashby."

He was frantic, searching and tossing things as he went. "Don't you hear it? How do you not...? You. Have. To." He was pleading by then.

Sgt. Michaels squeezed his tie clip, the voice stopped as other officers came to check on the situation. "Rich boy is hearing voices." They laughed as they wandered off. Sgt. Michaels spent the rest of the night kicked back in a chair where he was well within range to drive his prisoner to the brink of insanity. "Psst, hey Ashby, where's your girl?" He came out of the rack screaming her name. "Is she dead because of you?" By morning, Ashby was in a heap on the floor, sobbing for someone to make the voices stop.

CLAIRE CAME INTO THE Ashby estate with a maid service van, at the end of the day the house was set to start the second part of the plan. She lugged her gear out with a vacuum cleaner. At seven pm Bennett senior came in, his wife came out with a roasted chicken, a bottle of wine sat on the table. As she sat down, she sniffed the air. "Did you change aftershave or cologne?"

"No. why..." he sniffed, "Does the room feel cold to you?" He got up sniffing his way around the table before going from room to room. As he reached his study, he heard voices and threw open the door. Ashby II stood dumbstruck at seeing ghostly visions of Liam and Sophie dancing, her hand at the back of his neck, they turned and waved. He charged into the room as they faded away to nothing."

"Bennett, dinner is getting cold." He felt the walls and waved his hands over anything he thought could be the culprit before turning and walking back to the dining room. He looked over his shoulder a half dozen times during the meal. Later, as he sat in his study going over campaign notes he felt a cold whisper of a breeze across his back. Way earlier than normal, he headed off to bed. "Stress, my mind is all jumbled." His wife nodded and curled into her side of their king-sized bed. In the morning he drank a cup of coffee and made some notes. "Don't forget the dry cleaning, I'll be gone three nights next week."

"Where will you be this time?" She was fast growing tired of being alone.

"Charleston. Damn lawyers can't do anything halfway right unless I'm there." Ten minutes after he left, she was in the kitchen when she heard tires squealing on pavement and a horrific thump. Her coffee cup hit the floor and shattered.

A MEAL SLID UNDER THE door for Ashley. "Eat, no one wants to harm you or junior." She could tell she was on a boat from the rocking. The windows had been blackened so she had no idea where she was. Screaming for hours the days before left her with a sore throat. Scrambled eggs, bacon, toast, an orange and a glass of milk, it didn't smell bad. She went to the door and beat on it. "Could I have some ketchup for my eggs...please." A few seconds later two packages slid under the door. "Thank you." They, whoever they were, were taking care to feed her. She had a fan and blankets, a flat of bottled water and on a precise schedule, food was brought to her. For now, her logical side went with, she had no choice but to keep up her strength up. The next morning, there was ketchup on the tray.

SOPHIE TRIED TO GET on her feet twice before making it, staggering to the shower took everything she had. Ashby's trial had been moved up. She sat front row center behind the State Attorney whether it was a bond hearing or some new motion Ashby's lawyers tried to use. Always dressed in black, always calm no matter what was suggested. After she left, it was a different story. More often than not she ended up on a barstool at the frog.

Over the month, Sgt. Michaels ramped up on how often his prisoner heard voices until one day in court his mother broke with protocol and turned on Sophie. "This is your fault! If you had just gone out with him he wouldn't have hounded you. You became his obsession on purpose. Look at you, dressed in black like some witch."

Sophie was on her feet and had a handful of the woman's dress, she hauled her up so they were nose to nose. "Black has long been the color of mourning. I am deeply into that because your son killed my love, my life, my fiancé and left gaping holes in my heart. If you taught your little beast that not everyone will like him, any of the thirty-seven times I said no should have been a clue. He Lied. It came back on him. I transferred schools to be away from him so do not blame your lack of parenting skills on me you cheap wench." She let go with a shove that put the older woman on her backside on the floor.

Sophie left surrounded by her legal team with cameras in her face and questions being thrown at her.

Ashby and his legal team held court on the steps. "Half of her family died, we wonder what she had to do with that. We will be filing assault charges also. Keene beat them to the judge and got a restraining order. Mrs. Ashby was effectively banned from being in the courthouse if Sophie was there.

The voices invaded all areas of the Ashby home, at odd hours with chilly breezes and thermostats resetting on their own. A microwave turned on with nothing in it. The refrigerator held spoiled food even though it was still cold. Dead animals appeared in the yard. Mrs. Ashby ran screaming into the yard one morning, butcher knife in hand to cut down a partially burned scarecrow with a photo of Ashby III tacked to the head which had been hung in effigy. News crews filmed as she held it close and screamed Sophie was behind it, she was torturing them. Keene slapped the family with a libel suit before noon.

Claire was in and out on a weekly basis, after one visit the odor of sulfur seeped through the house with their son's voice coming at them, "I'll kill you both!" It was the last threat he had made to Sophie and Liam.

Ashby II began finding more reasons to go see his mistress. A video of their lip lock went out across the media. Combined with Bennett's voice yelling he hated her, his mother took to the wine bottle.

"There's more." Her words slurred to where it sounded more like 'derrsh moor', she struggled with the cork, falling against the stove and bumping the knob. She staggered out and on to her room. She finished off the glass as she watched the video over and over as she refilled the glass. Close to midnight, she went to the hall to set the alarm. Neighbors said the blast rattled their houses and blew out windows. Firefighters found Mrs. Ashby in the yard, severely injured. It was a member of the press who went to the mistress's apartment to break the news to the senior Ashby.

Sgt. Michaels turned the news on, watching the younger man collapse to the floor as he shrieked "Mom" repeatedly.

STATE POLICE PULLED in at the barn, Sophie's vehicle was parked cock-eyed. They verified the license plate and then walked into the barn. She was swilling Gator-Ade and brushing Mojo. Madge still didn't trust the beast, but she stayed close to his stall. "Miss O'Hara." Her eyes were bloodshot and she looked like hell.

"Yeah."

"We need to ask you some questions." Several minutes of silence elapsed as she waited.

"Are you going to ask or should I attempt to read your mind?"

He scuffed his toe against the dirt floor, "Where were you last night?"

"From seven-ish to right after midnight I was at the Flaming Frog, drinking away my woes." She chucked the empty bottle at a trash can and missed. Madge retrieved it and dropped the bottle into the can.

"We'll need to verify that."

"Knock your ass out, and tell Smitty thanks for calling an Uber for me." She brushed by the cop, patted her leg, and walked out with Madge. "Wonder why? Maybe I should get sober for a few days huh?"

JONATHON WENT OVER Liam's plans for the next few jobs, meticulous was the word he found himself using most often. In the margins, he would find notes, call Soph about the gala, check her schedule for two weekends from the 21st, remember to send flowers. He definitely had the woman on the brain. In a way, it reminded him of Chase. There was always notes around the office and they had to do with Charlie. One was to the point and hit home. Life is too short to be a numbers game. One is only given a few years. He pulled his phone out of his pocket and scrolled until he found the number for Olivia Fleming. Suddenly he was nervous, their only date and ended in near disaster for Charlie.

"hello"

"Olivia?"

"Yes"

"It's Jonathon Devilliers. I was wondering, if I could promise a much more mundane date, would you consider going to dinner with me Friday?" He ran a finger under his collar. "I'm in Charleston this weekend; spending an absolutely wonderful day picking out dresses on Saturday for a friend's wedding ...sounds perfectly annoying."

He chuckled at the summation. "As it happens, that's where I am."

"Well, in that case, Friday night?"

"Excellent, text me where to pick you up, and I really owe you one so dress to impress."

"Okay. See you on Friday." He sat there holding the phone for a few minutes. What he learned of Liam led him to believe the man wasn't prone to acts of stupidity. For far too long he worried about what the world thought. Sophie asked him if he was dating, when he said no, she told him to find someone and love them like you are the only two people on earth. Maybe it was time for a new perspective. He flipped the office TV on, Liam had been a sports fan, in the process of scrolling the breaking news banners jumped out at him. Front and center was a shot of Sophie leaving court from a couple weeks prior. Turning up the volume as he leaned forward, a live shot of the Ashby family home came on screen. "Oh hell. Please tell me you had nothing to do with it."

"I didn't" Jonathon jumped, nearly tripped over the chair, he held a hand to his chest. "But I won't say I was broken-hearted."

"You look like hell."

Sophie sipped her coffee. "Thank you. Feel like hell too." She sat down, sipping some more coffee. "I got the message, what do you need signed?" he flipped a checkbook around. With shaking hands, she signed for what seemed like forever. "Oh, it came in yesterday." She handed him a credit card for the company with his name on it. "You sir, are a godsend. I have no idea what Liam did on a day to day basis. The big picture, sure." Looking out the window and fighting tears, "I always figured we'd have plenty of time. I was all about showing my horse and maybe making the Olympic team. Seems so silly now."

"No, it doesn't Sophie. It was life at the moment. I also took the advice of both of you. I have a date on Friday."

"About time. Now, Madge and I need to go to the store and get her food. Take care." She held the edge of the desk as she stood. He had to give her credit for trying to appear normal, but, he also knew he would be making another call to Chase. "Oh, are you and Craig getting along okay?"

"Yes, Liam's remarks were right on target." She nodded and left.

LANDON'S HAND SLAPPED down on the desk. "Bloody damn hell. She better not have been involved in this." He backed up the video of the Ashby house explosion pulled from a dashcam of a passing car for hire. "One more funny little co-inky-dink... like some clown blocking me from Boonie's accounts. Literally." His bank of computer screens held his attention. Landon checked his watch and then leaned in closer. A mantle clock held his undivided attention. "Son of a bitch." A paperweight sailed across the room, crashing into the wall. "Oh Princess, you are so not what you seem." He typed in the URL for the bank he stashed the Ashby funds in. It was empty. Jaw hanging, he stared at the screen for a solid five minutes trying to figure out where it went. His next move was a deep dive into the dark web. "Oh little Princess and her pony, you are messing with the wrong villain. I'll have to teach you a lesson."

SITTING BACK AT HIS desk, Ace chuckled as he monitored Landon's search. "Silly boy. You don't even have a clue." Swiveling in his chair he followed along as Landon hit panic mode. One keystroke followed by a smile, "Three, two, one...let the games begin." His phone rang, the number appeared to be local, then it registered. Sophie. "Hello."

"Hey, I need info and I have to trust you won't go screaming back to my sister."

"Okay." The question hung in his tone.

"Went to court today, I sat where I usually do, but the only ones there were the prosecution, defense, me and the jerk. I overheard him say his hands were bothering him, he asked the judge for permission to have someone bring him gloves. His attorney had statements and records going back to his elementary school days..."

"Sounds like it was fairly serious." His brain hit overdrive.

"Right, but if it was that bad, could he have pulled a trigger? There was no bump stock found on the gun used. It's hot and humid here, if it bothers him so much, I mean I know he killed Liam, but maybe he didn't do the shooting and if that's the case—who did?"

"Did you bring this up to the attorney?"

"No, not to either."

He caught the tink of ice landing in a glass and the squeak of a corked bottle. "Are you in for the night?"

"Yep, huge storm brewing. Madge and I are going to camp out on the couch." Feeling as if he knew, "I also do not plan on using the stove for anything. I grabbed a pizza on the way home and I've been to the barn."

"Okay, lock up and let me go dig some. I know some people who might know."

"Thanks." He had a feeling her instincts were spot on.

"Now to do some research. These ducks may be quacking like crazy, but they aren't close to being in a row." Glancing at the clock, he dug in. He only had a few hours before reality came to call.

Sophie went to the bedroom, in the bottom drawer was a small lockbox. She opened it and pulled out Liam's gun. "Thank you babe. You made sure I had the tools to stay out of the fool's grasp." Sliding the clip in and checking to see how stiff the safety was, she went back to the couch. "Come on Madge." The dog and her duck climbed up to snuggle in with her human.

LANDON NEARLY DESTROYED his office, files had been dumped and tossed as he tore through pages and pages of information he had on Liam and Sophie. A late afternoon phone call from a financial reporter sent him over the edge. Someone bought out the majority of his stockholders. If he couldn't get the shares back from Liam's estate, he could easily be put out of business. All he had to do was find out who was behind DUWYK LLC. Sunset had come and gone and the morning was fast approaching when he finally fell over in exhaustion. Ace chuckled, he had watched the show from Landon's own computer bank. "Don't you wish you had a clue, or DUWYK, silly geek. Not as smart as you think you are."

DIALING HER NUMBER by memory, he waited in the dark. "Mmm. Cowboy, what's wrong."

"I need your professional skills, Claire has gone sideways. It puts a family member at risk."

"I read. That poor girl. I can be there in a few hours."

"Consider it a clean-up op."

"Gotcha. See ya later love."

"Lily,"

"Yeah?"

"Be careful."

"Oh cowboy...you just wait."

At eight a.m he got a text saying she was there and setting up. "That's my girl." He flopped over and turned off his alarm. "Sometimes being your own boss is a good thing." Bare feet slapping against the floor popped that bubble. Groaning, he crawled out of bed. "Stay out of the fridge, I'm coming to get you breakfast."

LILY SET UP SHOP IN a hotel in the city center, files already came in via email. She had to hand it to her cowboy, he was organized. "How did he ever get mixed up with the Beldman's?" she chewed on the end of a pen. "Poor Liam, lost his dad so young." Sipping her coffee, she read on. "Hmm, interesting. Mom and sister both somehow got addicted to opiates. Dr. Orphet, wonder how he found that out...I bet he's been playing in computer-land again. Let's check out the NPI number." Tapping of keys mixed with sounds from outside. "Six floors and this is a high rise building. Sometimes, smaller towns have it together." Lily sat up, grabbed her phone and dialed. "Hey Cowboy, I'm off to the county seat. If I'm right...we have a major oh shit situation. Call ya later.

Noah strolled out of Mrs.Peatree's, munching on some fresh caramel corn, he set off for the hardware store, enjoying the sunshine. Logan pulled up next to him. "Hey bud, how're things?"

"Going good. I got the inside of the treehouse done. I gutted the old travel trailer and I have it close to being redone...again."

"Fantastic news." He turned his head toward the radio and groaned. "Looks like I'm going to go play traffic cop for cows." Noah enjoyed the laugh as he walked on. At the hardware store, he picked out the screws needed and got a roll of screen, paid and sauntered off to his truck. Last week he added a chicken house and six hens, it felt good to see progress. People looked at him differently. Like, he was a real human instead of just a drunk hellion. Some nights still got him, he'd wake in a cold sweat, shaking, back in the heat of battle. Often, he would end up in the yard pounding nails into a board. Last winter proved the welds would hold, to the chagrin of many in town.

Looking around, he decided the yard needed a better landscaped area around the wet spot. Nothing super drastic, but some color was a good thing. Country music blared out of speakers mounted under the treehouse as Noah checked off boxes on his to-do list. He was a day behind, having spent the day before running over to Sutton

O'Hara's place to do critter checks. He was sad to hear Gilly was in the hospital with pregnancy problems. Especially when he knew several women popping out babies like tic-tacs and had no time or money for them. He had a long discussion with a cat on the subject. Fluffy offered no words of wisdom on the subject, and a bad case of mouse breath. Noah grabbed a can of neon orange paint and marked off where he wanted the plants. Smiling, he set to digging. "Yes sir, going to be nice when I'm done." At six he fired up the grill and tossed a couple of burgers on it. "Yep. It's been a great day." He went about building his infamous Garbage Burger. Two thin beef patties, two slices of cheddar cheese, bacon, lettuce, tomato, pickles and an onion ring topped with pepper jack cheese and a fried patty of macaroni and cheese. "Mmmm, ding-ding, dinner is ready."

Solar lights lit the yard area as the sunset. He leaned back in the lawn chair he made, he recieved an email from a place in Florida, scrolling through on his phone he found out they were opening a seaside retreat for vets and wanted to know if he would be interested in making a pair of chairs for an auction to raise funds. Someone shared photos of his work. He stopped reading there as he thought on who would have done that. He finally decided on his kid sister. As it happened, he had made an odd number and could spare two and still have three left. He emailed back if they had a pick-up person, they could do this. Noah sat back rubbing his belly with a beer in hand. He hadn't mentioned to his family he stopped and bought a six-pack along with groceries on his latest supply run. Listening to his parents or brothers whine he was heading for a life of alcohol abuse was enough to drive him that way. It wouldn't matter to them that it was the second one in as many weeks.

He started a list of supplies to spruce up his pond. Resorting to online for the new liner took most of the night to find one in blue. Stretching and scratching, he packed his laptop and phone up the stairs into the treehouse. Thunder rolled as lightning zig-zagged across the sky. Noah sat up to watch the light show for a few minutes before curling back into bed. "Mother nature is throwing a fit over something." Talking to himself was getting to be old, but there was a shortage of women in town.

His brother joked about finding him a mail-order bride, but in general, Trent didn't give him too much crap for fear it would come back and land at his feet. All eyes were on the Driscoll's now that the Monroe's were all spoken for, except Jesse and widowers were given some slack.

7

"Yeah Jonathon, thanks. We're trying to keep an eye on her without intruding but it seems the roller coaster of grief is getting steeper and deeper." He spied his wife staring out over the mountains, "Yeah bud, take care." Chase hung up, his face in his hands as he tried to find an argument they could use to make her come back. Without the threat of having her put under psychiatric care, they were out of options. The last thing he wanted was to have her put in the system in another state and not be able to get her back or to have her sever ties with them. Charlie understood where her sister's heart and mind were. If anything ever happened to Chase or their son, she couldn't say she wouldn't be in the same place mentally. If they gave her time, she would come around, Sophie could be a bit headstrong, a family trait. She needed to decide to make a move to put herself back on track...if they tried to push her, she would dig in deep and that was one war she didn't want.

She sat in front of Chase. "Let it go." Her hand went up, "I know, you want to "fix" her, the situation, and she has to do this on her own. As much as I hurt thinking I would never be your wife...you were still here. She doesn't have anyone. In no uncertain terms, her future, her world shattered. The man she loves still, she does with her heart and soul, every beat of her heart, every blink of her eye and we can't make a dead man live. I called her today," He stroked her cheek, after all their years, he felt her pain. "I made her promise to not drive drunk and used the dog to guilt-trip her." She pushed her hair back, "If they would quit jerking the court dates around, she might come home."

Chase sat with his thoughts, losing his mom at a young age led to reoccurring bouts of anger, grief, depression, he remembered it all too well. Cort had it the worst of the four boys. It took finding love with Rayna for him to move past the mental scars. Sophie was like his flesh and blood kid sister. If there was some way be sure. With luck, he thought Rayna might be able to offer some insights. He pulled the horseshoe off his desk and grabbed his keys. Chase stopped to kiss his wife and son and took off. The five-minute drive to his brother's home seemed like five hours.

Rayna dried her hands, looked up, her head tipped and then she jogged for the door and the driveway. "Hey Chase" she hugged and stepped back.

"Oh wow, what is it?"

"I need your insight. Sophie. I'm getting phone calls saying she's heavy into the booze and light on food, I lived..." his head shook, "I need to know if waiting her out is right."

"I can but try. No promises."

Chase pulled out the horseshoe. "She gave us this to hang over lil one's door."

Rayna took it, cold steel. Maybe. "I'll call or text if I get something." She kissed his cheek, "Now go home and make him a playmate, a cohort in crime."

He smiled, hiding his personal suspicions that she was not having an easy time conceiving, from the offhand things his brother said. "Thanks Ray." He drove off letting her contemplate the request.

Direct family was one thing. But this would be a stretch. Snapping her fingers she ran back inside and grabbed her phone, she dialed Sophie. "'Lo"

"Hey sugar, I got a quick question, the stuff you used for the pooch when she got sprayed, do you remember the name?"

"No, but the bottle is in the bathroom, hold on. Did one of yours get hurt?"

"No baby, I'm putting together a booklet of what to do if type situations."

"We could have used one of those. Here it is, I'm taking a picture and sending it to you."

"Thanks...Sophie, take whatever time you need to grieve. Don't you dare let anyone tell you what is right or wrong, Okay?"

"I'm alright today, yesterday was all over and tomorrow is a question mark. But, thank you. It means the world to me."

"You're welcome. Goodnight Soph." Rayna held the horseshoe, "maybe later." Two a.m. and Rayna padded out to the stock tank Cort installed.

"Hold up moon goddess." Hearing her giggle after the last few months was melodic. Naked and sliding into the makeshift pool had his motor running. "Damn woman, if I pass out, you have to save me from drowning."

"Brrr, water is cold, come hold me." Her request wasn't a problem. Sitting under the stars as she processed whatever his brother asked for was relaxing. She shifted and floated on her back staring at the full moon. In a flash she was on her feet, opening and closing her mouth like a fish in need of water. Sinking back into the pool, Rayna laughed until she had to wipe her eyes. "Is that a good laugh or a bad laugh but one you find amusing?"

"Maybe both." She wrapped her arms around her husband. "Do me. Out here. Right now."

He eyed the decking. "The super deluxe package or a quickie?"

"The my credit card would melt package."

"Wow. Okay." Whatever answer she sought, the moon improved her mood and Cort was not the kind of man to overlook a gift like her. In the morning, one of the ranch hands ran an oversized envelope over to Chase. Inside, she tucked the horseshoe and a note.

"Buckle up and hold on. This going to be a rocky road but in the end...happiness wins. As long as y'all can stay out of the way." Chase inhaled deeply and slowly released it. Wait and staying out of things was not his mainstay.

CLAIRE DROVE LIKE A madman cutting through traffic until she got to Landon's office building. "Rowley!" She kicked the door to his inner sanctum in, he laid splayed out on the floor. "Where the hell is the rest of the money? My husband will be home in forty-eight hours. You said it would be there." She hauled him off the floor, shaking him like a dog with a toy. "One way or the other or I swear to everything holy, tomorrow morning you will be a dead man if the money isn't there." For an instant, she saw fear in his eyes. "What happened?"

"Somehow, Princess stole the money from the king of thieves. " She sat down on his desk. "I know it was her."

Her laughter was bitter and worried Landon more than he hoped he let on. "A drunken, grieving, co-ed has outdone the master of thievery?" she strolled around the office, laughing until she stopped next to him. "Find a way, if it has to come out of your own funds or else." She turned and stalked past him, slamming the door as she left.

Lily watched Claire leave; she looked as irritated as when she entered the complex. "Hmm, someone didn't get what she wanted." Ten minutes later a ragged Landon Rowley exited the building. He ran several blocks to a bank and returned thirty minutes after that, looking only slightly at ease. "Well, well, Mr. Rowley. I wonder if your mama knows what you're up to." She sipped from a burger place soda leaving a rum raisin lipstick ring on the straw. "Oh yeah, you had her committed. Sweet child." She waited another twenty minutes, employees filtered out, most stared intently at their phones as they escaped. Landon staggered out, stopping to lock the doors before he made his way to his car. "Patience always pays off, that's what mama said. God rest her soul." Lily strolled along until she was under the recessed entry to Landon's office. She hobbled to the door, holding on to the wide vertical handle as she emptied something from her shoe. It was all a ruse she used to stick a magnetized disk in the bend of the door pull. With her foot back in her shoe, she walked on to the rental car, smile in place and greeting folks as she went. One more email and then she would need to call her cowboy to find out how he wanted to handle the situation. "Of all the jerks I have dealt with, this guy is the jerkiest jerk.

Sophie shook from pure rage, but she kept her mouth shut. The judge agreed to bond. Bennett Ashby III was alone except for the lawyers. His father was trying to salvage his reputation by staying close to his wife in the hospital. She had to admit, he looked like hell, probably worse than she did. Bennett asked about his fiancée repeatedly. Ashley was one more loose end to tie up. Find out what the hell Landon did with her. She stormed out, not waiting to hear anything else the judge or Ashby had to say.

A buxom blond leaned against Liam's truck, like most things, it would always be Liam's whatever. "Sophie O, Ace sent me." The statement took her back a bit.

"Okay."

"We need to talk. Is there someplace a little less conspicuous?"

"Meet me at the Flaming Frog, on their patio." Ace suggested he had friends that could help. He never said anything about sending them. How old was he? They played Solar Wheelz, but...her worst thought, Ace was a creepy old man living in his mom's basement. She whipped the big pickup into a spot and bailed. By the time she got to the door, it was all over the news. "Smitty, two racks of baby backs and two bloody Mary's please." She flipped him a credit card as she strode through to the patio. The blond followed close behind. They found a table in the shade, Smitty brought out drinks and offered his opinion on the judge. It was only a tinge better than hers.

"First things, tell me Ace isn't some dirty ol' man living in his mom's basement."

Lily laughed outright, "Lord no child. He's no kid, but he's not old and handsome as all get out." She reached a hand over the wrought iron table, "I'm Daisy" If it was a flower, she would answer. She always did. The food and a stack of napkins came out. "I like your style."

They tore into the ribs as Lily filled Sophie in. "It took a bit of excavating. The person you thought of as a friend, is the enemy in disguise. Landon Rowley was born Landon Thorpe. They, being him and his mama, moved to this area when he was in fourth grade. His father was Owen Thorpe, a hitman for Phineas Lang, a second rate wannabe mobster with a first-rate ego." Sophie felt chill bumps crawl along her skin. Liam's story of his father came to mind. "They relocated the next year; and moved back when he was in sixth grade. His parents got divorced. Mom took her name back and changed Landon's in seventh grade his father was killed for a botched job."

"Oh. My. God. He killed Liam's dad."

"You are quick, such a smart girl, no wonder Ace likes you so much." She sucked down part of the drink. Landon had his mother committed to Cooper Mills Sanatorium. His grandfather Thorpe was a doctor. He stole a batch of the old man's prescription pads and pretended to be his granddad. With his computer skills, he was able to change the ID number to match his doctor Orphet." She waited to see if Sophie would catch it. She did. Eyes wide open as she silently mouthed something that looked like an expletive to Lily. "He wrote all the prescriptions to Liam's mom and sister. Made sure they were hooked and then cut them loose." Lily slid a leather-bound, ragged looking, journal over to Sophie. "I...liberated this early yesterday morning. He's years into a love-hate relationship with Liam. At the moment he's running like a rat through a maze. I popped the front door locks remotely." Sophie got a visual of Landon running about with a rat tail and whiskers and smirked. "He removed some money from the accounts of a certain senatorial candidate. It was moved again. To Switzerland. Ace has the information for you. If you like, I can go sweep the house and make sure you and the dog are safe."

"Where do you work?"

"For the government. Ace too."

"Uh-huh. I have to go get Madgey from doggie daycare." Her phone buzzed with a message. *"Did my friend find you?"*

"Yes. So she's legit?"

"Def."

"Okay."

"Our favorite guy." 'Daisy smiled broadly. "I think if you'll follow me, I'm calling the cops and have them scope it out."

"That works." They finished their drinks and the last of the ribs, talking about nothing in particular. It was nice to not see pity in someone's eyes. Sophie caught the look on Smitty's face, sheer surprise in her leaving early and sober. With Madge in the truck, they headed for what was affectionately known as the marsh house. Force of habit had her checking out the yard and windows. A call to the cops was unnecessary; they rolled up right behind her in five cars including two from the state. Fighting to control her anger, Sophie sat on the swing with Madge next to her.

Lily walked to the end of the driveway to call her cohort. "Hey sexy, only got a minute. Cops are crawling the place, no clue what they are looking for. Your girl is about to go postal, she's called the attorney."

"Sounds like it is time to unleash the hell hounds. How did she take the news?"

Lily turned to look over her shoulder. "Not so good. She's liable to gut him."

"Not surprised. Keep me in the loop."

Walking back, Lily picked up on a bit of radio chatter. They were looking for a body. She whispered the news to Sophie.

Her head jerked up, her eyes narrowed. "Then they need to talk to Landon."

Sophie's comment set Lily back a step. "Do you think he may have killed someone?"

"Not any someone, Ashby's fiancée."

Lily's eyes bulged in shock. "No..." The word stretched out, "and here comes your legal beagle."

Keene came puffing up the drive, wiping sweat from his face with a handkerchief. He strode right on inside and came out with four cold bottles of water and Madge's bowl. "Stay out my ancient ass. It's hot and ladies need water...along with grumpy old men." He drained his bottle and then demanded to see the warrant and the one in charge.

Somewhere in the middle of the chaos and snapping of tempers, Sophie found herself ready to scream. So she did. Loud, long and to the point. "Shut Up! All of y'all." It was suddenly quiet. "Out, everyone. I can see straight through, no one needs to be checking out my underwear. I have pictures and I will file a complaint. Over and done. There is nothing here that you are searching for." Her next move was to call the police chief. He made the mistake of coming out to speak with her. Every last bit of pent up anger and disgust came out. Troopers stayed, mainly to safeguard the Chief. Sophie crammed her finger into his chest as she screamed, "If you had taken this shit with Ashby seriously, I would still have my fiancé, my world wouldn't have spun out of control and a good man would still be alive but you were too busy ass-kissing the rich dude to do your damn job."

Lily intervened and pulled her back, finally getting Sophie settled down by sidetracking her with Madge's welfare. She stayed with Sophie while the attorney had a field day with the press. He pointed out, loudly, that his client had nearly been killed and that her fiancé died. A productive member of their community and his loved one was treated as a criminal due to money and a criminal pointing a finger at her.

Once back in the car, she called her favorite cowboy. "This was a long day."

"How is she?"

"The term 'white knuckle' bring anything to mind?"

"Wonderful."

She filled him in on the tantrum, the attorney and the fact that the young lady used a jammer when she thought we were being spied on. "I had Decker sneak in and do a sweep, he found four bugs. He left two, two were used to determine who made them or issued the damn things. One was in their bedroom, makes me mad as hell."

"So, is Ace going to tell her or are you coming clean?"

"Ace."

She heard a ding in the background. "And I need to do it quick. Confirmation just came in on who owns an AR that I think is under the radar." Another five minutes and he was in game trying to make Sophie to answer. When option A failed, he went to text. She ignored that too. She was laser-focused on the journal taken from Landon's house. His writings over the years covered his rage at his mother for changing their surname to the loss of his father, which he blamed Liam for, to being jealous of the man he secretly despised yet admired.

Pages were neatly written on the women in Liam's life. One, in particular, made the hair on the back of her neck rise. Annalee Legare. Liam said he wondered what happened to her. She said she was going to the store and never made it. They found his truck on the side of the road, her wallet was there and the keys. The cops hounded him for months until the last polygraph test cleared him yet again. Annalee was the last serious relationship until she came along. Landon convinced his so-called friend that she ran off with some other guy. He swore he saw them in Myrtle Beach the same weekend. It became a sticking point for many in the area. She swore the District Attorney or Sheriff would make a public statement clearing Liam. Sophie ran the gamut of emotions. Madge tried to crawl into her person's lap and kiss away the tears. It would be hours later before she saw the text and sent one back. "*I know who, and I know who shot up the barn, killed my friend, broke the hearts of three other girls, scared the hell out of the others and I swear, sitting in jail for the rest of my life will be worth it. I will kill him.*" It was time to pull the plug. Seven hours to sun-up. He couldn't wait that long to call Sutton. This was a call he didn't relish.

SOPHIE TURNED ON THE news. Red and white letters heralded the breaking news. Mrs. Ashby died from injuries from the blast. She tipped Liam's flask to her lips, "Ding dong, the bitch is gone." She poked at the phone, entering Landon's number.

"Hello, Princess."

"You better make that Queen, because my next move puts you in checkmate."

Something in her tone made icy fingers run up his spine. "Whatever do you mean?" he really hated the road to the marina at night. He needed to concentrate and doing so was hard when you were being threatened.

"Which one first? How about Annalee being in your freezer? I see you're on the way to the marina. Is that where Ashby's girlfriend is, or her body? Why did you kill an innocent person at the stable? Are you that inept? I mean even a blind squirrel gets lucky now and then. You are in the police photos of the crime scene...do you know how common that is? All that you did and you are just...common. Mundane. And very soon, dead. I'm on my way and sitting in jail for life is worth watching you burn in hell Landon Thorpe."

BENNETT ASHBY II HAD everything and lost it. His party cut ties, his mistress walked away, he filed bankruptcy hoping the court would locate his money. When his wife was pronounced dead, he walked into the hall, pulled a gun, put it to his head and ended it all. Watching his father pull the trigger sent the younger Ashby racing out the door to his dad's car, heart racing he started the Mercedes and peeled out of the parking lot. Sobs wracked his body. Behind him, sirens blared. His foot laid heavily on the gas pedal.

Landon raced to the cove in a small boat. Liam's sailboat sat at anchor within view of the remains of the Ashby estate. He was in a panic. Running full out put him there in time to hear sirens when he killed the engine. He dashed below decks and grabbed a butcher knife from the magnetic strip on the galley wall. One swing and Ashley was free. "Get out, run for your life. Go. Go!" She wasted no time getting out of there. The water was only thigh deep, she made her way to shore in a minute or two.

Ashley heard the explosion but, had no idea what happened until she staggered out from behind an overgrown patch of bushes. She stood slack-jawed in the middle of the road looking at the devastation that had once been the Ashby home.

Headlights appeared out of nowhere, then the sound of squealing tires followed by her scream and a thump. Bennet bailed out of the car and ran to her side. "I'm so sorry, I'm so sorry, Don't die. Please" Police cruisers stopped, they faced all different directions as they ran up to him. She managed two sentences. One was Landon Rowley held her captive. The other was a simple. "I really do love you." One final gravely breath and she was gone. EMTs raced in trying to revive her and save the baby. Inside the wagon things went from action plus to silence. A cop came out, speaking into his shoulder radio for clarification, is a pregnant woman one or two homicides?

The straw that broke the camel's back. He screamed, primal, from the gut, maybe deeper. His voice was all raspy when he finally turned to the officer. "This is karma. I was supposed to kill Sophie. Landon paid me a million dollars, it's buried up there. I was supposed to run her over. But Boone moved too quick, I hit him instead. You ask Jared Stevens, hangs at the Frog. I told him. Landon threatened Ash then, If I didn't keep my word, she would die." Police were stunned, they let him ramble on for their body cams. "I loved Ashley. Landon said it was all Sophie's fault. Boone had not loved anyone and then she came along. If she didn't move I would have missed all of them. She tried to hold onto Liam. He threw her out of the way. I killed the wrong one and now everyone is gone." He sank to his knees. Gulping air as he sobbed out how sorry he was.

Sophie was at the marina with police when he motored in. They were crawling through his house with a hastily signed warrant. Police confiscated the gun used to kill Sara at the barn. Hard drives had been replaced, it got rid of some evidence, it would be up to Sophie what to do with them, but for the time being only she could say where they were. Landon was in cuffs when he turned to stare at her. "This is all your fault. If he didn't love you so much, you would be dead and not him."

Jared sat in the cell next to Landon. He overheard the cops talking. "Hello, Rowley. I was Boonie's friend. We're going to talk." That night, Landon used his own shirt to end his life. No trial, no answers. No exclamation point to the story. Jared was released early in the morning. When the officers pulled in to tell her before it played out on the news, she was outside with Madge. It was a good thing she wore sunglasses. The officer couldn't see the gleam of satisfaction in knowing Landon was dead. That afternoon the sheriff and city attorney along with several others held a news conference.

They cleared Liam Boone of Annalee Legare's murder with a public statement.

NOAH'S PHONE RANG TOO damn early for life to exist, not looking at it, he swiped the screen. "Yeah."

"Hey bud. I need a major favor."

"Sutton? Yeah bro, whatever it is."

His tale spilled out; "Sophie has been dragged out of the cemetery four or five times in the last two weeks, the bartender friend of Liam's said she's practically living in there and if I don't bring her home, I'm afraid we'll lose her too. I'd go but Gilly is back in the hospital, it doesn't look good and I'm scared shitless."

"Yeah man, I need to throw some stuff in a bag and clean out the truck." "Chase said he'd fly you out and his buddy, Jonathon will pick you up. I'll set up stops for you so the horse has a place to rest."

"Sounds good bro." He heard a car pull up outside his fence. Noah scrambled through his treehouse, gathering what he needed. "Hot as hell, shorts, socks, jeans, t-shirts, toothbrush and paste, deodorant, I'm dressed, hairbrush, feet in boots, keys, phone, charger, think I got it all." He charged out the door, stopping to lock it to keep his nosy family out.

Rayna picked him up and set out for the airstrip. "She's hurting. This has reopened all the old wounds." She blurted out what she could in the ten miles to their puny airport. "Charlie told me this morning. She's in a panic, between this and Gilly."

Jonathon took him out to the marsh house. "She packed some stuff to send home. I made arrangements to rent the other house. It's closer to town. Bigger." He glanced into the rearview. "I think she's trying to drink herself to death. I drove her home yesterday. Smitty said she was there when he opened, with the dog. Took a taxi in.

Someone has to do something." He dropped the keys he had refused to give Sophie into Noah's hand.

SUTTON HADN'T BEEN wrong; his baby sister was in a bad way. Dragging her out of the bar last night was a no-brainer. If it was turned around, he knew Sutton O'Hara would do the same for him. Right then, he had one mission. Bring Sophie home. Alive.

The aspect of her arriving there hogtied and in the horse trailer with Mojo and her belongings was growing with every second. She was still too drunk to drive herself. "Okay, fine. Bike in and I'll drive."

"I can do it, and if I die along the way, does it really matter?"

Noah sat back, in an instant, he knew he couldn't, wouldn't sugar coat anything. "Soph, I can't make this better. This is a journey that you have to take alone. Every miserable step has to be you picking up your foot and moving it forward and repeating it with the other foot. Every lousy step has to be you. Every bit of that heartbreak has to be you. Every tear, has to move you forward. Every time you miss him, every time you want to call him and remember, you can't, and you feel like you've been gut-punched...that is a step. Every first whatever is going to suck, Holidays, birthdays, whatever firsts women keep track of will suck, and they will continue to suck. Time won't heal a damn thing. It is there to give you a chance to be ready to face reality. No one can do it for you, you can't phone it in. Charlie, Molly, Shelly, no one can do this for you. I get it. It sucks. I know this. I held my buddy's hand and told him we'd be tipping back some brews and ogling women on a beach soon, grousing about how bad our teams were, how bad that assignment blew chunks, all while I laid in a pool of his blood and I knew by the time I was done talking he was dead. Married six damn weeks Sophie, I stood up with him, I was responsible for him and...he was dead." He paced from the bumper to her and back again. "I lost four men that night and had my own damn injuries to deal with. I know. First hand. Choice is yours." He pulled her bike into the trailer parking it next to the bent mass that had been Liam's. Shaking from anger, he stomped back out. "You can wallow in grief for as long as you want to, the only one who will be miserable is you. But, if you decide to drink yourself to death...I will kick your ass before you do."

Sophie wobbled in the breeze, his words struck a note, but, she'd be damned if she would let him see that. She tipped Liam's silver flask to her lips and drank, capped it, and shrugged. "Suit yourself." With that, she climbed into the passenger seat. Banging of the trailer gate signaled he finished loading; Sophie steeled herself for his tantrum.

"Alright your majesty, can you manage directions?" She pointed the way as they drove to the barn. Mojo trailered well, Noah could have done cartwheels as he went into his stall without a problem. "Figures. The only non-arguing member of this crazy traveling circus." Sophie grabbed a bale of hay, staggered, but made it to the truck. He let her carry two more bales, her tack box, and do a fill on a ten-gallon water tank. They were ready to pull out, he wasn't sure she could make a distance like they had to go. The trip was made in quiet, not even the radio. Sutton had arranged stopovers with horse people he knew along the way. Noah watched Sophie's handshake as she reached for a bottle of water. Pushing seven hours on the road without food, he knew after his recent excursion into building his treehouse that he could go another three hours and Sophie was the end of her rope.

8

Noah pulled in to a truck stop style gas station taking up eight spaces and a lot of shade. He came out with a couple of sodas and a bag of burgers. Sophie ran out of options, either eat or pass out. She took the offered burger, telling herself over and over she would not be sick. Eating went slower than drinking the night before. Halfway through the burger, she set the remains on the dash and eased out the door. The next few minutes were spent talking her stomach into behaving as she re-filled Mojo's bucket and hay net. She let Madge out on a double leash. "Sorry baby, I'm a bad dog mom right now. She led the pooch to the grass, breezes ruffled the leaves overhead. Feeling a bit more like a human, Sophie took Madge with her to the cab and took a few minutes to shove things over so Madge and her duck could hop in the back seat behind her.

"We have about ninety minutes until we hit the stopover for this leg." Sophie just nodded. Noah thought back to their younger days. Of all his sisters' friends, Sophie was the most level headed. She had always been all about horses and had been fearless. But, when she put her mind to something...she could be hell on wheels. He smiled as he remembered, Logan's temper ready to explode when she had instigated some sort of shenanigans, and her patting his cheek, saying, *"You're so cute when you're angry."* One time, the minister had a scout troop camping out in the back yard. A boy picked on her and the rest laughed. She used dental floss to tie the zippers together so they wouldn't unzip. The boys got a bit panic-stricken after twenty or thirty minutes of attempting to raise the zippers and not being able to escape. He thought the revenge play on her part to be hilarious.

Sophie was a born chatterbox, unlike the quiet, withdrawn woman riding with him. Her normally tanned skin went sickly pale. The bartender told him most of her meals were olives or celery in her drinks, maybe a handful of peanuts since her fiancé died. From what everyone said, Liam Boone had been a decent man. Unlike the louse Molly hooked up with. Their exit was next, he slowed and made a right turn at the bottom of the off-ramp. "Okay, there's the truck stop with the big green sign. Gonna pull in here and grab a few things." He glanced her way. "Soph, ya gotta eat girl."

"Not hungry."

"I know, how about if I get ya some soup. I mean, better than nothing." She stared at her finger. She picked a spot until it bled. Madge dropped her head on Sophie's shoulder. That distracted her for a bit. Noah called the landowners. End stall with a turn out area attached. Fridge and microwave in the office area and a couple recliners. The major plus, it had air conditioning. Mojo was happy to get out and move, Madge did her thing and then did zoomies waiting for food. She curled up in a chair with Sophie, Noah found a blanket in the truck to cover them. The landowners, Jim and Nancy, came out around eight a.m. with a carafe of coffee and some pastries. They also brought news. A heatwave was coming at them, it would be wiser if they could hang out until late in the day to leave, they already called the next place—the same there. Noah walked out with them to see where the water connection was. Explaining that Sophie's nightmares are not conducive to sleep and they would certainly rest up and much appreciated the offer was easier than he thought.

At five his phone buzzed, an invitation to supper. Sophie put on a brave face, Noah was surprised when she ate a bit of potato salad and some fried chicken. They loaded up shortly after the meal, Sophie swept the area looking for anything that could get left behind, especially Madge's favorite toy. She cleaned up, hauled out the trash and waved as she put the dog in the back seat. Noah's

"Last train to Clarksville," was almost funny. But nothing struck her as funny anymore. To Sophie, food didn't have flavor, colors were dull, life was just to be tolerated. It was after two in the morning when they pulled into a farm owned by Bubby Daniels. He referred to Sutton as Ned twice and corrected himself. He felt certain, the young woman in front of him was definitely related to his friend. She was a spitting image of his rodeo buddy.

"Well, y'all beat the rain, let's get everyone settled." Noah was able to pull right into the barn. They moved Mojo to a stall with outdoor access, he romped around the fence line a couple of times before coming in for food.

Noah grabbed his duffle bag out of the trailer. "I need a shower and I don't care if it's a hose duct-taped to a tree limb."

Bubby chuckled, Sophie hoped he hadn't gotten a visual of Noah and a hose. "Back here son, got a his and hers too." Bubby, with his rolling gait and barrel chest-arms out like an old west cowboy, led the way to the backside addition. Out of earshot, Bubby asked the million dollar question, "How is she son?"

Noah shook his head. "Bad. She's in a dark place." He glanced over his shoulder "If you could find a reason to stay close for a couple minutes...?"

"Certainly son, certainly." He ambled back out. Sophie had cleaned out the truck stall, put in new shavings and emptied the water bucket. "My word, you really look like ol Ned. Dang it, Sutton. I may never get used to the name." She half-smiled. "He developed a reputation as one hell of a bronc rider, darn near killed his fool self on a bull."

"I heard parts of the story. Thank you for letting us stop over." Her voice was soft, he remembered someone speaking about a soulless look, and that is what he saw in her. "Your brother said you show this big beast," he scrubbed the horse's nose. "How does he do?" Sophie pulled out her phone; she had a video she sent to Charlie.

He found her skill and knowledge fascinating. Not as a ruse, but honestly, and asked a dozen or so questions.

Noah returned in five minutes. Mostly shaved, showered, his long hair dripping down his back. Sophie excused herself, taking an armful of clothes and necessities along with Madge. "She sure don't say much does she?" Bubby stroked his chin as he spoke.

"Normally, she's chatty, can't shut her up. This is bad." They shook hands, Bubby pointed to the sky as he left. Clouds raced along. Noah turned on the truck radio to listen to the weather. He was all set to go find Sophie when she came running through, hurrying to get Mojo in and the doors closed. She did a check for fire extinguishers when they arrived, one sat close to her horse's stall. Madge whined and paced the area around them. Sophie worked to settle the dog, only to have her back up and pacing. She took duckie, as it was now called, to the truck and then tugged at Sophie's shoe strings to make her follow. Noah quietly watched, he went to the door, wind and rain whipped through the area. Mojo was one of six horses at the farm, when they all laid down, Sophie got worried. She didn't like the way the wind sounded and doubled up on leashes for Madge, one on her harness, one on her collar. She stood only to be grabbed by Noah as he raced them to a side storage room. "Tornado!"

She reached her breaking point, perched on a stack of feedbahs holding on to Madge, sobbing. Without thinking about it, Noah pulled her close. "Shh, it'll be okay." *Holy Jesus, there's nothing to her.* "We'll be okay Soph." He held her tighter, remembering when she was younger, much younger and wandered away from home. She walked to the cemetery and fell asleep talking to her siblings. He got dragged out to hunt for her. With a brother in tow, they took off on bikes, pedaling for all they were worth. It was just a flash of purple in the dusk, but they turned around. She sat on his handlebars, feet on the front fender, laughing into the wind. Now she was a quivering, crying mess. The roaring outside coupled with the cry of the horses drowned out all other sounds. The storm zipped past them as fast as the storm dropped in. Frantic to check on Mojo, Sophie launched herself to the door, in the hall the lights came back on as a generator kicked in. They were all back on their feet, munching away and totally unaware of the worry or the fact that she felt as if she aged ten years in those few seconds.

Bubby waddled out to check on them. The all-clear from weather channels and local news gave them a modicum of relief. "Yes siree, I got those whole house generators for here and the main house. You can run whatcha need to. I'm taking my old bones to bed." He strolled out, "You may have chainsaws for an alarm clock in the morning, think I lost some trees."

Sophie was already climbing into the bunk on the trailer. Noah wouldn't say he didn't trust her to not hurt herself, but he didn't trust her. He opened up a lounge chair, grabbed a pillow from the cab and got comfortable. Two hours later she was back out, stumbling toward the washrooms. Five minutes, ten minutes, he swore he heard the door open and close. Fifteen minutes later he sat up, "Soph?" he stuffed his feet in his boots and headed for the door. He ripped it open all set to yell her name, there she stood, holding a soaking wet kitten.

"Hold it, I still have to pee." She shoved the soggy fur ball at him. Its mew was bigger than it was. Sophie came back with a handful of paper towels. She wrapped the soggy kitty in those, held it close and glanced back at Noah. "I heard that pitiful cry, I had to find him." Bubby was organized, the storeroom they took cover in had shelves of canned food for dogs, cats, and a milk supplement for three other critters. "Well, I think a little sugar water and then once he's warm, we'll try food." Noah went back to his chair. She said more words in two minutes than she had since he pulled in. He was going to let her keep talking. Madge sniffed all over the interloper. Tipping her head and whining at Sophie. "I know, mama loves you, but he's a baby without a mama." True to her nature, when the kitty was put on the floor on a towel, she tried to keep the baby there.

Sophie found a plastic spoon and a lid, adding a bit of water to the canned food to make it mushier before going down for the foundling. He chowed down. "Poor little baby, can't be more than a couple weeks old the way he moves."

"He? Did you check?"

"Yep, kitty is a boy."

"What is that?" It was clear plastic and trimmed in gaudy hot pink, obviously used to house a small furry being.

"Hamster house, I took it when one of the barn kids little fuzzy died. We did a funeral in the flower bed. I was going to give her back the house, but they moved...military kid." She shrugged, "I figure a washcloth in here and he should be warm enough without the lid. I can put him on a shelf in there just until I'm positive Madge won't hurt him." She was back in the bunkroom before he could say anything else. But at least she formed real sentences for the first time since he found her at the Flaming Frog. If it gave her something to focus on other than her broken heart, he would haul in a dozen kittens.

Storm rain cooled off the area enough that they got a fairly early start, after a stop at a vet's office. Sophie spent an hour inside before she bounced out with a couple of small plastic bags and a mewling ball of fur. "Four weeks old, no worms, too young for shots, healthy and food." Madge crammed her head in between Sophie and the kitten, she licked his head, making him complain more. "Be nice to Mokie." Madge licked her ear, as if to say okay.

Noah was ready to beat his head against the steering wheel. Sophie was back to not speaking. Every three to four hours they made a pit stop to check on Mojo and refill water for the animals. He knew she still hit the flask, but they were spacing out. One of the stops was at a truck stop with a fried chicken place next door.

He headed that way, never imagining any kind of trouble. As he paid, Madge's barking and raising hell drew his attention. Rounding the trailer corner, he watched as Sophie took aim at some jerk who thought he was going to steal something from her. She was not even playing. Not from the size of the gun in her hand. It dawned on him in the breath before all hell broke out. Sophie was right-handed, the gun was in her left. The tweaker averted his eyes for a heartbeat. Precision aim. She stuck her knife in at the thumb joint. Before either man could move, her boot was meeting the guy's face. "I am in the mood to slit your throat. You better get the hell on out of here and don't try that shit again." She ripped her knife out of his hand as he caterwauled, wiped it on his shirt and slid the knife back into her sleeve. Acting like she was going to turn on him again, he jumped and ran. Back in the truck, she offered no explanation, he asked no questions. This was not the Sophie he knew. Ten hours in, and time for another stopover.

Dusty Fishbine regaled them with tales of Ned Greene and his rodeo days. They threw some burgers on a grill and popped open a couple cold beers. When she went to check on Mojo, Dusty leaned over, "How is she?"

"Pulled a knife on some dude that tried to rob her today, I know she thought about killing him. So out of character for her."

"Ned, durn, Sutton said she held her man as died," Noah nodded, "Sort of like us watching our buddies die in battle, but he was unarmed. Anything we felt then, she is now."

Gobsmacked. Flabberghasted. Totally blown away. Why had he not linked the two?

She was back with Mokie, trying to feed him from the bottle was like trying to paint the Tasmanian Devil's toenails in mid-spin. She rubbed his belly and took a damp paper towel to wipe him down. She fashioned a litter box out of a Styrofoam container and duct tape. "Well, think I'm going to turn in, I wish we had met under better circumstances. You have a peaceful night."

He made his way across the yard to the house. Noah waited as long as he figured was acceptable. "Are you okay? Today was a bit crazy." Sophie shrugged. "What was he trying to steal?"

"Madge. Looking for bait dogs." He sat up straighter then. One didn't move without the other and she let him live. Noah was amazed. "Oh, well, just deserts."

"Exactly."

She moved just right and he was out of his chair and had her by the arm. "What the bloody hell?" Sophie sported a bruise across the back of her neck spreading to the side. "Why didn't you say he had hit you?"

She was slightly stunned by the vicious tone of his voice. Reaching a handout, she rubbed his arm. "I'm okay." Sophie pulled a sleepy Mokie out of her shirt pocket and waited on Madge and ducky to go into the trailer.

He may have raised his voice to his ex-girlfriend, but raising a hand to a woman was something that burned his bacon. Noah wanted to go back and beat the punk to a pulp. Usually, his size was enough to back off most people, what Sophie lacked in size she made up in attitude.

They put more than fifty miles between them and two gates but he was uneasy. So uneasy he locked the outer doors and pulled the chair into the trailer. A gun case sat against one wall, he checked it. Remington, he liked the make. Shells were in the bottom of the foam, in cut out spaces for them, he loaded it, took the safety off and settled back to wait.

Four a.m. chimed on her phone. She had watched the bodies moving outside for close to an hour. The call to nine-one-one was in. Sophie pointed to the spot at the backside of the table. "Stay." The dog wiggled into it. "Noah, we have company." She crept out the door and locked it. He saw the baseball bat in her hand and had no doubts as to what she would do with it given the chance. Whispering, "I called the cops" as she crammed her feet into her boots.

Mojo nickered, they glanced at one another. To them, it seemed as if an hour went by as Noah turned the padlock on the door and lifted it, dropping it into his pocket and ever so slowly, swinging the lock-plate out. He held up three fingers and counted down. At one they sprang from the trailer, yelling.

Whatever Noah expected, was definitely not what he was met with. Two reporters, scared out of their minds, yelling as their hands went up. Sophie smacked the man in the solar plexus with the ball bat—pool stick style. He staggered backward and landed in a pile of horse apples. Police barged through the doors at both ends of the barn as Noah shoved Sophie behind him. Yelling from all sides stopped all at once when one of the invaders blew a whistle. "

Lady, and I use the term loosely, if you blow that thing one more time, the next time you blow it, you'll have to fart to do so." Sophie's eyes had gone to slits, making them appear more catlike.

"Who are you?" One officer, who looked to be about forty started pointing at the four people in front of him. "Howard Reed, I'm a reporter." He looked like he had been goosed by a ghost and was trying to do an imitation of an old comedic actor.

"Debra Snodgrass, I'm also a reporter."

"Noah Driscoll, I'm taking Sophie home."

"Sophie O'Hara and probably the reason these jackasses are here."

The cop looked back at the reporters and then to Noah. "Is that loaded?" he nodded toward the gun Noah dropped when he saw police. "Yes sir, it is. She tangled with some punk earlier, tried to steal her dog. We thought they were tracking us."

Sophie glared at the pair of misfit reporters. "I call b.s. and I want to see an ID that identifies them as true reporters."

"I think IDs on all is a good call." Noah and Sophie had to get theirs from the truck console or the trailer. She came out with it and Madge on a leash. She sniffed everyone and then squatted over Reed's foot to pee. When he tried to kick her away, he discovered what trouble was. Sophie went at him, he shoved her back and Noah sucker-punched him. Reed hit the ground and had the brains to stay there.

"We only wanted a comment or two from the woman behind so much death." Police presence was all that saved him. Noah let out something akin to a roar as he reached for the fool.

Sophie intervened pushing him back. "I got this." Phone in hand, she dialed Mr. Keene and filled him in. "No, by all means, sue the crap out of the paper." She walked away leaving them to wonder what else was said.

"We have rights, read the Constitution," Reed yelled after Sophie.

"What about her rights? The right to grieve in peace and not be hounded by a grade B rag calling its self a newspaper, and what makes you think she was responsible?" Noah stood next to a cop nearly as tall as his six foot seven frame.

"Well, she rebuked Ashby's attempts..."

"What? Did you listen to yourself?" The cop looked at Noah and back to Reed, "You are a jackass. Just because a man asks a woman out doesn't mean that she has to say yes to any part of it." He ran both hands along his head, "If I could arrest you for being stupid I would."

"He trespassed on private property," Noah had a smug look as he pointed it out.

Dusty picked that point in time to walk in. "Arrest them both. They listened in on a conversation with the young lady's brother. I told them then, they were not coming here to bother her. And any photos taken here are my property. It's listed on the sign, no photos without prior permission and a list of other items, so I'll take the SD cards."

"Dusty, you know it will be challenged in court and I have kids to send off to school in the morning. They can't arrest me."

"Oh, they can, and isn't your husband at work tonight?" she nodded, suddenly ill at ease. "So, you left three boys under the age of twelve at home alone."

Both were handcuffed and stuffed into patrol cars, Dusty spat a stream of juice from his chew into the dirt, "I never liked either of them." Statements were taken and things settled down.

Sophie looked at Noah, "For the record Driscoll, I can fight my own battles."

"I'd believe that if this trip wasn't the longest you've been sober since January."

She spun and slapped him across the face.

His head jacked back. "Feel better?"

"You do know I am not the one that asked you to play chauffeur, right?" she asked with her nose in the air as she turned to walk away.

"No, your brother did after you called him in tears, so drunk he was afraid you would die. Which just about ripped his guts out, he's worried as hell about you and his wife and she was in the hospital again. But, you have yet to even mention either of them. As his friend, it was an honor that he trusted me with you. Someone he would do anything for...you're a piece of work woman." He kicked a bale of hay, "You aren't the only one who has lost someone they love. Maybe you should call Molly. That ass she married beat her in a drunken fit and she miscarried...no, on second thought, better you don't talk to her. She has enough drunks in her life right now."

"You insufferable, egotistical, jackass! How dare you presume to..."

Noah cut in, he was over her and her attitude. "I presume because someone has to tell you the truth. Someone who won't sugarcoat the facts for the princess on her high horse."

"Do. Not. Ever." She took several deep breaths, "Ever call me princess. Ever." She ran out the back door of the barn.

His foot stomped on Madge's leash. "Nope, sorry pooch. You are not running off out there." He put her in the trailer. "It takes calling her princess to make her so mad she cries. Princess? Really? Women. Either you can't trust them or can't figure them out." His head turned, the hay bale he kicked had split open. "Damn it." Noah grabbed a pitchfork and scooped it into a stall. "Man you need to get a grip." Before he enlisted in the military, he had been into martial arts and yoga to stretch the muscles out. "Maybe I need to get back into something where I can beat the piss outta something and not go to jail." His hand ran through his hair. "Jeez, it is as hot as Satan's balls." He pulled his hair back and twisted it until he could tie it in a knot. He walked out back, Sophie was sitting on the top rail of the fence, a white horse came to say hello, it rubbed its head against her until she gave in and scratched his ears. "Why?"

Sophie's brow furrowed in confusion. "The princess thing."

"It is what Landon used to call me."

"Okay, that makes sense." She gave him a look like she was ready to go toe to toe, "No, it does. I wouldn't want to be tied to him either." His head tipped, "I don't remember there being a white horse out here earlier."

Sophie's voice was low, "I don't either." Her head rested against its nose, like she used to do with Mojo. "Is Molly okay?"

"No, but pride keeps her from saying anything."

"I thought I dreamed the conversation with my brother." She kissed the end of the horse's nose. "Liam was different from any man I have met. Losing him was like losing my siblings and Judd all over again, all at once. It brought all of them back and took them all away again." She shook her hair back. "I bet Hannah is the posterchild for unhappy camper because you went on this expedition."

Noah's fist-bumped off his forehead, "We broke up. She broke up is more accurate. Before my last deployment, the day I hit the hall, she married Bob Carpenter." He wasn't so sure Sophie's eyes weren't going to fall out. "So I either worked my ass off or got drunk. I know all about crawling in a bottle to self-medicate. To numb yourself."

"Bob?" her head swayed side to side. "He's got to be hung like a horse, cuz that man is as ugly as dirt is gritty."

"Sophie!"

"Don't even...Bruce is the only one in that family with any brains or looks and it seems like he got all of both." The horse bumped her, "It's true. Steal something from someone, get caught with it in his hands and then have the brass to say he didn't steal the thing."

The horse's head dropped. An alarm on her watch went off. "I gotta check on Mokie." She hopped off the fence and jogged inside the barn.

Noah looked at the horse, back to the barn and back at the horse. "She's...complicated." The horse threw his head in the air like he agreed. "Mokie is a dumb name for a kitten. And I'm talking to a horse. I need to sleep." As he walked inside, the horse let out a long whinny.

9

Pieces for a metal shelf lay scattered about Charlie on the floor. He son, Elijah, raced his toy truck in a playpen close by when Rayna came in. "Hey lady, how ya feel?"

She sighed, "Tired all the time. Doc said this will pass. At least I'm not tossing my toenails."

Rayna surveyed the mess in front of her. "What is all of this?"

"I'm putting up shelves so Sophie can store her stuff." Side-eyeing her sister-in-law, "What."

"Uhm" her face scrunched up before her words raced out in one long string. "She called me for the new number for Dudley's storage and the lakeside Inn."

"What? No! She needs to be here where we can take care of her."

"Honey, love ya like a sister...but that is the last thing she needs. Yes, she's been through hell; but she needs to do this without feeling like a bug in a bottle."

"But"

"Charlie, we both know you would mother hen her," Charlie sighed. "Granted, your henning would be with the best intentions, but you would drive her batty. Granted, slower than Wanda would, but still."

"Okay, first, is henning a word? And you may be right, but sending Noah for her, I see that as a recipe for disaster. He's still dealing with crap from the army and Hannah. I mean let's put the two most fragile people in a vehicle with animals, road stress and all. We could well get a call to go bail their dumb asses out of jail."

"Trust me, they will be alright." Rayna had an air about her, like she knew more than she let on, but Elija deciding he wanted to be the center of their attention distracted her.

"WELL DAMN," SOPHIE muttered under her breath before she started tapping away on her phone. She would repeat the phrase a dozen more times over the next hour.

"I give, what's up?"

"Trying to find a storage room and a place to stay; there are no storage facilities for a hundred miles in any direction. Lakeside is full, Granny Martin's is full, and the only other option, one of the Lewis's is renting a room...probably full of vermin like them."

Noah snorted coffee out his nose. "Ow damn, that hurt." He glanced at Sophie, "Ha—you almost smiled." He stuck his tongue out at her.

She rolled her eyes and shook her head. "Typical boy." She plucked Mokie from her shirt pocket, holding him and the can of food still took a bit of doing. "I think you need a real kennel. Crazy Cat-en." He meowed and rubbed all over her face. "Can I ask you a question?"

"Sure." Noah flipped someone off when they yelled about the speed limit.

"We did see a white horse...right?" Dusty stared at both of them like they had lost their collective minds, insisting he didn't own a white horse. His were all bays, except for his granddaughter's palomino.

"Yes. We may be slightly crazy but we both saw one. I think he wanted to mess with us." With the radio on low, they covered another two hundred miles.

"Noah," he looked her way, "how much longer before we need gas?" "About a quarter of a tank more and I'll be looking." He glanced back at her, "Need a bathroom?"

"No. I have the munchies"

"So, gas with gas, gotcha."

Shaking her head again as she muttered, "Boys."

Noah quickly got used to her being quiet. If he thought about the situation long enough, he could probably make a sensible argument against her logic. But, he understood all too well. He blamed himself for the loss of the men he served with. Over the years he tamped down the hurt until it became like someone trying to pack five pounds of sand into a two-pound bucket. Something had to give. The give had nearly been his sanity. How many nights did he sit with a pistol in his hand ready to end it all? He lost track.

Not like he would tell anyone, but every time he contemplated suicide, a voice stopped him. A whisper, slightly breathy, and calling his name. It always seemed so real he would search for the source. He had five or six years on Sophie, at the moment, he couldn't remember which. If he couldn't grab onto all those feelings and wrestle them into a bag, how was she supposed to? He tried to drown the memories, but someone taught the bastards to swim. To tread whiskey, to spit beer like a naked nymph in a fountain; and most annoying of all, was when they laughed at his attempts to shush them. Not too many people would understand. An O'Hara would, they were introduced to death and despair practically from the crib. It really wasn't fair for her to lose anyone else.

Life seemed to hold a grudge for some people. Like Stephanie, she beat cancer, found her dreamboat and he died in the sands of a foreign land. He promised her, her love would come home. He never said it would be in a flag-draped box. Sophie's hand on his arm startled Noah out of his reverie. "You okay?" She didn't turn his way, she didn't have to. The hitch in his voice was a give-away.

"Not yet." Truer words had never left his lips.

"Heard that." She leaned back, Madge's nose on her shoulder, Mokie curled up on her chest.

"I have an idea." He flipped on the signal for their exit ramp to a gas station. "You need a place for a while until the family is convinced you got your stuff in one sock." She was nodding along, "I did something crazy," her brow inched up.

"Do tell."

"I built a tree and a treehouse. I can slap something together for the horse, why don't you stay at the treehouse? I own an ancient Silver Bullet I remodeled, I can live in there. You'll have space, everything is new and if anything breaks...well, I'll be close by."

"You built a tree? You do realize they grow in the outdoors?"

"Not tall enough, not fast enough."

"This house is safe? No hazard to the critters?"

"Or you."

"Okay. Give me a minute to figure this out." Noah pulled up next to a pump and bailed out. Sophie swiped a credit card, inhaled deeply, turned and walked to the store.

"The hell?" Noah was mystified. He would swear she was ready to cry. She came out with two bags, one with sodas and a one with food. He caught her trying to wipe away a tear. "Hey, what's up."

Head shaking, Sophie's hand was up in front of her, as if she was trying to ward off him or a thought. "I got out and was immediately hit by the lack of everything I have come to love. The smell of salt air, sounds of seagulls arguing overhead, the aroma of low-country cooking, and it.."

Noah dropped an arm around her shoulder and pulled her close. "It did seem pretty cool." He watched the dial spin, "And gas was cheaper."

"Yeah." He squeezed her shoulder. "You're gonna be okay Sophie. Everything's gonna be okay." Looking out over the parking lot as he went on, "Not today, or tomorrow, or next week, but you will pull through this and patch your heart up. It will always be a little broken, but it will work again." The pump cut off, he rattled the nozzle in the tank to shake the last drops as Sophie climbed up in the cab. They agreed to make the last stop instead of driving straight through.

Sutton's friend left a note with a cooler in the barn, "Wife went into labor, grill is outside. Here's a couple steaks and some potato salad. Do us a favor and make sure everyone has water. Thanks, Henry & Sally."

"Aww, how sweet. Damn it. Tears suck."

Noah chuckled, "Naw, just a sign the patches haven't all stuck in place yet." He snagged the cooler and headed out to the grill. Sophie dug some paper plates out of one box and found silverware in another. She carted it out with bottles of lemonade. "Nice setup, grill, picnic table, away from anything flammable ."

"Uh-oh, the wheels are turning."

"Could be. Property is a work in progress. " He poked at the steaks with a thick index finger. "Almost." Noah cooked as Sophie worked out some of Mojo's kinks on a lunge line before turning him loose in the paddock. Madge was tied to the table leg. After spending time with her, he would bet her heartbreak ran as deep as Sophie's. Testing the steaks again proved he perfected the method, "Ha. Didn't burn me this time." He turned to yell, but she was washing off the dirt at the spigot. They got through the first half of dinner in relative silence.

"Okay, so, you built a tree." Sophie was still trying to wrap her head around that part.

"Yep, sure did."

"How ?"

"I-beams and worked out from there. The "bark" is textured concrete. Painting it was a bitch but I got it so it looks sort of like a tree." He spun his phone around to show her the pictures. "It's only fitting you stay there for a while, I got the idea from you." Her brow cocked in an unasked question. "When you were home for Charlie's wedding, it jogged my memory. I remembered you and Molly talking and the thing about a treehouse. I always felt a bit gypped as a kid too...so I built one."

"Amazing." She chewed another bite of potato, "And the trailer is?" Noah moved a pile of potato salad around on his plate to be the fence and a piece of steak for the tree and explained there was a deck connected by a spiral ramp and where the trailer sat, where he could put something for Mojo and the pond. "So you fenced in a pretty large chunk of land?"

Nodding he answered, "Yep, sure did. I needed room to work and since no one had tried anything like this, I needed to be sure I had space to goof up and fix it without hearing "I told you so."

"And you aren't going to try to be my keeper?"

"Nope, you're a grown woman. However, I will not allow you to harm yourself." He set his fork down, folded his hands and rested his chin on them as he organized his thoughts. "Day before I flew out, a friend called. A guy we served with became one of twenty-two who take their own life. Suicide is an epidemic. I called my guys, and a couple of the women, just to touch base. To listen to their words, let the inflections and tones sink in. Then I went out and turned a log into toothpicks. I can't save them all, but I can remind a few they aren't alone, someone cares. I've been a pallbearer and honor guard too damn many times. We walked through hell, I'm not afraid to walk a few more miles with someone who needs a shoulder. I refuse to lose anyone else."

"You're a good man Noah." His phone rang, breaking the spell.

"Noah, Dusty here. I wanted to let you know...I saw the horse. Don't have a clue where it came from. But I swear it was like he was stickin his big ol horse tongue out at me. I went to grab a flashlight to go check it out and poof, he was gone."

"Strange. But thanks for calling."

Neither of them said anything for a few minutes, in unison, "No way."

Madge crawled into Sophie's lap, a paw on each shoulder, nose to nose. "I know baby. Hop down, mama give you a nibble from my steak okay?" she moved, but lacked the happy dog tail. "Here baby, mama got yums." Madge sniffed and gently took the bite, licking her lips after. "Such a sweet girl." She tossed their plates and empty bottles. "Okay Noah, you at least are not clueless as to what my life is like now. I will accept your offer until I can get my feet on the ground and my head screwed on somewhat near straight."

"Thank you for allowing me to help." He waited until she climbed into the cot in the trailer before he walked back out to the picnic table and called Sutton.

"Hello Noah."

"Yo brother, how's your lady?"

"Doing better. Question is, how is my sister?"

"Well, so far we took shelter from a tornado, adopted a kitten, saw a horse no one else did, had an argument—she packs a mean slap and she's moving into the treehouse, I'm taking up residence in the Airstream."

Both men were quiet for a minute. "Well, it may make the most sense...she agreed to this?"

"Yeah, in the last twenty-four hours she hasn't had any liquor that I know of." Noah scanned the parking area by the barn as he spoke.

"I heard about the reporters. Sophie was adamant about putting them out of business."

"Yeah. Not surprised. Some punk tried to steal the dog. She pulled a knife on him."

"Draw blood?"

"A bit. So what is it with you old rodeo dudes? We pull in, there's a bag of charcoal, starter fluid, and a cooler with a couple of steaks and some potato salad, right along with a real short honey-do list. They're at the hospital having a baby."

"I didn't think Sal was that close. I'll check on them in the morning. Call us when you get to your place. Take care man."

"You too." Nights were cooler on the west side of Nebraska, rain was due in the next few days, he overheard people talking about it at the gas station. Small towns, they run on weather reports, gossip, and hard work. There were a few more things for the list, but they all had that in common, he missed the mentality when he was overseas. Half smiling, he remembered a night waiting for orders when he made a list of everything he missed about home. The Fourth of July picnic, Halloween in town, high school football games, hunting and fishing with his brothers, sitting out in Parsin's field with a beer and a bonfire; those usually ended with a midnight skinny dip session in the creek with his girl. The occasional northern lights, the rodeos were on the list too. Other guys in the unit had strip clubs and bars on their lists, fast food and parties. "God, I feel old." Noah was set to go crash out when his phone lit up. "*U up?*"

His jaw dropped, "*yes sir.*"

"*How close 2 home r u?*"

"*Tomorrow sometime* "

"*How is she? Logan told me.*"

"*Rough but she's tough, O'Hara's r strong.*"

"*Feel like jawing some and tipping back a couple cold ones? Please say yes, folks r drivn me nuts.*"

"*Hahaha, sure thing bro, I'll hit ya up when we get back.*"

"*Thanks bud, appreciate it.*"

"*Anytime man, anytime.*" With his mood vastly adjusted, Noah stood, stretched and headed off for his chair.

IN THE MORNING, SOPHIE noticed his mood seemed lighter. The homeowner was back, he brought coffee and gas station sausage biscuits, but she wasn't going to turn her nose up at either. Madge was still in the dumps, they were at the picnic table, Noah overheard the conversation between her and the dog. "Poor baby, you miss dad, don't you? They say doggoes don't understand, I say they are a few fries short of a happy meal. Yes ma'am. Doggies know. You're going to need to remember, I'm your human now and I love you enough for two people." Immediately her tail swished. "What? You just needed to hear someone say I loves a puppy?" Madge licked her nose, "Eww, you need a doggy breath mint."

Henry came over, "Sorry to bug out on ya like that."

"Hey, priorities. Now, spill the beans."

He laughed at Sophie, stared at her for a moment, sipped his coffee and finally spoke. "Wow. I am blown away. You really resemble Ned...dang it, Sutton. Your eyes are a little lighter but other than that, man." He shook out his arms and stretched, reorganizing his thoughts as he did so. "Your brother introduced us," he glanced at the tabletop and back to Sophie. "Our lil man took his mama through five hours of hard labor and then out he popped, in the sac. I was all freaked out but the doc let my sister-in-law snap a couple pictures before he split it. All seven pounds even and twenty-one inches was all curled up in there, and he has this butterscotch color wad of hair on his knobby head." He gulped a bit more coffee. "Women are amazing. Soon as she was done cryin over how perfect he is she started in, "remember to empty the dishwasher and turn the hose on the garden." There was a whole list of things. I only heard half, just looking at her with our son. I thought I was gonna cry big old alligator tears." He looked at Noah, "You got kids?"

Noah had been transfixed by the story, so into the emotions and the soul of the teller that the question caught him off guard. "Nope, not that I'm aware of." He unwrapped a biscuit, "I'm not sure there is a woman out there with my name on her to-do list." He half-smiled. Sophie acted like she hadn't witnessed the flash of pain or heartbreak.

"Ah, you'll find one. I thought I was a loner for life and then boom." He chugged back the rest of his coffee, "Gotta jump on the list and go pick her up. Man, my momma said she was in for a week and Sally is coming home after a night. Women are strong."

He waved as he strode off to the house. "Yeah, he's still on cloud nine."

Sophie nodded in agreement, "You're in a good mood."

"Luke is home."

"Wow! How is he?"

"He says okay, we'll see."

"Broken body, broken-hearted, jaded, spirits in shambles...we sound like a modern-day three musketeers."

"I prefer to think of it as we are in different stages of healing."

"Ever the optimist." Madge snuffled at a spot in the dirt and pawed at it. Sophie went to investigate. "Whatcha find baby?" She dug a finger in the dirt, "Spent casing." Madge shied away from the brass shell. "It's okay baby, it can't hurt anyone now." She set it on the table.

Noah picked it up, "probably used on coyotes, thought some were singing in the distance last night."

"Alright, let's get this circus on the road. I have people to piss off." She stopped at the door to the truck, resting her head against it.

"You okay?"

"We were planning this trip, load up Madge, go properly meet my family. I swear I have been cursed. First Judd, then Liam, I don't have a safe place to go."

"Nope, Judd was his own worst problem. Once you get honest with yourself, you'll see it too. You took his keys, you had no way of knowing he had a spare stashed in the truck. Hell, his dad said he found a dozen hidden around where he parked and in the thing. Getting out of the truck when you did was smart."

"I still wish he didn't die out there."

"We all do. The only positive thing to come of it was his dad got his life straight." He opened the truck door, "Madge isn't going to know what to do, all the cows and sheep around us."

"I'm thinking the first time she hears an elk bugle, she'll be in my armpit."

He snickered, "I would happily pay to watch you try to shave that pit."

"Boys."

His laughter echoed in the barn

SOPHIE LOOKED AROUND, the yard area was probably close to an acre not counting all the buildings along the fence. Madge wandered over to the pool. He was not fooling her. He may have made it, but it was still a pool. She followed Noah up the winding entrance to the treehouse. While it looked roomy, the place was also empty except for a folding table, a recliner, and a TV. In the master bedroom, she stopped and pointed. "Yep, a round bed. Bought it for thirty dollars at a place in Grand Junction; brand new too.

"Okay then." In one end of the bathroom, there was a large clawfoot tub with a small wood-burning stove and a good-sized window. On the other was a party shower. That was her classification for one with five showerheads and as many different lights that could also keep time to music. It left her wondering.

"The only thing I paid real serious dollars for was the range. Everything else was free or close to it."

"I'm sending you out shoe shopping for me."

He snorted, "Still can hardly get shoes on Charlie and you are the opposite." He looked around, "So, you ready to unload your stuff?"

"Yep, let's do this." Two hours later they were done unloading, a round pen had been set up and Mojo was happily watching Madge. Sophie sat down on a wooden crate on the deck, one mass text message sent out to let everyone know she was home. Except for gram, she got a phone call. After the tears and a promise that she was okay, she was able to hang up.

"Luke is coming over, his parents have turned into hovercrafts." Noah looked in the freezer.

"I'm calling Ray, have her take me to Spirit Lake. Anything ya want?" "Chips and dip." Before she could dial, Rayna knocked on the gate, it echoed across the yard and set Madge off. She ran to Sophie, not chancing the hairy guy to properly defend her human.

"Hey y'all, just me."

"Come on in woman" Noah trotted down the ramp and met her with a hug.

"I was fixing to call you. Need a ride to Spirit Lake, gotta fill father Hubbard's cupboards." Sophie turned to Madge, "You be good, mama will be right back. Maybe I'll even bring you a piggy ear." Happy dog wags were her reward. They were on the highway before either one spoke.

"So you two are going to start the rumor mill spinning...am I allowed to be evil when I shut them down?"

"I was about to suggest Voo-doo dolls and then hang 'em on a roadside tree and light those bitches up."

"Ooh, I like that. Logan probably won't but that's okay." She cut a glance at her passenger, "Have they put all the pieces together as to what the hell happened?" If anyone was going to understand it would be Rayna, but there was always a tiny chance that everything could backfire.

With that in mind, "Sort of, the person Liam knew as Landon Rowley was actually Landon Thorpe. The son of a bad, third rate, hitman for an equally bad wannabe a mob boss. He shot the wrong man and ate a bullet for his efforts. It appears Landon had a love-hate thing with Liam for years. He had his own mother committed; boy was a hot mess drama king. He wanted me dead, figured his ol' buddy would hurt like he did. This was after he kidnapped and killed Liam's first fiancé."

"No way."

"Yep. He held Ashby's pregnant girlfriend or fiancée hostage on a boat, let her go when he knew the cops were closing in. She ran out in front of Ashby, he slammed into her with daddy's car...he killed them both, Landon committed suicide. I lost the man I had dreamed of because some bitch boy was jealous." Tears danced along her eye rims.

"Damn. That is a truth is stranger than story."

"Yeah. At least Noah doesn't give me the sad eyes full of pity when he looks my way. He gets where I'm at."

"He was in bad shape for a while. Logan's jail was his second home, then poof. He had the treehouse underway and was busy from sunup to dark most days. I think the only thing that left more people with their jaws hanging was when Field's middle son came out and had a knockdown drag-out with his daddy. They 'bout beat the snot outta each other. Eastman had to stitch up both of them. I think the ol' man is ready to let bygones be but Richie is still not even looking his way."

"That is crazy. I mean...never mind, look at Wanda the wonder mom." Rayna pulled into a front-row spot. "I have a feeling Noah eats like a caveman."

"I don't know, he did spend some time in Logan's home gym with him." Sophie made a major run on the veggie aisle and through the meat case. From there it was the freezer section and then down the center of the store to fill in the gaps. Then it was a treasure hunt to locate a real litter box and litter for Mokie, pig ears and jerky for Madge and a twelve-pack of Sunset Bay Pale Ale. "Luke is escaping his folks tonight. I figure a few beers and some food can't hurt them."

"What about you?"

"I've developed a fondness for bourbon. Besides, they probably want to blow off guy steam. And, I have furniture to push around." Rayna caught her up to date on all the local gossip on the way back and helped carry the never-ending grocery bags up to the house.

"She a beauty." Madge was all happy tail and tappy toes. "But, how did she get that name?"

"Old dish soap commercial was on some special. Every time they said Madge, she turned to the TV." She dug into a dozen bags before she came up with the bag of pig ears. "Look what you got. Piggies." She held one out, Madge scurried to the porch to chomp on it. "Thanks Ray. You have no idea how much I appreciate it."

"Anytime. Y'all can load up and come over for dinner anyday. I still cook for a herd." She stopped by where Noah was cleaning a grill. "She's still not in a safe place metally. But, she's trying."

"Last thing the fuck nut said to her was that it was her fault, she was supposed to die not Liam. Screwed her head all up. Good thing he offed his dumb self or I would volunteer for the job."

"I think I'd volunteer to help. Take care, I gotta head home and see what trouble Cort has gotten into." As she left, one side of her lip curled up. "Yep, you just keep that mindset son."

LILY WALKED AROUND the corner and waited. "Creature of habit. Think you'd know better Claire. She waited until the car was parked before strolling up to the window. Claire would be found ten minutes later by her husband. Lily took delight in scrubbing off the "floozy make-up" with baby wipes as she watched from across the street. Screaming kids and a weeping military man...one loose end with the potential to do them in. Cowboy never needs to know. If they picked her up on security cameras it wouldn't be her usual M.O. Her look totally changed to jeans, a t-shirt and dark hair with a temporary tattoo peeking from under her sleeve. Usually, she went platinum blond and tight skirts. Now there was nothing to keep them apart.

DILLON AND LUKE ROLLED in at six-thirty. They were sitting around a table Noah made from heavens knows what. Sophie threw a batch of salsa together along with a giant dish of baked buffalo chicken dip and hauled them down with chips. It took her a bit to escape from her brother. Now and then they would hear something crash and her cuss, once the dog scooted outside and spun to make sure nothing was coming after her.

"I offered to help and she shut me down." Noah held his hands in the air as he spoke. "Stubborn woman says she can do it so I'm going to let her". By the time she was done moving boxes and sliding furniture around, they were ready to drop steaks on the grill.

"Come on sis, we ain't had dinner together in forever." She rolled her eyes and groaned. "Okay," she looked at Madge, "You coming baby? He stinks but he's my brother." She picked up ducky and followed her human. Noah steered the conversation away from things he knew would have Sophie in tears. As it was, he felt she was on the edge most of the night.

When she went to check on Mojo, Dillon leaned over, " How is she really,?" Noah shook his head. "Damn. I thought she was dealing some b.s." He sat back in time for Sophie to not suspect anything.

"Remind me, tomorrow, I have to track down Madgey's food and load in some hay." Noah plugged it into his phone. "You guys have a goodnight, I have some stuff to unpack." She planted a kiss on her brother's forehead and hugged Luke before making her way up the ramp, Madge right on her heels with her toy.

10

The guys traded war stories, made a pact to check in on each other every week if not more and to get Sophie to a better mental place. With three of them, maybe they wouldn't be so obvious.

Days turned into nights which turned into weeks. Eventually, Sophie came around to where she could say "Liam" and not cry. Perspective had taken a new spot on her shelf of tools to deal with grief. Some days were still harder than others. Some were meant for celebrating. Like the day she went with Chase and Charlie when they found out baby number two was a girl. They went to Mrs.Peatree's for two dozen pink chocolate dipped popcorn treats. They boxed each one in a box with pink and blue ribbons. Watching the reactions as they handed them out to family and friends gave her a bit of hope.

Eight weeks later, in the middle of the night, Sophie's phone rang. Her shortest conversation ever. She raced for the door, shoes in hand, one arm in her jacket. "Be my sweet girl Madgey, mama's gotta go. There's a baby coming." The door banged behind her.

Noah threw an arm out, effectively snatching her out of thin air. "Whoa, where's the fire?"

"Charlie's in labor."

"Let's go." He shut the door and ran for the truck. On the way, he snorted, glancing over at Sophie for an instant. "Does it seem like everybody we grew up with is hatching out kids? I feel old as hell, kids I used to toss out in the lake are now changing diapers and making play dates...whatever the hell those are. Yep, old and like I got left behind."

"You were in the Army, in a battle zone. You didn't get left behind, more like you were thrust into an alternative universe. You've had a fair share of shit to deal with and I came along and totally threw a monkey wrench into your world...besides, you have time."

He wanted more time to talk with her, but the hospital loomed ahead. They ran together to the third-floor maternity ward. Her dad beat them to the floor, Wanda had been asked to not come. Sophie was fine with her mother being absent. Sutton strolled in with Gilly on the phone so she could be with them in a different way. They paced the hall, played a 'I'm bored to tears' version of musical chairs; where they sat, got up, moved, sat and repeated the process. Finally, Chase's voice carried over everything else. "Oh my god, she's perfect."

A panic stricken Charlie's voice rose. "Why isn't she crying? What's wrong? Is she okay? Someone say something!"

Sophie bolted into the room and stopped in her tracks. "Look at you, checking out the world while your mama is so worried."

"Charlotte, she's okay." Sophie followed the nurse to the strangest looking baby table she had ever seen, as soon as the baby started to chill—she started to fuss.

The nurse took her to mama, Charlie burst into tears. "My baby, sweet baby girl." Chase was at a loss, she hadn't cried when their son was born and now she was sobbing. Sophie wiggled in across from her brother-in-law.

"Hey sissy." She kissed her sister's head. "She's okay. She's just chill. And she needs a name."

Chase brushed Charlie's hair back, "Heather Kaye. Seems like the name is gonna be a Monroe thing. Jess started the line with Layla, Beau followed and now...our turn." Their pediatrician checked over the newest Monroe. Sutton weaseled in to let Gilly join in by phone. Walt came in after everyone calmed down. He had news, but it could wait. Right then all he wanted to know was his daughter and grandbaby were healthy. Sophie and Noah were the last to leave, her face hurt from grinning so much. They made cinnamon apple pancakes and a pile of bacon which they chased down with a pot of coffee before they gave up and crashed.

Madge wasn't sure what the deal was, but she had mom and the big hairy dude in her sight and both fed her bacon so dog life was all good. Mokie stretched across the back of the couch taking in everything. Napping sounded like a plan.

Days were cooling off some, nights were definitely chillier. One of those nights, when sleep eluded her, Sophie made some hot chocolate and sat by a window, cracked open as a precaution with the woodstove. Noah softly padded across the yard and over the lower deck to the hot tub. His jeans dropped to the towel on the flooring, he turned to throw a leg over the side, Sophie inhaled so fast, she whistled. "Sweet mother of mercy, I heard the family trait appears to be large...intentions. " She looked at Madge, "That's like a mastodon bone." Her cheeks went bright red. "Okay, it is just because I've been close to a year without any sort of sex." He stood and leaned to adjust jets, leaving Sophie to bite on her knuckle. "I can't do him. He's my friends' brother." He swung back around, illuminated by the full moon overhead, she got a grand view of his equipment. "I would love to know what he's thinking about. What would he do if I joined him?" She shook her head. "Transference, something the all-knowing shrink would say."

Transferring emotions had been one of their topics of discussion before she quit going. "Day-um, Imma of the opinion, transferring some of this to some of that would be a good thing...no one ever said you had to love someone to indulge in a little sex with them."

In the hot tub, Noah got the distinct sense of being watched. One hand-stretched over to grab the military-grade flashlight on his jeans. Scanning the outside area of the yard as best he could gave him nothing. "Cluckers would be fussing if something was out there." He felt a bit better, but still had a sense of unease. Mokie stretched on the windowsill, Noah was tempted to stand up and wave his goods at the cat, but with his luck Sophie would pick that moment to let the dog out and see him. He didn't need a hot tub, he needed a cold shower. She started working Mojo again. Her tight riding pants and those boots led his imagination down a path guaranteed to get at least him in trouble. "I mean, after all, Sutton said to go rescue his baby sister, not go drag her ass back and...yeah, I gotta be the world's worst friend."

SOPHIE CALLED MELISSA, she needed to see how Lis was handling life as a widow and dating. An hour spent talking to her and staring at what needed to be accomplished left her exactly in the same place mentally she started at. Noah answered a bro call. "I need help" was a sure-fire way to get him where ever the friend was. Luke bought a small place and thought a ramp might be easier to traverse until his leg healed more. Getting up and down was still an issue.

Noah had enough to do, she could swing getting hay in. Sophie toed the backhoe, "Strap and lift the bale and swing the bitch into place. Once the first one is in, I can shove the round bale with this. Guess it's a good thing no one was ever around to say "you can't do whatever." Yes ma'am this is a plan. Not a great one, but still."

Feeling the need to blow out cobwebs, she rode her Harley over to Rayna's. The first few miles she fought the urge to hyperventilate. A sign with Mardi gras masks and beads painted on it reading "Monroe's" sat at the end, back far enough if a jerk with a baseball bat went after it, they'd be in the ditch. Before she got her helmet off, she was surrounded by Rayna's crew, most of which had known her for her entire life. She felt the love. "Okay guys, let her breathe, come on girlie. I hauled out lunch stuff."

"THANKS RAYNA, I WANT to get this home to Mojo and Dillon can grab one when he comes out. If I can fit in a third I'll let you know when I come back for my bike." She hugged her friend, "Promise, I'll be careful with the truck."

"Not worried about the green beast. Mileage rolled over at least twice and I think twice more before that." They listened to elks bugle, "Man, they sound close."

"Yep, Noah and Trent were talking about how the fires have animals all sorts of places they don't belong." She climbed into the cab, buckled the seat belt and fired up the old truck. She was closing in on a year since she came home. It seemed more like yesterday at times. As she drove her mind wandered, to what she could have been doing as Mrs. Liam Boone. Some days she struggled to remember his smile. Some days every nuance seemed to be burned into her soul.

A flash of tan caught her attention and brought her back to the immediate space in time. "Shit!" Sophie locked up the brakes, the back tire blew out, exaggerating the slide of the truck. And then, the world tilted. Like she hovered some place high above as the truck tipped over, one roll, almost righted, slid on two wheels before slamming back down. She bounced off something and stopped upside down. She hung there for a second before the stench of gas got her attention. She wore a small pouch with a multi-tool on her belt. "Please...yes.has a blade. She sliced through the seat belt and crawled out the window. Patting her pockets until she found her phone, she yanked out the tan case with horseshoe print, her phone, she yanked it out, "Lucky me, screen didn't break." She scooted another few feet, "Damn that hurt. Put my...put my head down for a second. Nausea go away."

Through the brain fog she recognized the sounds of the elk call out again, brakes squeal and someone yelling. "Oh hell, it's Sophie!"

"Come on kiddo, hey Soph...come on, eyes open."

"Is she hurt ?"

"Looks like a little PvP with the bull elk over there. I'm more concerned with why he's still standing in the same place."

"Okay, my brother is on the way. Noah is with him."

Words swirled, PvP is a gamer term. What the hell does Jesse know about... "Ace"

She mumbled, but, he heard her. "Hey Peaches, you ready to sit up?"

Peaches, her gamer name. "Yeah." He helped her get upright. "Damn elk. Stupid tire." She pushed her hair back. "Damn it, Rayna's truck."

"She won't mind. I can promise you. Did you hit the elk?"

"No, slid. A loud bang and roly-poly time." Luke scratched his head.

"The elk fell over."

"Take the shotgun from my truck and go see what the deal is."

"On it." It wasn't a jog, his gait was more of a hop and skip as he cleared the space between the truck and elk. Luke yelled back, "Someone shot him, and not well. From the blood puddle, I think he slowly bled out."

"Split it with ya." Jesse read recognition all over her face.

"You're Ace."

"How hard did you hit your head."

"Nope, it's you."

Logan and Noah pulled up, blue lights spinning down the light bar, "We'll talk later."

Noah was on a run, to Jess it was like the running of the bulls, panic laced his words until he landed next to her. "Sophie, "

"I'm okay, smacked my head...again is all."

"Okay sweet cheeks, tell me what happened." Logan squatted in front of her. "Stupid elk just stood there. I hit the brakes, heard a loud bang and slid until I turned into a roly-poly and then these two goofballs showed up."

Jess checked the back tire, rummaging through the pieces until he found the one. "Yep, buckshot in the tire. It appears like someone was doing a little poaching and then our girl there ended up in the middle of the act."

"I want the damn thing, but I'll share." Sophie held a knot on her head, "Ow."

"Yeah, you need to dig the pellets out of the tire so we can match them up. Do you remember seeing anything?" Logan looked around, she wasn't sure at or for what. But, everything was a little scrambled. "A man standing by a bright red truck, way too clean to belong to any of the farms or ranches."

Logan strode over to the SUV and radioed in. It wasn't long before deputies were scouring the county looking at bars and motels for a bright red truck. His second call was for an ambulance. When they rolled up, Sophie was on her feet, wobbly, but on her feet and giving Logan more details.

She was fine while the EMT did a cursory check, when he said "We need to take you in," she lost it. Flashbacks to Liam being loaded into an ambulance and the race to a hospital. Someone called Rayna, she skidded to a stop and ran across the two-lane road, her door hanging open. Sutton and Gilly pulled up, stopping only when they spotted Rayna. Sophie went into panic mode to go along with her injury.

Noah whistled loud enough to deafen sea life all the way off the California coast. "Hold on, Jesus," His head shook, "pay attention to her." He held his hand out. "Come on babe, I won't put you in there...promise." She stared at him, but stayed rooted to the spot, hyperventilating, looking for a place to run.

"No." Gulping air, she tried again, "Not going in there."

"Cool, I'm not a fan either."

One of medics tried to ease up on her. Noah snarled at him, "Back off ass hole." He still had a hand out. "Come on. You can trust me. Been there, remember?" He inhaled deeply and exhaled, like when shooting the enemy except this held far more importance in his view. "C' mon, we need to brainstorm getting the hay bale to the storage room."

Her eyes darted all over. Not listening to Noah, the EMT made a grab for Sophie. He was met with the heel of her palm to the end of his nose followed by a shriek. Her booted toe connected with his shin like she was kicking a field goal. Noah dropped him with a fist to the jaw, scooped her up and carried her to the rolled truck. "Sshh, I got ya, no one is going to put you in the box baby. Promise."

No one knew what to do, they stood there like statues as the medic moaned in pain. Gilly waddled over, both hands on her belly. "Soph, here." She placed her sister-in-law's hands on her extended belly. Baby number three was wiggling all over. Sophie's jaw dropped, her gaze went to Noah first.

One move. His words. Plain as day.

Everyone there understood in an instant. As far as Noah was concerned, Sophie had been moved from friend to a category she might not be ready for, for a long while yet. "Sutton and Noah can take someone's truck and Rayna can come home with me. They won't let anyone force you to do anything. We both know I'm right. Okay?"

Sophie nodded. "Did you find out yet?" her voice barely over a whisper as she moved her hand to track the squiggly soon to be relative.

"No, we can positively say, peanut has a butt. I told your brother it has to be a girl cuz if it was like him, it would be showing off everything."

No one moved, breathing was a maybe as they waited. "Now, walk me back to the car, so we can take you to a doctor." Sophie held on to Gilly's arm as they trudged back to the hodge-podge of vehicles. Rayna met them at the car door, kissing Sophie's cheek and then helping Gilly buckle up. "Keys are in the truck, keep me in the loop."

They waited until all three were in the truck and pulling out. Jesse and Luke loaded the elk into their vehicle and headed for Luke's place to get knives and bags before driving over to the compound, as they referred to Noah's place. Bart rolled in with a tow truck, he righted the green beast truck, strapped the round bale to the flatbed and ran it out to Mojo.

"Yep, my calling in life. I am the O'Hara whisperer." Gilly patted her belly.

Rayna laughed so hard she almost peed herself.

Dr. Eastman met them at the emergency room, first to treat the EMT, followed by Sophie. "Alrighty miss, bright light." He checked her pupils, the knot, reflexes, "Which one of you broke the guy's nose?" Sophie looked at her feet. "Mmhm. Fight or flight mode." He pocketed his glasses, "Sophie, you have PTSD and need to talk with someone. You could have hurt yourself, Noah, anyone in range. Not intentionally, but out of fear. I have treated you since shortly after the accident. Trauma, not treated. More trauma because of your mom, add more when Tammy died and a million times more when Mr.Boone was killed. Your psyche can only take so much. I do not believe in throwing pills at everything, but if you think..." her head was shaking no, "Excellent. You need to talk it out. I'll have Janey text you a list of providers. Now, with the knot on your pretty head. I would say minor concussion. You will most likely be sore and bruised for a few days. Hot bath or shower, take it easy and eat some of the beast. Come see me in a week." He turned to Noah, "Keep an eye on her, she gets groggy or acts strange, bring her back here." He stopped at the curtain, "Check with Grace Lightfoot, she makes a concoction, does wonders for muscles."

Sutton fought his fear as the gamut of emotions raced across his kid sister's face when Eastman said she needed to talk to someone. Gilly wouldn't be able to sidetrack Sophie with the baby bump much longer. His phone dinged, he pulled it out of his shirt pocket, half-listening to the nurse go over the instructions in detail. It was Luke and Jesse. "Elk is in a cooler in Sophie's truck."

"Cool. Let's ride." With a minor crab step, she was on her feet and moving. Halfway home she sat up straight. "We need to get milk and did the hay make it to the yard?"

"Hay would be a yes. Gilly said Bart moved it. And do you have a particular store you use?"

"Never use Crabtree's. Gas is watered, everything is old, even the candy bars are gray."

"Okay, info worth knowing." Sutton pulled into a gas station store across from Crabtree's, Noah ran in giving him a minute to play big brother. "Where did you learn to fight?"

"Lessons, I had a stalker and needed an equalizer."

"That man loves you baby sister."

"Be real."

"I am. I saw the look on his face as he belted that ambulance jockey. The way he tried to talk you down. He may not want to admit it...but I know that look. Same one I used to give Gilly. You could do worse." He looked her way, "When you're ready, just remember that."

Noah came bouncing back out the door, laughing at something. He yanked the truck door open and climbed in. "Hoo-we." He wiped his eyes as he spoke, "Guy in there thanked the ATM and then put all he had into pulling open the cooler door—walloped himself. Put a big ol crease in his forehead, took him to his knees, he bit his tongue and he was yelling that someone hexed him."

"Oh boy, sounds like a Moby regular." Sophie wanted to shake her head, except it hurt.

Sutton chuckled, "Sounds like he's been into the bathtub gin." He dropped them off with the reminder to check in tomorrow. Trudging up the ramp, Sophie could not believe how loud Madge whined at the door. "If anything happens to me, you have to take care of her and Mokie."

"Why me?"

"Because you are the only one who would love them like I do."

Noah stopped her at the door, pulled her in close and held on to her. No words, no one watching, judging, two hearts beating, a gurgle from a starving belly and then a chuckle. "I'm hungry too. Go dig out a couple pans and I'll go grab the cooler and cook us dinner."

"You're on." She dug out a heavy cast-iron skillet, a sheet tray, and a couple other saucepans. "Okay, that gives you a choice." Grabbing a dish towel, the next stop was an ice pack and a chair she brought along. Mokie hopped up to rub on her before moving to the window sill. Madge raced down the ramp, peed while turning and flew back up to guard her human. Every time she shifted, the pooch sat up to check on her.

Finally, Noah backed through the door. "When someone says cooler, what do you think—just use your hands." Sophie held her arms out straight and flipped it to be sort of even. "Thank you. I thought I was off." He grunted as Jesse's ninety-five-quart cooler slid through the door.

Sophie peeked from under the towel. "Good grief. That is closer to a cooler on steroids."

"And the boys packed it full."

"I'm sorry."

"What for?"

"You're probably going to catch a load of shit for slugging that bozo, and I am zero help around here right now."

He crouched next to the chair. "You do plenty. You did scare the hell outta me but..." he saw it in her eyes, the twitch of her lips. "What?"

"Liam told me that a couple times." She took a deep breath and exhaled slowly, "Jonathon called, the cops said the fingerprints on the bullet fragments picked up by the jackass, I guess as a reminder, matched Landon. They dropped the murder and attempted murder for the attack at the barn. Ashby is still in jail though. On the other side, Landon's mother was released. They have her in like a halfway house to acquaint her with more modern technology and the like. He had her locked up for over a decade."

"How do you feel about that?"

"I questioned his involvement before, some physical issues would have made it hard for Ashby to do the shooting, I think I'm okay with it. He has other charges that he probably won't walk away from. In a weird way, we're almost in the same boat. They want me to go back for the trial."

"Anyone else know?"

"Nope. And there is more you should be aware of, but I want food first."

"Sounds like a plan." Noah made room in the freezer for the beast, dropped a couple of elk steaks in the skillet and started some water boiling for potatoes. His humming from the kitchen made Sophie smile.

She whispered to Madge, "They really are a lot alike." Not missing a beat, her head whipped around to see Noah and back to Sophie, almost like she was questioning her person's sanity. "other than this one is built like a gorilla." Madge's doggy brows moved in a canine version of Morse Code. "Silly girl, I love you." She climbed up in Sophie's lap, sniffing toward the kitchen. From where she sat, she found the clunk of a knife meeting a cutting board, comforting, as Noah sliced something and the sizzle as it landed in a pan, in a few minutes she was sure the something was mushroom gravy she smelled. Her phone buzzed, it was Shelly." *Just so you know, Noah's ex left her husband. Said she should have never left my brother. Can I beat the beotch?* "

"*Yes, you may. How did you find out?*"

"*Was at Moby's, cute cowboy butts to watch. He was in there drowning his sorrows. They're both a waste of time. How's your head?*"

"*Sore, your bro is making dinner...it may hurt 4 a week.*"

"*Ha. Go figure. Hugging U, feel better.*"

"*Nite.*"

"Hannah left her hubs. Said she should have never left you."

He hustled around the corner waving a wooden spoon in the air as he spoke. "That hoe-bum gets close to me and you're around you gotta promise to make her go away. I don't care how or what you say, just let me know so the story jives."

"So, I could tell her she can't have you back because I need you to play princess with me, cuz you make a fantastic woodland fairy and it's okay?"

"I can even be a naked woodland fairy wearing sparkly wings and jewels on my toes but be careful where you attach the bells." He wasn't sure what brought that out, but the sound she made sounded slightly rude and made the dog jump. "Dinner will be done when the buzzer dings."

"How can a buzzer ding? Either it is a buzzer that buzzes or it's a dinger that dings."

"You know what I meant." He dragged the cooler out to use as a table so they could sit in the living room area by the open door. "Beast, mashed taters, green beans, mushroom gravy, and biscuits."

"You're hired." Her eyes closed as she got the first bite of biscuit dragged through potatoes and gravy. "Yum."

One small act, made Noah extremely happy.

"How's your leg, I saw you working it yesterday, today, whatever."

"It's tight. Last winter it dogged me all the time. I expect it to do so again." He ate a bite of steak, "How are you feeling?"

"A bit stiff. Dumb thing. I must have come around the bend right as he shot "

"Lucky he didn't hit you."

"I almost think he already shot it, the elk didn't drop and he started to take the second shot when I came 'round the bend and he pulled it and killed the tire."

"That could be."

They both tried to sneak bites to Madge, fussing at the other for spoiling her. Noah loaded the dishwasher while Sophie walked out with Madge "Well girl, we shall see how forgiving one can be." They came in as a light wind blew through. "brr, won't be long before we're ass deep in snow.

She curled into the chair as Noah got comfortable. "Now what's so drastic that made you sound so ominous?"

"You are so kind and generous; it's in your nature. I think I always knew that. Liam was much the same. You let me cry when I needed to, dragged me out to do the things I should and let me come to terms with his death in my own time. I will never be able to thank you for being there. But, when Liam died, I wasn't just a broken sobbing mess. I was flat pissed off and wanted vengeance. I was behind Ashby's fiancé getting grabbed by Landon. At the time, I had no idea he killed Annalee," she looked up and realized he had no clue. "Liam's former girlfriend, fiancée, was going to be. It messed him up. He thought she simply disappeared." She shook her head, "Her body was in Landon's freezer. I was behind the people who rigged their house to hear Liam's voice and whatever else they did. I didn't care about them as people, I wanted him to hurt like I was. I wanted his heart to crumble like mine had. From what I was told, nothing done should have caused the Ashby's house to blow up. That seems to be the hand of fate. I was behind the photos of senior with the kids being released, they were all doctored. We, as in Landon, emptied their bank accounts and then Ace, a gaming buddy," she wouldn't give up Jesse, no matter what. "moved them so he couldn't blow through the money. Landon paid a guard to torture Bennett with recordings of Liam's voice, paid someone to wire the house so it seemed Liam was haunting it, paid someone to hang a scarecrow of Ashby in effigy and for the press to be there when mama went a bit cray-cray. We think he was planning on doing some more and sinking me...thing is, I didn't care."

Noah drew designs on the back of her hand with a finger. "If I had watched the woman I love, heart and soul, die, the person who did it would have been found in a shack in the woods. Skinned alive. Heart carved out and stuffed in their mouths. No mister nice guy about it. Not even close to it. You need to cut you some slack. This Landon dude could have said no. He was an adult. Thing is babe, no one really knows how far they will go, until it happens."

"You are very forgiving."

"Two sides to every coin babe. Ashby the elder was as crooked as a snake on a hot road. Things were coming out daily that from the pucker of that brow, you knew nothing about. It was a matter of time before he went to some country club prison. And junior had been accused of date rape in New Jersey but they bought the girl off...you were not aware of that either."

"I didn't...nope. That's nuts." She fidgeted in the seat. "Think I'm going to take a shower, dinner was great. Thanks Noah."

"Anytime." He pulled her to her feet and waited to see if her world would spin, satisfied that she was okay, he hugged her. "Just glad you weren't seriously hurt."

"Pssht takes more than a giant beastie in the middle of the road to take me down."

11

Less than a month later, Sophie harped on Noah for an hour, he finally gave in and got ready. It was just dinner and cards with her brother. His pregnant wife was bored. They rolled in to the little ones crying and Sutton yelling. Sophie about ripped the door off the hinges, her intention was to beat the crap out of her brother. Instead she handed kids to Noah, "get Eastman here yesterday."

He dialed as he held wiggly little people. Doc must have had a career as a moonshine runner in a former life. He tore down the driveway throwing gravel and sand as he whipped the wheel around. "Call Donna" was the next order.

He followed the order to the letter...sort of. He called Rayna and blurted out "Soph said call Donna, I don't have the number. We're at Sutton's" He didn't get out another word. In a few minutes Rayna and Donna arrived to claim the oldest two O'Hara offspring. Each held one when the screech of new life rent the air. Movement stopped. Talking ceased. Until from inside came a mighty cry of satisfaction in an "I told you so," from Gilly.

Sophie appeared in the doorway with a blanket-wrapped bundle. "Look." Tears sat ready to spill, awe in her voice. "Oh my god, she is perfect." Dark hair curled around her head, a button nose like her mama. "I bet she has her daddy's eyes."

Sutton stepped up behind his sister, while everyone focused on the new arrival, he saw the look on Noah's face and made a mental note to talk with him. If anyone was a match for his wild-child sister, Noah was the one. His grin got bigger at the thought. "Now, boys, be nice to your sister."

They leaned over to peek at their tiny sibling. "Dadda, she widdle." Followed by "Beebee" from the other tot.

"Thank you, Donna, Rayna. We truly appreciate your help." He got the usual wave of the hand and a noise sort of like a raspberry as they loaded small O'Hara's into car seats.

"Donna is in her element when it comes to kids...who would have thought." Noah let the comment hang, with Sutton nodding in agreement. Inside, Doc was explaining to Gilly he had a feeling about this one and stocked everything he might need in case junior decided to pull some shenanigans.

"So what is my darling niece's name?"

"Uhm...we figured peanut was another boy. They won't do for a pretty little miss like her." Daddy rubbed a finger down her cheek before answering his wife's call for assistance.

They had to work at not making fun of her older brother. From down the hall, they heard Gilly, "Sutton, women have been squatting in fields pushing out babies and going back to work for ages. Just keep me steady."

Doc's laughter faded out as he entered the room. Noah and Sophie sat side by side staring at the new one. The not so covert glances between the parents and doc said the same thing. Gilly parked in a recliner with her feet partially raised. "She went from zero to a hundred in three steps. All I could do was hit the floor and yell for help. Thank our lucky stars you guys got here when you did."

Noah, still in awe, responded, "That's crazy dude. No wonder you did the rodeo thing, nerves of steel."

"Not so much bud, I was never so happy for a sister to bust through a door." His grin was what Sophie needed to see. "So, whatcha think sis? You got suggestions?"

She stared deeply into the small one's eyes. Noah offered Emma, but Gilly pointed out there was about fifty in the area around them, same with Olivia.

In a whisper, Sophie answered, "Isla Nicole."

Sutton and Gilly traded glances. "I like it," in unison, followed by chuckling in stereo. Doc inked up tiny feet and pressed them against a certificate. While the ink dried, he filled out the rest and signed it. Sophie handed her niece over so doc could do some tests.

She headed for the kitchen, dialing her phone as she went. "Hang on, adding gram." She made certain they were both on the line, "Baby is here." Charlie nearly scared the dog out of his fur. Chase raced into the room thinking something was wrong. "Boys are at Auntie Donna's Camp for wayward O'Hara's." Her comment got giggles from all. I'm making dinner for them for tonight, one of y'all has tomorrow." Charlie looked at the phone, silently questioning when her baby sister got so bossy. Sophie handed off her phone, she thought the parents should give out baby details. She did a once over of the fridge, gathering ingredients. "Here, slice these." She handed Noah a knife and a box of mushrooms. While she cut meat into bite-sized pieces and added oil to a deep skillet she went over the steps in her mind. She grabbed a tube of tomato paste, poking the hole in the seal with the cap was a nuisance. "Okay, stir this while I dig out the gravy stuff."

Gilly sniffed, "What are you feeding me, it smells marvelous."

"Beef stroganoff." She checked the pan, opened a box of beef broth and added some to the pan, "My secret for super tender meat." Noah nodded, he knew hers was better than he had anywhere else. "Some tomato paste," he kept stirring, oblivious to the elbowing and nods from the threesome with the baby. "add the mushrooms, some of this, makes the gravy darker and some sour cream," she shook a pan with green beans. "Okay, we're dropping the noodles, I can stir if you can pull the plates down." She looked up, "Doc are you staying? I made plenty."

"Love to." Sutton and Noah pulled a table in so Gilly could sit with them more comfortably. "Oh my goodness, Sophie this is wonderful." Doc speared a mushroom, "You two made a good team." Noah came close to missing his mouth, Sophie ignored it. Fast moving conversation, a sense of light-heartedness, and seeing her brother beam made the night for her.

With the meal done, Sutton saw his chance. "Come on Noah, you can help me feed so I can get back in here faster." Both men sprang up, moved the table back, and went out to take care of the animals. Noah lined up buckets at the spigot filling them and then putting them in their appropriate pens. "Man, I am so glad you guys showed up early. The boys were fighting, baby decided two contractions was enough to exit...that was a hot mess."

"Sophie had been ridin my ass like an old mule, "Come on I want to leave now, kind of like she knew." He laughed, "Then she stuffs those wiggle worms in my arms and says call...like I got a spare hand."

"Well, you did it."

Noah stopped moving, as if it just registered; he had. "Guess I did."

"Does my kid sister have any idea you're in love with her?" Noah felt seasick, he didn't want to duke it out with an old friend and he sure as hell was nowhere near ready to admit to anything when it came to Sophie.

"We're friends. That's it. I understood the pain when you lose someone. That is all there is."

"Uh-huh. I call bullshit." Noah's mouth opened, Sutton's hand went up, "Let me just offer this up. You could do far worse than my baby sis, and she could certainly do way worse than making you a legal part of her equation."

"Thanks...I think." He looked around, "You guys got what ya need for a couple days? Bread, milk, Charlie's bringing chow so you'll be set for dinner, you need someone to come by and help with the animals? The four-legged ones, not the squiggly worms. You need an army for those."

"Naw, we had a baby, not a blizzard. But, come spring I'll be adding on. I'll need help then."

"Call, I'll be here."

Noah and Sophie cleaned up and made sure mama was comfortable before she broached the subject, "If y'all didn't really like the name, don't agree to it to make me feel better. The year hasn't totally sucked. I mean, I got to be here for this. And Charlie's new baby."

Gilly had a horror-struck look, "I love it, so girly and yet kind of strong and it is pretty. I kept hoping for a girl, but I thought it was another boy. We were arguing between Blaine and Kent. Both were guys he used to ride with who got hurt."

Sutton chimed in. "Sis, it is a perfect name for her. Now stop. Your year may have sucked a big hairy one, but there is only so much I'll sugar coat. My kid's names are not on that list. Isla is as beautiful as you and her mama. She needed a name to match."

On their way home, Noah sighed, "Sophie have you talked to Doc about your neck and shoulder?"

"How did you know?"

"You grimace and roll your shoulder."

"Do I?"

"Every time."

"She's beautiful."

Noah's grin spread, "Yeah, she is." Dawn would be creeping out soon. Sophie tossed and turned and resorted to muscle relaxers she had from before her world went to hell. Still sore and stiff she shucked her clothes and eased into a skimpy bikini with an oversized sweatshirt. She grabbed a towel and headed down to the hot tub. Madge was Noah's early warning. His mouth went dry, he was naked as the day he was born, legs folded back close to his body, steam nearly obscuring him. It was dark as dark could get, not a light from anywhere except a few stars peeking out from behind clouds. She didn't notice him, her towel landed with a soft ploof on the table his jeans were on. At the last second, she spotted them. With her brain in hyperdrive, she pulled her sweatshirt off. Noah was fairly certain he was going to swallow his tongue. *god almighty. I may have a heart attack.* He swallowed hard, trying to move the lump in his throat to go one way or the other.

Great granny. Yeah, it has been a while since I had sex...okay, over a year but that doesn't mean I need to jump by BFF's brother. Even if he is seven kinds of hot and thanks to spying and Hannah, I probably know more about his anatomy than I should. "Are you alive?"

"If you don't stop taking stuff off I may not be."

She stepped down into the hot tub. "Oh my word, there's even jets. How the?"

"I found the places to hit."

"I guess." Her head rolled, causing her neck and shoulder to throb like she had just taken a header off Mojo. "ahh, ouch."

"Feelin like the beast got in a gnarly kick?"

"Feelin like the truck tried to beat me up."

He chuckled, "can't be as bad as ol' Chase when he rolled his jeep trying to run down Charlie after she found out Mike was bangin Chloe."

"He should have figured out she was on Cochise, she was going to run it out of both of them and then she'd be ready to talk. Silly boy." She rolled her shoulder trying to work out the knots.

"Yeah, but you can't tell me he didn't enjoy her playing nurse."

"I didn't think they would ever figure out life and get together." She sighed, "Watching Gilly with Sutton is like some cheesy romance novel. Their little ones have him wrapped around their tiny fingers."

"Like Luke around Mac Granger. He's always been about her. Lunkhead. She's overseas right now." "Yeah, she joined the Navy right before I graduated, maybe sophomore year. Seriously, you're done with Hannah?"

"Over and done. Luke told me one of the Fletcher's said she had been with him most of my first deployment. I don't need a woman like her."

"So what do you need?" It was leading and she knew it. Problem was, she didn't know if she was ready for something serious.

His mind was racing. Go big or go home had always been his motto. "You." His voice was low and slightly gravelly.

"You're asking for trouble." He chuckled. "Baby I have never been afraid of trouble. Besides, you're as honest as a person can be, life hands you some shit but you always err on the side of love. Like your sisters, you can set a man to smoldering in the blink of an eye, or taking off a sweatshirt."

She rolled over so she could see him better. His hand was outstretched. What was it Liam whispered, "promise me you'll live your life to the fullest" she put her hand in his and let him pull her closer. Her hands framed his face as they kissed, slow and deep only to do it again and a third time because, three's a charm.

"I can tell your hesitant." Noah lifted her chin. "Your call, your speed, just remember I'm fine with whatever you need to do."

"Noah..." he watched a plethora of emotions play across her face.

"Come here babe." He wrapped his arms around her, knowing in a heartbeat, it could be like holding lightening. Quicksilver had nothing on her.

"All I've done is cry on your shoulder and here I go doing it again."

He kissed the top of her head, "I don't mind. Especially when I'm holding you close." Noah lost track of time, he wasn't sure how long they had sat there. "Babe, we need to crawl out of here, we're turning into prunes."

With a sigh, she sat up. "Noah Driscoll, you are a one of a kind." She kissed the middle of his forehead before she climbed out.

DEACON WATCHED SOPHIE drive off, rumors and gossip thrived in a small town. Generally, he stayed away from the hall, but too many things had been said. He needed to find out what the score was. He drove into the parking area and climbed down from his four-wheel drive. "Yo bro, you alive?"

Noah stopped what he was doing, "Deacon?"

"Yep."

"Well bring your sorry ass on in here."

Deacon was as tall as Noah, and as solidly built. It was like two rams meeting. "I figured I better come hear it from the horse's mouth. Lots of stuff is being said."

Noah drained a bottle of water. "Yeah, most of it is b.s."

"But, she is still living here."

"She is, and I hope she stays."

"Are you willing to wait?"

"Let me try to explain this." He leaned forward, hands wrapped around the bottle, "We both, you and I, know what it feels like to watch someone die. See their blood in a pool you can't escape, listen to their last raspy breath...and so does she. Sophie hurts, her heart is broken, her soul is shattered. It's a day at a time. But I can wait. She is sarcastic, hilarious, quick-witted, not afraid to call me out. She's a bit of a daredevil, hard as nails, soft as a breeze. Sophie is a challenge on a daily basis. Some days she needs me to let her be alone with her thoughts and some days, she wants to bagass outta here and the people around us. Even if we only drive to Spirit Lake. I had one of the old school yell and fight nightmares not long ago. Letting the dog out, she heard me and came beating on the door until I answered, she sat with me while I pounded the hell outta some nails. Until I was ready, she let me work through the anger. I took her out the other day, she put about a dozen boxes of ammo through my

Smith & Wesson. Murdered those cans and buckets a few times." His head shook, "She's strong. She's beautiful and she may be a few years younger but she's a hell of a woman."

"I heard she was right next to him."

"She was."

"It's like some spirit thing has it out for the O'Hara's. Especially her. She was tight with ol' Judd Lawson too."

"Yep."

"So you two are occupying a space," his hand waved around over his head, "But not a bed."

"Correct."

"If I was you, I'd be trying to change that. She's a hottie."

"I won't push her. When and if she is ready, I have no doubt she will let me know in no uncertain terms."

"Okay, so you said you needed help with something." The brothers were off on a new task. Close in age, Deacon was satisfied his brother wasn't getting taken in, not that he believed an O'Hara would do so and he knew where his brother was in terms of his own mental health.

SOPHIE DROVE OVER TO Jesse's. "Okay, Ace." He stared at her, trying to think of a way out. "Your PvP gave you away. Only a gamer would know player-v-player." He could have kicked his own ass at that point.

"There are things, that if anyone knew, would put my kids in danger."

"She said you worked for the Government."

"I did, before Elise died, that was how she died. She was targeted. Everyone connected in any way has been eliminated."

"Because of Layla and Parker."

"Yes."

"I can understand that, but why did you find me in-game?"

"Charlie was worried, she's family now. Which meant you had to be kept safe. You wouldn't tell me, but you'd grouse to friends."

"Sneaky."

He smiled, bringing out his dimple. "You okay now?"

"Yeah."

"He's a good man."

"I know."

"Does he make you happy?"

"Very much so, but I'm not ready to go there yet. I told him so."

"I appreciate an honest woman."

She hugged him. "Still gonna kick your ass on that level."

"Ha. We'll see."

She got back in her truck, no longer did she think of the Dodge as 'Liam's truck', satisfied with what she found out, she was off to finish her list. Two more stops, one at the bank and then on to the most important one. Sophie turned down a driveway with a sign reading "Maison Lamou." And below that, "Monroe's." Beau was herding little people, he held them in check until she was out of the car with Madge. Daisy came racing up to greet both. "Beau, fatherhood looks good on ya."

He hugged her tight. "We were so sorry to hear about Liam. 'Nay was so torn. She wanted to stay with you but we were so wrapped up with mister man here, he hoisted his son, "Come say hi Sabina." A towhead blond ran up, "hi" and raced back to the swing. "and the chub, is Daniel, or chunk master slobber." He wiped his son's chin and then wiped his fingers on his pant leg. "We've been afraid to come over. I'll put it out there. We hound Charlie for news, but we didn't want to say something to make you any sadder...I'm sorry. Lousy friend aren't I?"

"No. Not at all. But, don't be afraid. I need to know I can talk about him, us and not freak someone out." Her hand sat on his arm. "Now where is your wife?"

"Her studio, have fun." He pointed the way. Sophie was a little jealous, she'd admit to it. Going into the huge pole barn, it became evident that Evonay had mad skills. Pieces were hung on walls waiting to be shipped, or stacked against the opposite wall. Madge and Daisy followed her into the small, neat office.

"There you are. Come here Shug, let me hug on you for a spell."

"Lord, I have missed you. I only met you at Charlie's wedding but I feel like I have known you my whole life."

"Same girl, same. Now come sit with me, tell me what we're going to create." Evonay was excited for her friend, to be out and to be creating something special with her.

"I don't know how much gossip is out there."

"Oh, plenty. Want me to tell ya what ya don't know you been doin?" They both chuckled.

"Thing is...Noah swallowed his fears and said he's way more into me than I ever thought was possible." Evonay was about to dance in her seat. "But, I'm not quite ready to go there." Her friend's face fell. Evonay wanted a second chance at love. "No, now wait...I'm interested but I'm not quite ready yet."

Tears rimmed the blond's eyes, "Oh cher, you loved Liam with your soul. I wish I could take that pain and send it far away."

"I did. Now I'm at the guilty stage." Every emotion Evonay felt played out in her expressions. "Never play poker, my friend." Sophie squeezed her knee, "I feel guilty for having feelings for Noah and I swear he gets this without me saying it."

"Smart man. He knows a good woman when he sees one."

"You are too sweet." She played with her necklace, "I have some hard choices to make soon and before I do anything, I want to be positive he's on the same page as I am. So," she pulled out a simple pencil drawing, unfolding it and placing it in front of her friend. "I want rings made, like a backward promise ring."

Evonay's fingers traced the lettering. Croi go croi go deo. "What's it say?"

"Irish or Gaelic for heart to heart forever."

"Oh my gosh. Yes, let's do this." She grabbed Sophie's hand and dragged her out to her supply bin. "Do you know what size?"

"Sort of." Evonay turned to see what she was doing. "Almost." Her finger went into a shiny metal circle, she pushed it up with her thumb as she held it to Madge's bone tag. "Just a hair larger." Evonay handed her a different one, it went through the trial. "Yep. Twould be the one." She shoved her hair back as she stood up. "Good girl Madgey."

"Okie Dokie, what about you?" Sophie held out her ringless finger. It seemed strange to not see her engagement ring. On her way, she stopped at the bank and put it in a safe deposit box. She got as far as the door before she went back and put it in a box in her bag. "Okay." She rummaged through three different bins before pulling out a box from candy Beau bought for her. "Here we go." They put the dogs in the office and headed to the workbench. "They ain't sexy but they keep your eyes safe." Evonay handed safety glasses to Sophie. In her high tech workshop, Evonay took the pre-cut rings and sanded them smooth before locking them into a laser cutter. As they finished that part, Beau came in with a tray, he flipped the light switch to draw her attention. "Back here babe."

"Well come this way, I brought lunch." They went to the office, sure enough. Half sandwiches, soup, and salad, with her raspberry lemonade; he even remembered the napkins and dressing. Before he got out of there he gave his wife a kiss that made her toes curl.

"Shoo, you won't be happy unless I'm half nekkid and Sophie is beet red." He laughed heartily as he escaped the office. "That man," her sigh said it all. "The black is rather a smelly process."

"I muck out a stall on a daily basis. Horse is so full of crap he could be a politician."

"Ahh lawd." She got a bite and hid it behind her hand, "Gawd I missed you girl."

"Ditto." They caught up on all the dirt while they ate.

Right down to the one close to home. "...and then Rachel walks up to Trent and says, "You aren't good enough for me, with your stinking ass cows." And throws her hands up and walks out. I thought Shelly was gonna feed her a door, but her mama slowed that roll."

"I don't get it. Monroe's, Cole's, and Driscoll's were in that line for looks and hearts a dozen times. They are loyal and honest, and hot as hell. They work hard, they provide for others too. I give up."

"Now tell me again how you don't know."

Sophie dropped her head to her hand. "There is knowing and really knowing. He did say I had to defend him from Hannah seeing as she left her old man." She dropped the napkin on the tray. The finishing touches took another couple of hours before she polished them.

"There we go miss. Now, go slap a ring on that man."

By the time she got home, she had talked herself out of it. "He wanted to get laid, hell I wanna get laid. But that doesn't mean it's going to happen." She muttered to Madge as she drove the last mile. "He's going to think it's silly and childish. But, it sounded like such a cool idea at first. Damn."

12

Juggling groceries, Sophie set one bag down to open the door. Mokie stretched out along the hand rail. A sack of flour flipped out of a bag, taking several other things along. She gathered everything, setting them on the railing until she rearranged the grocery bag. The cat sat up, sniffed the flour bag and decided to chew on the corner before sharpening his claws on the end. "Mokie. Bad cat." He met her glare and gave the bag a swipe. "Look out!"

Instead of moving, Noah yelled back something sounding like "what", but it was drowned out by the 'whomp' when the bag smacked him on the head. Flour spilled down his face as the bag tipped and fell.

Sophie ran down the ramp, her hand covering her mouth. "Oh, my god." He resembled a snowman with a five o'clock shadow. His cheeks puffed up and then he blew the flour off his lips. "I said lookout." He turned to look her way, what started as a giggle turned into laughter until she cried and laughed some more.

The first time since he picked her up, she allowed a smile and the sounds of pure joy and amusement to escape. A year plus. It took the whole year and then some. But, finally, he glimpsed a light in her eyes. "I'm happy to see you take mirth in my flour-ness."

"I'm sorry." Her head shook as she took in the scene. "Poor Noah, are you hurt?"

"No, I'm fine." He shook, like a large hairy dog ridding its coat of something that didn't need to be tracked through the house.

"Flour-ness isn't a word."

"Is in Noah-landia."

"That's not a place."

177

"Says you." He stuck his tongue out at her, immediately wishing he hadn't when flour dropped on it. He swore and spit which made her giggle again.

"I gotta call Rayna, she needs to grab more flour." She ran up the ramp, more sounds of mirth drifted down to him.

He shook his head sending flour everywhere. Noah stood there for a minute, nothing hurt, yet. He turned to look at the cat. "You're him aren't you? Her man." His eyes narrowed as he stared at the cat. Mokie stood and walked down the rail until he was at eye level, put a paw on Noah's nose and meowed. "You know, she's always gonna be yours. I'll never have a chance." With a paw on each side of Noah's flour-covered face, Mokie proceeded to carry on a one-sided conversation with the man. Flour fell around his feet, he pointed at the cat, "Don't you run off, she'll be even more broken-hearted." He glanced around to be sure no one was listening. "I'm telling you...she loves you. I'm somewhere under chopped liver." Mokie stuck a paw in the middle of Noah's forehead, meowed in several tones and then stalked off to the house. "Uppity cat," Noah mumbled as he shook to free himself of the rest of his covering.

Rayna pulled in twenty minutes later, Noah still wore a combination of sawdust, which Sophie referred to as man glitter, and flour as he ran wood through his mill. By dark, he was stiff as some of the boards. Moving slow, he put away his tools and cleaned up the area. They carried down trays of cookies, on the third trip, Rayna noticed how Noah held his head. "Are you okay?" She looked up to the railing and back to where flour still marked the spot. "That's a pretty fair drop for five pounds, and can do some damage. "

"I'm okay, I worked straight on without a break and a fair amount spilled first. And I tensed up at impact."

Rayna drew a circle in the sawdust with the toe of her boot. "Talk to her." Sophie bounced down the ramp with the last box. At her vehicle, Rayna turned to her young friend, "Talk to him. I think he's hurt from the bag hitting him and I think his spirit is in need." Holding held her knuckle between her teeth, she nodded. "See you tomorrow." Sophie stood at the gate, waving as Rayna pulled out.

The same thoughts wandered through her mind the day before, he seemed more reserved, more sheltered in what he shared. "Maybe I should find my own place and give him back his. I don't think he planned on me staying more than a few weeks, let alone over a year, and now I'm talking to myself. Great." She trudged back in the gate, looking around the space, she realized had become home to her. The mere thought of leaving made her incredibly sad. Wiping a tear and mentally beating herself up, she missed Noah standing next to her.

"What's up Soph?"

She looked around the yard, "I just realized how much I'll miss this place."

"Then don't leave." Everyone viewed him as large and in charge, but she saw the silly, soft-speaking man who brought water to butterflies and made his friends kids fly through the air after he sugared them up. The man who had his phone plastered to his head as he scribbled down information on one of his guys with a note to send help.

"Noah, it's been a year. Actually a little longer. I don't think you planned on an extended stay when you offered your home to me."

He sat on a log, "At the time, no. I didn't think you would stay more than a few days and then you'd bug out for parts unknown. I'm so used to seeing you and Madge every day," he rubbed his neck, flinching as he touched a couple of spots. "You can stay as long as you want. I promise, you being here is not hurting my feelings."

"Hmm, your neck is hurting, you need to see a doctor."

He smiled or tried, the result was more of a grimace. "I'll go when you agree to stay. At least for another three months."

She pulled her phone out of her pocket and scrolled until she found Dr. Eastman's number and hit the icon. "Mrs. Eastman, Noah got hurt. No ma'am, power tools were not involved. The cat knocked a bag of flour off and smacked him in the head. Yes ma'am. Thank you." She was up the steps and back down in a flash. "Get in the truck bitch."

"I guess you did adopt the south as home." Her brows furrowed in her usual confused expression, "I heard that line is foreplay in the south."

"Pfft."

"I'm offended."

"My ass is offended. Blackmail, bribery, whatever to make you let Doc give you a once over... boy, if you ain't hurt, you will be 'cuz I'll wallop your ass."

He laughed at her. "Baby, I've got nearly a foot in height and a hundred and forty pounds on you."

"Don't forget, I have equalizers. Women don't play fair "

"That's for damn sure."

She glided into a spot in front of Eastman's office. When Noah reached for the door handle, she saw the flinch. "You are hurt, you dip stick, you should have said something." She raced around the truck and took his arm, "Step up." Once inside, Noah explained how he was injured with Sophie filling in the parts he left out.

"Okay, x-rays first." Eastman's x-ray room was more of a cubicle than a room, but for emergencies, the cramped space worked. He shot several sets of film. Noah wandered out to wait. It wasn't long before the doctor was back. "Good thing you're built like an ox. You have two bulging discs. You'll be down for about six weeks. Rest, ibuprofen, after three or four days, start stretching." He flipped through his notes, "You do yoga, go with beginner moves and if you have access to a hot tub, aqua-therapy would be excellent for loosening the muscles." He disappeared and came back with a collar. "Wear this for the next seventy-two hours. He handed her a small paper envelope, "for pain, enough for four days."

"I was about to ask, knowing hard head here, he doesn't keep any around and wouldn't let anyone go find something." Sophie stuck her nose in the air. "Driscoll must be old English for stubborn as hell."

"Name is Irish."

"Okay fine, Irish for stubborn as hell."

" We're not stubborn." The doc snorted, Noah tried again, "Just firm in our beliefs."

"Like concrete." Dr. Eastman snickered as he followed them out.

Janey, his wife, walked across the street. "They haven't figured out they're in love yet, have they?" She linked her arm with his, a contented smile in place.

"No, not yet. Amazing how two smart people can be so slow minded."

SOPHIE REPEATED THE story at Hope's baby shower the next day. They chuckled and asked if he felt better. Before they left, Evonay did her best to allay her friend's fears about staying and the ring. Elloise Driscoll caught up with her before they headed home. Standing on the porch looking out over the horizon, her benefactor spoke low enough for theirs to be a private conversation. "I heard from Coach Fern, she thinks you could get back on the circuit and make the Olympics."

"Yeah." Some odd something tipped off Elloise, Sophie's world was not as right as people thought.

"For as long as I can remember; the Olympics was your dream."

"Was." She took her time, sorting emotions and searching for the right words, "Thing is, I'm no longer sure the public arena is what I want. I had very specific goals that did not involve a man, until they did. Then he became part of the dream and it was shattered into a bazillion tiny pieces and so was I."

"And now?"

"I don't know."

"I know my sons, Trent may never love again after the wench he...anyway, Zach is coming into his own, Cade is Cade and sees each new woman as a test, Ethan is good-time Charlie, but Noah is patient. He wouldn't let you stay if he wasn't interested. I quietly take in him and all the nuances a mom picks up on, like how he watches you and see the signs. He's invested and he will wait you out. He's also not tied to this town, don't be afraid to make him follow you."

"We'll see what happens. At the present time, I don't have a clue what I want. It's a relief to sleep without reliving the day, to ride Mojo out to the wash and back, to not be in fear twenty-four/seven."

"I can believe that. You may not think so, but you've done alright. People are learning from watching you and Melissa White."

"She came to visit the day after I came home. We check in on each other every few days."

"Sort of a widow or may as well be, but still in love battle buddy."

"Yeah." As Elloise Driscoll left, she stopped to hug Charlie, she whispered something to her which made her face light up. Hope limped out, one hand on her belly, one on her husband's arm.

"Something made sis a happy girl."

He nodded as he stepped down. "I'm betting it has to do with Sophie and the ox."

"Is that nice?"

"No, but have you looked at him? He's huge."

NOAH DRAGGED SOPHIE over to a Juniper Springs carnival sponsored by the Sheriff's Association. They ate corndogs and funnel cakes and rode some rides before heading for the games. One row was shooting competitions, whether water or pellets, he wasn't sure how she would react. Sophie was fine and better when the bands began to play. It was the start of a once or twice a week outing. Even if it was only a run to Spirit Lake for groceries, he turned the outing into a lunch date. People whispered behind their backs before, once they were seen together in public...the whisper became more like a dull roar.

Both families backed out and shut their mouths. Their fingers and toes may be crossed, but no one was going to risk saying something to make them go their separate ways. One night they went into town to meet Beau and Evonay for burgers and to shoot a few games of pool, a couple whiskey on the rocks and a few dances turned into a month-long gossip fest. All the while, Sophie and her former coach were emailing on a daily basis. Coach Fernsby had been tapped to be the US Olympic Equestrian Coach. Dressage would make a huge part of the games. In the near forty years, she coached, never had she the pleasure of watching such a well-trained pair. Sophie would need to hit the circuit to prepare, soon. After the year she had, she wasn't sure if the world arena was still her dream.

"Coach, I'm just not sure. I know Mojo would be ready in a month. But I don't know if my head is in the game. Liam became such a part of barn life, my soul hurts somedays when all I'm doing is saddling Mojo for a ride, sounds of gun shot, screaming horses, the scent of blood, and flashbacks to losing Liam fill my head and I am on the ground trying to breathe."

"Think about it."

Noah got a call, someone had a family member with some great wood, some, expensive and hard to find. He just needed to go pick it up. "So take the trailer, pull the panels and use the rolling horse house to bring it back. If ya hit rain, nothing is messed up." He took Luke for road company.

Sophie turned to Shelly, Charlie, Rayna, and Evonay for advice. Molly holed up and closed herself off from everyone. She felt bad for her friend; she sent the pictures of him kissing someone else at a restaurant in Spirit Lake. The man was a snake. The lowest of lows. "I would so love to hit him with a sledgehammer. Super glue his man parts to a post...where he has to stand on his toes to not rip it off. In an ant bed. Jerk." Sophie gave in, her belly growled enough, she had to give in and go eat. Chocolate didn't cut it. Looking at her ring, she noticed the caked on gunk from giving Madge her heartworm pill. "Oh crap, well it looks like it'll wipe off." The dog wagged, she spied a butterfly and bounced that way, bumping into her and knocking the ring out of Sophie's fingers. "Madge! Oh shit, I gotta get it back." Her tennis shoes came off, "No, sweater says dry clean, damn it." She peeled it and her jeans and was into the water. Noah wasn't supposed to be back for a couple of days. She was in a panic. Plunging back into the water, she kept repeating, "Pond is not a pool" as she felt along the bottom trying to find the ring against the rocks.

Noah was happy as a clam when he pulled in. The wood gifted to him would make twenty flag boxes, far superior in quality to what the Exchange carried. Plus there would be plenty left over for some other projects.

Something flashed, he saw Madge on her belly at the edge of the pool. Sophie. He charged that way, not bothering to shut the truck door. She surfaced again, grabbed a breath of air and was back down. Just as he was preparing to dive in, she bubbled up. "Got it." Teeth chattering, goosebumps all over, she turned into Noah. And yelled "Ahh, dammit!" Her arms pulled in close to her body, "You scared the hell out of me."

He jogged to the trailer and fished out a towel from the laundry basket she left inside. "You're going to be a popsicle. What the hell were you doing in the pool?"

"I had gunk on my ring, tried wiping it off, Madge bumped me and the ring fell in so I had no choice." He wrapped the oversized towel around her and gathered her castoff clothing.

"What are you doing back already?"

"Woman, I swear to all that is holy, you scare me one more time..." he scooped her up and ran up the ramp. "Come on Madge, let's get your mama inside." She beat him to the top.

"I can walk. And I thought the pond had a heater."

He let her feet hit the floor, but held on to her. "Sophie, there was no way I could have lived through your walk up here. You're half-naked, soaking wet, and damn fine looking. On top of which, I don't think you're ready to have some lug like me sniffing around you."

Her brows furrowed, trying to sort out what he was saying while her teeth chattered like they were castanets, left her in a fog. "Are you hinting or suggesting you might like me? As in a serious, permanent type, relationship sort of thing."

There it was, out in the open. He could run, or come clean. "Yeah." Considering their closeness, "Maybe you should go change and then we can talk."

Sophie padded off to her room, her mind in a whirl. "He likes me...damn. Am I ready for this?" she whispered to her reflection. Turning on the hot water in the shower, she bit her lip. "He's been wonderful...mostly." She adjusted the knobs and stepped in. "I mean, it is comforting having him around. But, I should be able to say I love Liam in a different way than I do him and I'm not sure I do. Hells bells, now what do I do?" Warmed and clean she turned off the water and grabbed a towel. "It's time for reinforcements." Mokie jumped up to the counter, meowing away. She scratched his ears, "What's your opinion Mokes? Is it okay to consider love? I swore I would never do that again. It hurts too much to lose them. Is it time to move on?" he stood up on his back legs and stretched so he could headbutt her. "You're so silly." She decided on a text message to Rayna.

"Help."

"What's up girlie?"

"He likes me. He?"

"Noah."

"This is good yeah?"

"I don't know."

"What does your heart say?"

"It's confused."

"Mmk. Try this. Picture Noah not in your life anymore, in any way."

"God, No. I don't want to lose anyone else."

"I didn't say dead, just not there."

"It'd be the same. I don't want to lose him, but I don't think I'm ready to go forward."

"Tell him. Luv ya chickie, now go conquer the mountain."

"Thx." With an exaggerated sigh, she walked out to find him playing disappearing toy with Madge. Mountain. It was appropriate.

"Okay, now that I am no longer freezing. We need to talk." Noah couldn't decide if it sounded good or not.

SOPHIE'S PHONE RANG, ordinarily she would ignore all devices until her afternoon coffee break ended, but her dad's face popped on the screen. "Hi, dad."

"Hi, Punkin. I wanted to tell you before word gets all over town. I moved out and filed for divorce." Her jaw fell. "Don't get me wrong, I still love the Wanda I remember. From before. But, I can't live with this one and she refuses to seek help. Too many years, too much said and not done, too many things what can't be erased. Neither of us is stepping out, I'm just done."

"I can understand that dad. Are you staying with Gram?"

"Yep. She offered and I accepted."

"Winter will be here soon. I feel better knowing you'll be there."

"Well Punkin, I'm heading over to tell Sutton. You take care now."

"You too dad." She hung up and slowly sank to the couch. "Dad filed for divorce."

Noah stopped moving. "Whaa?"

"Yeah. Isn't that nuts?"

"Yup."

Sophie couldn't sit still, she got up and went to the bar cart. Standing in front of it trying to gather courage she turned to the fridge and grabbed two beers, "Come on big man," Noah thought he was hallucinating. There was no huge, sparkly ring on her finger. She handed off the bottles for him to open. "Okay. You dropped a bomb on me the other night...but honestly, it's not a place my mind hasn't already gone."

Noah was sure he was running a fever.

"I'm not sure how it happened, but one day it was like a lightning bolt and I'm starting to babble." She chugged back a quarter of her beer. "I'm still not ready for a full-on commitment, but I have some major decisions I have to make and do so soon and I want to know you're with me, that you'll wait. That you have my back," her finger went to his lips. "So, I took an old custom, turned the sucker inside out, went to Evonay and we made these." She pulled a velvet bag out of her pocket. "Think like a reverse promise ring. I need you to swear, you'll be here and ready when I am positive I can move forward."

"There's two." His brows furrowed as the realization of her words sank in.

"One for me, to remind me, when the world shits all over my path, I have you and one for you to remind you, I'm not on the same page as you, but I am turning them as fast as I can."

"Really?"

"You think it's stupid."

"No, I'm so amazed someone put so much thought into something made for me. This means so much to me. I am honored and I most certainly will wait you out." She slid the ring on his finger, amazed when it fit. He took hers and held the band so he could read the words, "Wow, you did your homework girl." He slid hers onto her finger. "Now, what decisions?"

Sophie laid it out for him. "I'm going to pitch a training center to some folks that Chase knows and if it flies, I'll be looking for a place close to here where we can build. The plan is to tap Beau and Micah for construction and plumbing...and Chase doesn't know what the project is."

"That will drive him batty."

"It is. But, I have court and the lawyers say I need to be there and I have some personal business to take care of while I'm there."

Noah sat listening, turning the ring. "You want company or want me to take care of the critters."

"Critters, but don't be surprised if I freak and call you to come save me from myself."

"Do I get a kiss to go with this or a secret handshake or something." Listening to her giggle did his soul good.

"Yeah, silly man." Sophie crawled into his lap. One kiss turned into twenty.

"This is like being a teenager all over again, hole up and make out."

"Driscoll, you are a hot mess."

13

Sophie came off the plane, dragging her suitcase behind her. She took a deep breath and exhaled slowly, willing her nerves to settle down. "Ah, Liam. Why did you leave me?" she fought the tears threatening to take over. All she could think of was coming back from Charlie's wedding and him running to meet her. "I'm beginning to think this wasn't such a hot idea Madge." A car and driver waited for her. "Let's go check on Jonathon."

"Good Morning miss, I'm Richard Mobley, I'll be your driver." His Aussie accent and smile offset the solid muscle from the way he moved and the fit of his uniform. "Mr. Monroe asked me to check, there is an event, Jones Feed Store will be closing early, should we go there first?"

"Yes please." Madge stared out the window as Mobley twisted through construction traffic. The closer they got to the barn area, the more Madge seemed to stretch. "You remember don't you baby?"

Jones' Storefront hadn't changed in the least. Mobley exited and came around to open the door in an instant. Madge hit the end of the leash but didn't tug. She trotted right up to the counter. "Madge!" Ted looked her way, his face lit up when he saw Sophie. He came around the corner to hug her. "How are you, sweetie?"

"Doing okay. Some days are better than others. Do you still have her food?"

"I do. I couldn't bring myself to quit carrying the brand. Then some star said this is what he feeds his dog and now everyone wants the stuff."

"Go figure, yeah?" Ted nodded in agreement. "I'm going to get half of a pallet."

He waved one of the boys over to haul bags out to the car. Being the arrogant soul and lacking brain cells, he wised off to Mobley.

Not being one to horse around, he picked the boy up by his collars. "Mr. Monroe pays me well to be sure his family is safe and gets where they need to be. She is my client. However, I am an expert in small arms, several forms of martial arts and spent time in the MMA. If you entertain the idea too much longer, they will transport you to hospital and a dentist when you get out."

Ted hugged her again and gave her a bag of cookies for Madge. "Was really great to see ya, sweetie."

"Nice to see you too Ted." She needed to make four more stops before she was delivered to the Marsh House. Jonathon had been quite happy to see her, they spent an hour going over things before he asked her about buying the big house. "Get the house appraised, make an offer."

He seemed mildly surprised. "I love it here, didn't think I would. Olivia does too.

"Oh, Olivia huh?"

She smiled he sat back. "I can definitely tell you and Charlie are related. How are they?"

"Like you don't keep him up to date." With Chase, no rocket science was required.

Jonathon had the grace to allow his cheeks to take on a little color. "Touche'"

In the morning, with new toys in her old house, Madge stretched out in a sunbeam to wait for mama. The house no longer smelled like her man friend. She went from room to room and couldn't find him. Not a trace.

Sophie drained her cup of coffee at the door before entering the courthouse. What happened turned out to not be much of a trial. Bennett apologized to her repeatedly. "Hate me, you deserve to. I understand what I took from you. I was an idiot, spoiled, and it took a crash landing to realize I wasn't the king on high." He turned to the judge, "Your honor, save the time and money. I am guilty. Every charge."

The jury was out for an hour. They handed a slip of paper to a bailiff who in turn, gave it to the judge. "Mr. Ashby, the jury has found you guilty, and recommended twenty-five years to life without parole." He turned to the jury box. "Ladies and gentlemen of the jury, I am going to poll you on the verdict." He adjusted his glasses and read from the form. "On charge one, murder in the first degree. The verdict was guilty. Do you agree this was a unanimous decision?" One at a time, they agreed. "On charge two, Vehicular Manslaughter in place of Vehicular Homicide, was this a unanimous decision?" Again, they all agreed. "On charge three, Aggravated Stalking..." He went on through the list, assault, breaking and entering, homicide of an unborn fetus, and driving while under the influence. I am going to do something unorthodox. It goes with the rest of this fiasco and sentence you to twenty-five years, no parole, fines totaling five thousand dollars, and a ten-year probation where Mr. Ashby must speak to youthful offenders, a lifetime ban on profiting in any way from this and a lifetime restraining order for the victims of these crimes. Mrs. Boone, do you have an issue..."

After that she wasn't sure what he said. Not until her lawyer bumped her. "I'm sorry, the name is Miss O'Hara, I never got the chance to marry Liam." Her lawyer cringed when she admonished the judge, she missed the reaction, focusing on Bennett; he seemed to have aged a decade. " You'll still be young enough to do something with your life. Not likely but..." She made eye contact with the judge. "Yes, I do have an issue, your honor. My life was turned inside out. I watched the man I loved bleed out over my feet and I have his smirk" she pointed to Ashby, "forever ingrained in my mind. I have an issue. My personal belief is he should be put to death as Liam was. Slam a speeding car into him, let him sail through the air and bleed out. I would attend. I think this is not fair or even appropriate, and has not even a minuscule chance of being useful." He contemplated her words for all of thirty seconds before his gavel met the block of wood. One segment of her life was over. She walked out, straight and tall.

Once in the car, she pulled her phone out. "Flaming Frog please Mr. Mobley." Sophie sent a text to Noah. *"Court is done."* She sighed as she typed.

"U ok?"

"Strangely, I think so."

" Miss you"

"Miss u too. Will call later." He sent back a heart, the text made her smile. "Come in and eat lunch, Smitty makes the best burgers." He hemmed and hawed and finally gave in. Over burgers and hand-cut fries, Sophie looked to Mobley, "I need to be at the cemetery at nine a.m. Once they are done, we're ready to roll." She emailed her old coach with her plans. While Coach Fernsby was not happy, she understood. In the morning Sophie bagged up Madge's toys and her food, she pulled some more items to take back to Wyoming and loaded everything in the car. The drive was quiet as they traveled through the misty morning. Mobley pulled down the narrow path used by hearses. As before, he opened the door and stood where he could scan the area.

She took Madge over to a headstone. A man walked up with a large bouquet of flowers and shook Sophie's hand. Mobley checked the time, deciding to wait a bit. A work crew was next on the scene. He watched as the headstone was removed, and decided to call then. "Boss, she's replacing the headstone. Some guy is here, old man."

"Replacing the headstone?"

"Yes, after I drop her off I'll come back by to investigate."

"Drop her off?"

"Flying back. "

"Court date is?"

"Yesterday. Twenty-five years."

Chase didn't say anything for a minute. "Yeah let me know."

The new headstone had an amazing likeness of Liam sitting with Madge next to his Harley. In his hand was a heart-shaped rock with her name emblazoned across the middle. His dad was moved next to him on the side once reserved for her. On the other side, a simple casket was lowered in, a new stone was placed. Annalee's name and dates and a line from a poem were engraved on the front, on the back *"Home at last."* Sophie stood arm in arm with the man. She knew his name was Daxton and he was nearly eighty. He spent every dime he had looking for his daughter. When her friends quit, and the law stopped, he kept on. She didn't tell him she arranged for him to collect the reward check.

"Part of my heart will always be yours Boonie. I'm trying to do what you said. I still miss you." She kissed her fingertips and touched his name, Madge nosed the new stone, licked Liam's image and then followed Sophie to the car. "Can we drive around for a few minutes?"

"Yes Miss, whatever you need."

She guided him a few times, softly sobbed into the dog's fluffy coat, when she was done she spoke quietly. "Thank you, I'm ready now."

At the airport, he loaded her luggage and boxes onto a cart. "Miss O'Hara, anytime you need a driver slash bodyguard, yell and I'll come running. You are quite a lady."

"Thank you. You're very kind." They walked to the steps, Jonathon gave her a bright blue envelope and admonished her to have a pro read over the contract before hugging her.

Together, she and Madge walked up the steps to the plane. "Okay, Madgey. Back to Whitehall. Is it home now?" she wagged her tail. "I'm still not sure." She sent Noah a text. *"On our way."*

"Everything done?"

"Yep."

"C ya soon baby"

"Yeah. Madge is wagging."

"Ha,"

Mobley went straight back to the cemetery. "Okay boss, can you see?"

"Yes."

Moving slow so as to not make his boss seasick, he scanned from one side to the other. "According to a story in the paper, she paid for the dead girl's funeral and marker. Class act boss. Even arranged for Mr. Legare to be given the check for finding her."

"She never said a word to me or Charlie."

"Maybe the guy she's been hanging with?"

"Could be, Thanks Richard, you earned a bonus."

"That's not necessary boss, she's been a dream to escort."

"No drinking?"

"She invited me to lunch with her and the dog. Patio dining, I didn't feel right leaving her alone when I would be two blocks away."

"Yeah, a block is a bit far if anything happened."

"She drank a little more than half of a bloody Mary and ate a monster-sized burger."

"Hmm. Okay. Head home." Chase sat drumming his fingers on the desk, he might need to go talk to Noah after all. He was derailed by the sight of Elija on the floor with his baby sister. "It's like she's patting him."

Charlie nodded, "It's been like this for an hour." "She really is just chill, let me sit down for a minute and tell you what your sister did."

"Oh no." her brows wrinkled, her hands went to her face.

"Nope, she's has a heart of gold. In fact, she proved so today."

NOAH PARKED IN FRONT of Betty's Blooms n Blossoms. Sophie's text said they would be in the air in a few minutes and she would be back in the hall in a few hours. A tiny bell rang when he opened the door, "Hello. Be right with you." Betty hustled out from the backroom. "Noah, how wonderful to see you."

"Good Morning Miss Betty, I need a bouquet of flowers." He held his hands out to show her the size he wanted.

"Certainly dear, what kind of flowers?"

"Six of those purpley pink roses and then a hodge-podge. So it looks like wildflowers or grabbed from a garden."

"For Miss Sophie?"

"Yes ma'am. She's coming home today."

Her fingertips covered her mouth, "Oh my, I heard about the trial on the news. That poor baby. O'Hara's are always getting slapped by fate. But, in the end, they sure seem to come out ahead. Look at Hope, Charlie, and Sutton."

"Yes ma'am. Fate does like to throw some curveballs at them."

"Please tell me you're going to be her knight in shining armor. There's enough turds in a tin cup in this town...and a real shortage of decent men."

Noah ducked his head, trying to smother the snicker. "Well, we are at the considering stage. Right now, she still hurts. If I tried to rush her, I'd be on par with the turds."

She patted his arm. "Oh Noah, can you reach up there and grab the pink box for me, please? It has ribbon in it, not heavy, just too high." He chuckled a bit as he pulled the box down and set it on the work table. "Thank you, now, she likes these, Peruvian Lilies, some Statice, hmm, she doesn't like white, I think a dusty pink Daisy, and a purple chrysanthemum." She pulled buckets as she spoke, Noah drifted with her vision. "Dear, do you have a vase?" His head shook vigorously. She held up two, "Round or square?"

"Round."

"Clear, or amethyst?"

"Purple." She added in some greenery, measured, snipped, added some powder to help preserve them and tied an oversized pale lavender ribbon around it.

"There you go Noah. Seventy-two dollars." He flipped a credit card over and then slid it across the counter. "Gossip is Walt filed for divorce."

"Yeah, bit of a surprise." He took the vase. "Thank you, Miss Betty." He strolled out and anchored the vase into a box on the floorboard. Once home, he took them into Sophie's room and left them by the bed, shutting the door on the way out. "No sir mister cat. You are not eating those." He moved a load of towels to the dryer, "No wonder women hate housework, it's boring as hell." His nose wrinkled, "Pee-you. Cat you got a rank ass. My god, son." He chucked the litter into a doubled trash bag as he held his breath. "What crawled up your out door and died? You should be ashamed." Noah was still shaking his head and making faces. Mokie stopped in mid paw wash and meowed at him before continuing with his clean up. "Okay, dinner is ready to go on the grill. Bath stuff for her is in there, Mrs. Peatree's treats are in the jar, wine is in the chiller, whiskey rocks are in the freezer, beer is cold, I'm cleaned up, yep. Time to get my lady." Noah took one more look around, there was even a new toy for Madge. He drove out to the airport, the forecast was for snow by the end of the next week. He expected a shipment of pellets in before then. Mojo's barn had been insulated some. Noah pulled in to a front row parking spot and pulled a bottle of water out of a cooler. He checked the time and opened the truck door. He hadn't thought about a relationship with Sophie, not in the beginning. Slowly it just felt right. Thinking about the hot tub kiss made his toes curl and another part hard as a rock. Readjusting himself behind the cover of the door left him muttering to himself.

In the plane, Madge suddenly sat up and she began to whip her tail side to side. "What's up baby? You see stuff you know?" she whined and pawed at the window. "Okay, hold on. We're almost there." They coasted in, setting down easy and rolling to the end of the strip making the turn around to taxi back to the marked spot on the tarmac.

Noah stood outside the doors of the ancient concrete block building. Old Sam emptied a trash can and put a new liner in, passing a few pleasantries with the younger man. It occurred to Noah, old Sam had been old when he was a small child and by that point should probably be ancient Sam. Stairs were wheeled out and locked into place, the door opened, Sam dragged out a cart. Noah knew what it meant. More stuff came back. Madge barked from the top step and nearly dragged her human down the stairs and to the big man.

"What's up Madgey?" his voice went to a falsetto which Sophie never heard before. "You happy to be home?" she licked his nose around ducky. "Aww, you decided I'm okay finally? Guess who bought you a new toy?" She spun around in circles.

"You bought her a toy?" Sophie's hand rested over her heart.

"Yeah, I was in Juniper Springs and the vet has a dog shop. It's a green and red candy-striped bone." He saw the expression, the blinking eyes, *shit, now what did I do*, his mind was in hyperdrive trying to figure it out.

"She had one, red and white...she dropped it in with Liam." Noah stood up and walked to the wall, he didn't know what to say. Sophie startled him when her hand touched his back. "That is so sweet, you thought of her. I'm not so sure she hasn't looked for it a few times. And you swore to me, you knew this was not easy. I can't love with a fragment of my being. I love with everything I am."

"I'm mad at myself, and I wouldn't have you any other way." He kissed the top of her head. "So I'm not in the proverbial dog house?"

"Nope. And I need to make a pit stop. Come on." She led the way out to thank the crew and helped drag the cart to the truck. Not that he needed assistance, she just liked to feel like she helped.

"Where are we stopping?" He tossed in another bag of Madge's food.

"Trying to decide between Rayna and Sutton." The tailgate shut, tonneau cover locked, the dog waited at the door, tail wagging.

"Up ya go baby," she went right to the backseat. "Jonathon made an offer on the big house, I brought it with me I need an opinion on whether or not it's a viable one."

"I thought you'd go to Chase."

"Too close to Jonathon...not that I don't trust him."

"What about Beau?"

"Oh! I forgot, it's close to his line of work too."

Noah reached up and hit a button, "Call Beau."

Two rings in, "Hey Noah. What's up dude?"

"Sophie wants to come over and run something by ya."

"We're at Rayna's and she's hollering for y'all to come here." Sophie nodded yes.

"Okay, be there soon." He made sure to wait for the call ended notice. "She knows so much about so much, she scares me sometimes."

Sophie laughed at him. "Mountain of a man is scared of little Rayna?"

"Hell yeah. She's sneaky and well able to kick butt."

"Oh good grief." They pulled in and found a spot close to the others. Madge led the way, as soon as she saw Chex and Daisy, she started to hop; making the couple erupt into peals of laughter.

Dinner plates sat stacked at one end of the table, a pile of silverware next to it. Hugs came from all sides, it struck Noah that as far as present company was concerned they were a couple, not spare friends.

Cort handed him a beer, "How's the project coming?"

Noah tipped his bottle taking a swig, "All the annoying little projects are done. Got the ventilation cap in on the horse barn so he should be warm this winter, put insulation panels in around the bottom of the trailer so no frozen pipes this year and the pellets are being delivered Monday."

"Yep, you've been busy. What about the major ones?"

"One and I'm down to rigging the solar panels for the artificial sun lights."

"Man if that works, let me know. Ray has is nagging me to build a greenhouse."

"No problem."

Sophie pulled the papers out, "Okay, Jonathon wants to buy the big house. I'm not going to live in it so I see no reason to not sell it. He put this together for me, but really, I have no clue."

Beau shuffled papers, "Comps for the area, stats on the house, appraisal, offer," he read over it once and then went back over the documents. "He attached a personal note. "*Sophie, several pieces of furniture appear to be quite old and in the family for an extended period. Also, there are several art pieces that your sister should evaluate. I'm having them crated and shipped to her. Some other things appear to be family items, I'm sending those to you in the next week."* His comps and the appraisal are in line with his offer. One point nine million to five and a half million for most of them, this one appraised for one point seven and he's offering one point five."

"Yikes, what's the payoff?"

"It appears Boone owned the property outright."

"No." the word stretched out, she snatched her phone and beat feet out the door to the swing. It had been moved from Rayna's old place, Sophie always loved it. She dialed as she strode that way. "Jonathon. Hey. I was looking over the offer, but can't find a mortgage company on the paperwork...What?" She was silent for a minute, "No, he never told me. Landon delighted in dropping little bombs and he never mentioned it either." She stared at the stars, "Yeah, thanks, and yes I would love to have those. Thank you." She sat there, pushing the swing with one foot.

"Is that good or bad?" Rayna whispered from behind Noah.

"Not sure." Noah leaned into the screen door, pushing it open. Hands in his back pockets, he strolled out. "Hey, sexy one. Are you okay?"

She patted the seat next to her. "His grandmother left the entirety of her estate to Liam. There hasn't been a mortgage on that house in over fifty years. I'm sure he probably didn't know its worth, but oh my god. Or maybe he did know."

"He might have knowm but it didn't matter because it was hers and he was going to keep it."

"Could be. We stayed there a few times but Charleston was an hour out of where we were so, not that often." She tucked a stray lock of hair behind her ear. "If I sell it, I can build my training center and not have to worry about investors...or I can put in a majority and save some so we can travel."

"We? Does that we include me?"

"It does."

"Dinner is almost ready."

"Yeah, we should go in, cuz son you look good enough to...let's go in." his laughter echoed across the yard.

"Well, one of them is happy." Leave it to Evonay to find a silver lining.

They trooped in, trading one-liners. "He owned it free and clear, it was his grandma's."

Beau glanced back at the paperwork, "Wow, the deal is fair. Prices in that area are pretty steady."

"Thank you, Beau, I appreciate the input." She stuffed it all back in the envelope and made way for the salad bowl that Sabina could have sat in, and a baking dish loaded with lasagna. It was an easy night, one where everyone relaxed and let life be as it would. Laughter flowed freely, and stories rolled out, happy to be shared. Dogs begged, the toddlers danced and sang and everyone knew no matter what else was going on in the world, inside those walls, was love.

14

They pulled in late, Madge watered several patches of grass before racing up the ramp. She dragged her case up, Noah carried the one box she said couldn't wait until daylight. He set the box in a corner and handed a badly gift-wrapped present to Madge. "Here girl, I got ya something for being such a good dog." She spun in a circle, her lessons in 'gentle' kept her from snapping up the gift, Moving slower, she took the gift and went to her spot, where she tore into the paper, freeing the toy.. She tore into the paper, freeing the toy. She let out several small yips, when she bit down and the bone squeaked. A second one sent her all over trying to find what made the noise. Mokie ran out for his head rub.

Sophie yawned and leaned into Noah. "So sweet of you."

"You need to rest, I'll come make breakfast and you can tell me what you think about several projects around here." He kissed her forehead, "happy to have you home." He jogged down the ramp and to his hideaway.

Sophie wandered into the bedroom, exclaiming over the flowers. "Noah, how did you...? They are beautiful." In the bathroom, she discovered all of her favorite bath products were replaced with new bottles. She filled the tub and sank in, "oh my stars, big man, you are a love." She posted a picture of her bubble covered toes to social media, tagging the shot with "ahhh someone knows me so well."

OVERHEAD, A HUGE FULL moon filled the sky. Cort held Rayna in the bed of their truck. Babies were a hit or miss with her. Some days she loved on any of them and other days she couldn't even glance their way. She chattered on until she turned to face him and planted a kiss on his lips. "I love you."

"That's good, cuz I love you." She pulled her shirt off. Cort figured out she planned the assault...she didn't wear a bra. Rayna placed his hands on her breasts and kissed him again, long and slow.

"Mmm," the kiss broke, "Get naked woman." She stood up and dropped her jeans. In the moonlight, she resembled some fairy goddess. Following her instructions, he took her every way she wanted until she turned into a pile of jellied bones and he wasn't much better. "Man this getting old shit is for the birds."

She slapped his ass. "Not old, seasoned." He helped her back into her clothes. "I hope Sophie and Noah are having as much fun as we are."

"Now Ray, the man says they are just friends."

"Really? With matching rings?"

SOPHIE SLEPT LIKE A rock for two and a half hours and was wide awake. "Ugh, not this crap like Junior year all over again." She paced the room, before giving up and wandered out to the kitchen. Drinking from the milk jug was allowable in her viewpoint. Madge sat at the window, head tipping one way and then the other. Sophie eased out the door. Noah sat on the deck for the hot tub, steam rising, cross-legged, eyes closed. "What are you doing?"

"Meditating."

"You are naked."

"There is no law saying one must wear clothes to meditate."

"It's cold and you are naked."

"I'm warm." He wasn't about to tell her that between the heater next to him and the heat from the tub, he was close to being steam cleaned.

"You didn't even take a towel with you." She scooted back through the door and around the corner to the laundry. With a couple deep breaths, she shucked her underwear and then ducked into her room. She stashed Liam's condom case in the bedside, one more thing she didn't want to part with. She yanked a couple, tossed the case back in the drawer and strode back out to the deck.

"You can join me."

Sophie padded that way, at the halfway point she heard the heater. "No wonder you're warm." Patting the pouch on her sweatshirt, the packages crinkled. She dropped towels on the deck, stepped over his leg and sat down. His eyes nearly popped from their sockets when her bare ass touched his leg. Rotating her head and being so close to Noah meant he heard the crunch of her neck. His hand slid up her spine under the sweatshirt. It was slight, but he caught her intake of breath. "I did something while I was there."

"Yeah?"

"Yeah. Annalee's dad couldn't bury her. So when I replaced the headstone, I also paid for her burial"

"Something happen the headstone?"

"No...just time and perspective." She drew circles on his arm, "Her dad spent every last cent he had searching for her. So, when I found out Crime Stoppers was going to cut me the check for my tip," she snorted, "I don't think a phone call saying "hey she was killed and her body is in the freezer" counts as a tip, but anyway. I asked them to give the money to her dad instead." She wiggled trying to get comfortable and was met with his solid dick which nearly caused her to stumble over her words. "If I had not met Liam and fallen in love with him, and been treated like a queen...I could see myself in the same situation as Molly. He showed me how a confident man treats a woman whether she's having a good day or a bad one, if she is afraid or mad which is perfect for me now."

Noah wasn't sure where this was going, he was focused on breathing and not going caveman. "Because now I have something to judge by, I can tell a quality man from a bone head. I also am of the opinion, you are one of the quality men."

"Wow, thank you." He was baffled. How did that come from a trip back for a trial?

"I believe you will have my back. I will do the same for you. On the way back, I wasn't sure how I would tell you everything running through my head, and then I questioned if you even cared. But when Madge saw you and reacted with the same happy tail and was as excited to see you as with Liam, and you bought her the best toy not even knowing the back story...well, I booted the voice making me question everything, and chewed away at my confidence. You were right." Noah's eyebrows and hairline came close to meeting. "Judd was his own worst enemy. He partied like a rock star and had the brains of a rock. He never cared about anyone except himself. My sympathy to his dad and kid sister but, life goes on."

"You sound like you may be ready to go forward with me."

"I am." She tipped her head back, "and I am freezing my nipples off."

He patted her thigh, "Hop up." It was closer to a crawl up. Being the incorrigible soul, he reached up and squeezed her ass. The last thing he expected was her to lean back into his hand. Noah stuffed his feet into his work boots and shut down the heater. "Come her Soph," she executed a little bunny hop into his arms, wrapping her legs around him. Instead of going to the treehouse, they went to his trailer. He spun and sat down. One hand at her neck, one running up her back as he moved in to kiss her, his breath at her ear gave her goosebumps. "My queen, how far are we going on this journey tonight?"

She pulled the condoms out of her shirt pouch. Instantly, his heartbeat kicked up several notches. "Arms up." If he went any slower sliding the shirt up her arms, a snail would have beat him. "Head back." Noah never knew the sensation of her hair dragging over his tender places could be so hot. His fingertips skated over her skin, touching but not touching, so close Sophie swore he possessed magic fingers. The feeling in the pit of her belly took her by surprise. His fingertips floated over her throat and collarbone. Her breasts felt heavy as his finger traced around her nipple and back up. Sophie ran her hands up the sides of his face, pulling him to her kiss.

Backing away from his lips and slowly opening her eyes, she whispered, "I want you." Grabbing her and the condoms, he pinged off the door jam, swearing at it. She was sure he set a speed record for getting a prophylactic on. Noah slowed down, he wanted to explore the delectable treat before him. Kisses, touches, his tongue running over her skin investigating her, followed by his fingers sliding into her, made his heartbeat so hard he was positive she could hear the thud. Sliding down the bed, he positioned her legs over his shoulders to taste her.

Sounds of satisfaction made him drip. He slid a thick finger inside her as his tongur danced over her clit. She tugged on his hair, unable to speak. Noah held her hips as he eased into the most exquisite, hot, wet, place, he suddenly understood nirvana. His lips closed around her nipple, she arched her back, gasping at the deliciousness of being filled by him, her fingers tangling in his hair, holding him to her breast. "Sweet baby Jesus. Noah,"

Giving in, he pulled back and slid in until his balls met the soft skin of her ass. She spasmed around him, causing Noah to groan in satisfaction, her nails raked over his shoulders and they were gone. No turning back, no mind-changing, like a run-away train theywere racing full steam ahead. Watching her face turned him on in ways he never imagined. Her cry of satisfaction brought his roar of ecstasy, fulfillment, and an understanding. She gave him all of her, heart, soul, body, mind and he was ready to shed a tear or two. "Don't beat me, I'm gonna screw this up, I know it. But, babe I have had a few women and not a one felt like this." Resting on his forearms as he kissed the end of her nose, "my lord woman, you're gonna turn me to a pile of mush."

"You do know, as soon as the people we know and love, figure this out, they'll be all over us to do the legal thing."

"So we do what any self-respecting teenager would do...deny, deny, deny, until we're ready for the next step."

"And a few? Remind me to buy you a dictionary."

Snickering, Noah divested himself of the spent condom, grabbed clothes and carried Sophie back to her bed.

Madge's yip at the door woke him up, he opened the door to let her out. "Man I am starving." He wandered to the kitchen, they shared the space most of the time since she moved in. Slowly, he turned in a circle. Realizing the dream house, the escape, the passion project had always been about what she might want in a place of her own. Cabinets were placed where she could reach the contents, steps were built into the kick-plates of bottom cabinets to be sure she was able to reach the top cabinets.

Sophie leaned against the door frame, arms crossed as she watched Noah. "Are you lost?"

"Epiphany."

"You just discovered you were in the kitchen?"

"No, that I am pretty sure I built this place for you." His voice gave away the surprise. "All the little extras, I pictured you stretching and not being able to reach, or needing a spice and it was easier to have a pull out next to the stove." He finally faced her. "I never even realized I did all the things with you in mind until this morning."

"The hand of fate, now make me breakfast and then I need to go to Spirit Lake."

"Want some hairy hulk to tag along?"

"Yes. That would be wonderful."

"Biscuits and gravy?"

"Sounds delish." She didn't look up, she was busy signing the contract from Jonathon. Their expedition to Spirit Lake included looking at property on the way back. "New Jersey is home for the equestrian team, but once you get this side of the Mississippi, there isn't much for training on the top level. This could potentially bring more of the horsey set to the hall, and along with that, money." She sent a note along to Jonathon, he texted her as soon as he read it.

She read the text out loud, *"I'm in. I know three others, we're all in for a rock each."* Sophie needed to sit down for a moment or two. "Is that a lot?"

"Million apiece, plus whatever Chase throws in."

More and more it became a Noah and Sophie thing in conversations. Invitations for the Cattleman's Ball came addressed to both parties. They strolled in at eight p.m. arriving shortly after her sister and brother-in-law. Her hand in his oversized mitt put an end to most speculation by the single guys. They could only gaze longingly at the dark-haired beauty attached to Noah's side. Rayna and Evonay were regaling Gilly with their antics from a previous year. Charlie wore her favorite green Grecian goddess dress, the last time she wore the gown, she almost died. But not being superstitious, she donned the creation again. They looked like bookends, Sophie stood not too far away in a black dress covered with emerald green rhinestones.

At the bar, Cade, Trent, and Deacon Driscoll stood side by side. "Yo bro, are you ever going to marry the woman?" Cade needed to needle his brother. Some things never change.

"When she's ready," he tipped his bottle in greetings to Luke.

"Appears someone already put a ring on her, check out her hand" Deacon was too busy checking out the one his brother wore.

Without saying a word, he strolled over, took her hand and kissed the back.

"Thank you for taming the family beast. He is much friendlier now." They traded jabs until she threatened to find a marrying kind of woman with his name written all over her. Once back to the safety of the brothers he calmly asked, "Your idea or hers?"

"Hers."

"Legal?"

"Not yet."

"Good, cuz man, you go and pull a Beau and we'll have to duke it out."

"Yeah. Okay. I'm gonna leave you ugly fucks here, I got a beautiful woman waiting on me." He ordered a drink for her and then strolled to her side.

From the banquet room, Hugh Monroe and Tyler James turned to Gus Driscoll. "My bet is by this time next year, they'll be hitched." Tyler nodded in agreement.

"Praise the Lord, pfft. He has a warped sense of humor. Elloise asked for a miracle and he sent that firebrand. It's a wonder they ain't set the countryside a fire."

Tyler shrugged, "They keep looking at one another like they are and they could torch the whole damn place."

More than one person commented on the heated glances and flirting during the night. When they hit the dance floor, more than one woman needed to fan herself. "Who is more moonstruck, our brother or Beau and his wife," Trent commented to the other brothers.

Deacon snorted, "I think he nailed it, you're all a batch of jealous bitches." He set his beer bottle down and went to find a willing dance partner.

BY THE END OF THE YEAR, Sophie bought a chunk of property. Trent freed up a section of land, giving her a hundred-year lease for a dollar a year. There would be a few concessions for him, but nothing major.

New Year's Eve, Noah took a chance. He bought a ring, currently in his pocket. Whitehall was throwing a bash. He arranged for a horse-drawn sleigh to pick them up and do a loop through town. Noah moved to sit across from her. "Sophie, I practiced a million ways to say something and do not remember a single one. I love you. Marry me. Have babies with me. Make me build another tree. You're my missing piece. My salvation. My everything." He opened the box, the ring may not have been as grandiose as Liam's, but four carats of diamond on a rose gold band was nothing to sneeze at.

Charlie hauled her camera out for the first time since the bombing. Through the telescoping lens, she watched Noah pull a box out of his jacket and her baby sister jump in his arms. She snapped away, tears rolling down her cheeks. Evonay stood by her side, "Aw Shug, what's wrong." She turned with a finger to her lips and showed her the images. Both hands slapped over the blond's mouth.

"Ian, drive us through town please!" He threw birdseed out shouting "She said yes" as loud as he could. They stopped long enough to grab an offered bottle of champagne and a couple paper cups.

Deacon and Luke held hands out to their particular sibling. "I told you so, pay up" was the song of their people. Sophie's version of an evil giggle worried him some. She pulled Noah's head closer to hers. "Watch them freak." She looked at where her sister stood with the James women and Evonay. "What do you think about May?"

"You pick a day and time and tell me what I need to do, and we're all good." She giggled again. "This is going to be hilarious." Ian stopped next to the gaggle of women. "Ladies, put your heads together. This show goes down in May."

Ian pulled away leaving them yelling "wait, hold on" and Evonay laughing so hard Beau needed to hold her upright.

SOMETHING MUST HAVE been in the air. Molly filed for divorce and threw her ex's stuff on the curb. Walt's divorce was finalized and the next day Wanda left town.

Sophie, Evonay, and Charlie set out for Denver and Boulder, seventeen shops and nothing. At the last shop, Sophie held the saleswoman's hand and spoke clearly. "Do not bring me anything with poof-balls. Nothing with an Egyptian theme, nothing see through. This is the wedding, not the honeymoon, nothing short, nothing so wide the dress needs a zip code, no feathers, and nothing with a train so long I could take small children and animals for a ride." Forty-five minutes later she came out with her hands in the air. "Obviously the dingbat doesn't understand English. Every damn thing I said no to, to start with, is what she brought me."

Sophie and Rayna made a weekend trip to New York City and found nothing. Hope went along with her baby sister to Atlanta and she zeroed out. The only positive aspect had been lunch with Jordan Granger. Chicago became the hunting grounds for Sophie and Shelly. Nothing there. "Girl, love ya madly but this is March and you are getting married in May."

"I know. I know. They just aren't right." Dallas, Houston, San Antonio, and Phoenix all fell in rapid succession.

Evonay came squealing into the drive, yelling out the window and blowing the horn. "Come on Sophie, I think I found your gown and Chase is holding the plane." She grabbed her purse, kissed Mokie, Madge, and Noah and hauled ass to the car. "This place is owned by Fabiana Boudreaux. You'll love her." On the flight, they went over her lists. She was right on schedule.

They walked into a boutique in the quarter, "Evonay! Cheri, you came home."

"Only for the day. You have a wedding gown I think would be fantastic for my friend who is getting married in May." She emphasized the month.

"Non. That is no time."

"Exactly so we gotta hook a girl up."

Fabiana sized Sophie up. "No poofiness." She walked around Sophie, "Sleeves?"

"No."

"Straps or strapless?"

"Yes." Fabiana walked all the way around her, snapped her fingers, grabbed Sophie's hand and jerked her through the dove gray draperies to the back. Evonay, hot on her heels.

Fabiana unzipped the bag. "This was two seasons past. I held it because I love it." Cap sleeves, scooped back, form-fitting from the waist up, tiny rose designs in the lace ran in rows and a barely-there train. Sophie gently touched the material, it was softer than anything she ever felt. Her fingertips hovered at her lips. Evonay crossed everything she could and not fall over. The woman hustled Sophie into a changing room, prattling at her the entire time. "I knew it. Perfect fit." Like a magician, she pulled the brocade curtain back. Evonay sat in the lounge with a glass of champagne. The poor girl next to them came out in a dozen different style gowns. Her entourage picked them apart.

Sophie came out, bottom lip caught in her teeth as she looked at her friend. Gasps from the other party made her look over. "Be-you-tee-ful"

Evonay set her glass down, her hands clasped in front of her. "Is it the one?" she waited a second. "It is gorgeous." She was close to begging, "You will knock his socks off."

Sophie whispered, "I feel like a princess again, like when I was little." She stood in front of the mirror, seeing three sides. Fabiana waved her people in with a stand mirror. Like when she was a child, her hands were in front of her lips. She spun to see her friend.

"Well?" she snapped a picture and sent it to Charlie. Her phone rang in seconds. "Hang on, putting you on speaker." She hit the button, "Okay."

"Peanut, is this dress the one?" the hopefulness in her voice made Fabiana smile.

"Seventeen total cities, more than a hundred dresses, and I'm in love."

"Buy it. I don't care what it costs. If you love it..."

"I do Charlie, I feel like a princess again. This dress is amazing."

"Baby, get the dress. Love ya."

"Love you too Charlie."

"I know your sister is dancing 'round them young ones and they think mama done lost her marbles." Sophie dabbed at her eyes, "Don't you dare cry. If you do I will and this place ain't big enough for two ugly cryin' women." That made her friend laugh.

Evonay looked at the other bride to be, finger waving as she spoke, "honey, they ain't wearing the dress. You are getting married, not them. You get the dress that makes you feel special and if your mama pulls the old 'I won't pay for it' crap again, you tell this wonderful lady, she can call me and I'll pay for the damn thing." The young woman was off the small stage and into the back room. In a few minutes, she was back in a simple white gown with a ribbon belt. Her smile had Sophie cheering her on.

"Are you wearing a veil?"

"No, a tiara. For the complete princess effect." It was meant as a joke, until Fabiana brought out several.

"Yes, hair up, some flowers, and this." Silver with faux emeralds, a little dramatic buy Sophie loved the tiara. She went to change as the old friends caught up.

"You were smart in calling me cher. She will be the most beautiful bride in...where do you live?"

"Wyoming and yes, she will be."

They stopped to say hello to Rayna's Aunt Fred, bought some small gifts for the bridal party and enjoyed an early supper at a small café. "I can't believe she stocks Cinderella shoes."

"I know. It's all you dreamed."

"With a dream man too."

They were back home in no time. Like a child, Sophie bounced all over. Noah laughed at her antics, Mokie was as impressed as a cat gets; he stretched, rolled over and went to sleep. Madge was happy because her humans were happy. When they were really happy, they gave extra treats.

15

"Okay, so we booked a venue. We need to finalize food and pick a cake, and if I don't give my girls a color so they can buy dresses...they're going to hang me."

"What's your choices?" she flipped the stack of swatches at him. "So whatever color, is the same one for the guy's ties and stuff, right?"

"Yep."

With a devilish gleam in his eyes, "I like this one."

"Carnation pink." She leaned forward, Molly and Shelly look fantastic in the color, Evonay would look great in it, Melissa will be beautiful in it and Lara looks gorgeous in anything. Okay. We have a color. She dropped one in each envelope with a short missive. *"Dear Friends; This is the color. Long dresses, please. Y'all are the best judge of style right for you and your body, I want you to feel as beautiful as my dress does. Our itinerary is included. Can't wait to share my day with you. Love ya. Sophie. xoxo"* "Why pink?"

"Because my macho ass brothers once said they wouldn't wear pink for any reason."

Rolling her eyes, Sophie muttered "Boys" as she dug out her shoes. "So, cake. Let's go slay the beast."

Jesse was at Rayna's, Sophie strolled to the fence he leaned on, keeping an eye on Layla while she fed chunks of apples and carrots to the horses. "Told ya I'd beat ya."

"I'll take ya on the next level." He looked over her shoulder. "You love him?"

"Yes."

"You guys are making women all over town jealous."

"Poor things."

"Everything is okay? This is what you both want?"

"Yes."

"Thank our lucky stars." She slugged his arm.

"Seriously, I waited until I knew the time was right. Everything was done, over, and I could face the future with a smile. Noah patiently waited for me, never pushed, never yelled, never tried to guilt-trip me...he let me mourn in my way and kept telling me if I needed to cry or scream or whatever, then that is what I needed and it was correct. Not many men would do anything close."

"True. I'm happy for both of you."

"Thank you. Now I need to go reel in the cake mavens."

"Good luck with that. You'll need it."

Rayna had been smart enough to do mini cakes, the size of half dollars with all the flavor options. Noah gobbled down whatever they put in front of him until the tenth one. "Why can't we do different flavors for different layers?" Noah looked between the women. It obviously held merits.

LUKE CAUGHT UP WITH Noah, in town "Hey man. Congrats."

"Thank you."

"You okay" he rubbed his thigh, war wounds, the bane of his life. "You looked like your mind wandered off to nowhere kosher."

"When Hannah broke up with me, I almost went someplace else. I would have missed this. I wouldn't have this woman ready to marry me. Hell, I'd probably be dead."

"So, you're happy and ready to do this?"

"May can't get here fast enough."

"In that case, I am excited for you both. Now, about the job..."

SOPHIE SAT WITH HER list, staring out the window. Her father pulled a chair out and sat down, "Second thoughts babycakes?"

"No, I was trying to decide if I would be this happy had it not been for Liam. Then it turned into, would I have been this ecstatic if I was marrying him? He will always be this tiny part of my heart and I will never forget so many things but this feels so wonderfully right. If the fates decided I needed to be honestly loved and not just a piece of ass for some guy, did they have to arrange for the revelation to be so painful?" she sipped her coffee, sighed, "Probably wished you didn't open that can of worms."

"Not at all." He tugged on his mustache, "When you were a wee bit of a girl, you would take it in your head to go talk to your siblings at the cemetery. We always did the freak out and run about trying to find you." His hands came up with a shrug, "It was silly to think you would be someplace else...there would be adults racing about like chickens with their heads cut off and here would come Noah. You would either be on his handlebars or when he got that ratty dirt bike, on the back of it. It's like he was always there for you and neither of you noticed."

"True, and yeah, I never thought about it." Her lunch order was served. "You have a bachelor thing to go to. Just remember, no strippers rubbing all over him."

Her dad laughed until he had to wipe his eyes, she realized how much she missed the sound. "He told us, if there was a stripper, he'd leave." Walt pushed his chair back and kissed his youngest daughter on the forehead. "You have a good time tonight Punkin."

Not trying to eavesdrop, Sophie overheard Almira Winger say, "Lord have mercy. Walt is still good-looking for an old man." And her coworker retort, "and I'm surprised you can see that far old woman."

Invitations went out and the RSVP cards came back. Noah had some older relatives and Army buddies coming. A few are going on whatever the bachelor excursion is. Luke and Logan are in charge so she didn't feel as though she needed to worry. Their venue decorations consisted of simple bows to hang on the ends of the bench seats.

Goldie and Frances were a hoot. They bought a parcel of land at auction. At one time it had been used to house something with the military, but she couldn't remember what. They spent two years turning the enormous building into mini destinations in one long hall. They had a Caribbean theme, a Hawaiian room, one for Christmas, one for the Solstice, and a Halloween room. They finished each other's sentences and punchlines to jokes. The cake would be ready, and yesterday they baked twenty-five hundred pink macaroons with huckleberry, blueberry, or bourbon honey cream filling. Packaging them without Chase and Noah trying to sneak one was frustrating and the cause of many jokes. Gifts for the wedding party sat in bags, wrapped and ready to go to the reception. Food, all lined up and ready. Dolly Brown was coming to help with hair and make-up. Some of the church ladies would be on hand to help wrangle little people and love on babies. Two of Charlie's friends volunteered to take pictures and her sister would have to get a camera in there at some point in time. She ate the last bite of chicken salad and gathered her belongings. "Thanks ladies, it was nice to sit and relax for a minute." She paid her tab, threw a five on the table and strolled across the green to her car.

Evonay put together something for the women. Their wedding shower had been a blast, she had a feeling this was going to get far more risqué.

THE GUYS GATHERED AT Hoof-n-Horn Lodge, owned by the Cole brothers and Sutton. The lodge butted up to a stream known to be freezing cold all year long. Angus Driscoll flipped a fly line into the water. Across from him, Walt O'Hara was easing into the stream. Horseshoes clanged against their posts, country music came from speakers hidden about in the landscaping. A pair of grills and a flat top sat waiting to be fired up. Brooke left everything food-wise ready to go except what was going on the grill. Jovial one-liners flew about. Dust flew behind Beau Monroe as he pulled in, stereo cranked and a loud "yeah boys" as he exited the truck.

Trent and Deacon went about setting out targets for hatchet throwing and cans for shooting. They ran a timed event. Event was a loosely used term, it was someone with a list and someone with a stopwatch. Hit a blue thing, green, etc. until the allotted time expired. He with the most hits wins. When it got dark they would change over to poker. According to Gus, "men could be men, burp, fart, scratch their nuts and no one was offended...unless you ate pickled eggs and drank a beer. Pickled egg an beer farts offend everyone."

Evonay put out the word, it was going to be a lingerie party for Sophie, the theme was sexy. Champagne cocktails interspersed with tea, coffee, and sodas for the pregnant ones. The Driscoll women, Charlie and Hope, Rayna, Donna and Melissa, Brooke, Gilly, and JJ found seats as Sophie came in with Lara and Madge. She dispensed pig ears to Daisy, Chex, and her own pooch along with kisses.

The guests munched on tiny, fussy, sandwiches and sweets. Lara had never owned a shy bone, she dragged in a dress bag. "Okay ladies, this isn't a mini fashion show. I can't decide and our wonderful bride said "whichever" so, I need an A or B." she followed Evonay to a changing area. Both dresses were the same shade of pink, one was a halter neckline and the other was softer looking with a sweetheart neckline and wide straps. The majority said B. "Now, let the fun begin."

Evonay made an offhand comment to JJ about no trashy games at their party and then it all went sideways. First one and then the other piped up with games they thought to be utterly ridiculous.

Elloise Driscoll rolled her eyes, "Toilet paper anything is just wrong."

"If I wanted to play bingo, I would go to the church," added another.

"Pin the penis on the groom." Lara held her drink to the light as she spoke, "With his me-maw, and great grandmother present." Her story won the night.

"You know, I think we could wrap that penis in the toilet paper and have a weenie roast." They watered Elloise's next two drinks.

Lara's gift needed some explaining. "Well, baby oil. Slippery, need I say more? Twister game because, yeah. And, because you need a spinner...Alexa. She's already programmed to call out a color for you."

Mother Driscoll set them askew, "Silk sheets, Oh my Gawd, they will actually fit, Yes! Thank you Elloise."

JJ glanced at the package. "A round bed?"

"Yep, Mr. Thrifty bought it for next to nothing at a going out of business sale. He said it still had the plastic on it."

"That would be like a whole bed of corners." His great aunt seemed puzzled. Everyone else was amused. Massage oils, incense, lotions, his and hers robes, Tiny silk nighties, lace-up corsets, body paints and a CD of make out songs and a sound machine rounded out the gifts. "

Alrighty ladies, Charlie, you can't play this one, but draw what you thought she would pick." She handed out cards with a Brides head, hand, and bouquet printed on it, and then a bucket of colored pencils and regular ones were placed on the coffee table. "Everyone draw what you think Sophie's dress will look like." Sophie went through them all, laughing at some, complimenting all. When she got to one, she slapped it to her chest. "Damn you, Charlie. I really thought about it." She dabbed at the tears which came with the memory of Tammy and the blue camo dress. She turned the card around and offered the explanation, a chorus of "awws" followed. Everyone won a prize for something, Pulling the heartstrings was Charlie's, best flowers, most original idea, and on to the end.

"What's in your purse?" everyone focused on Evonay. "If you have what I'm looking for, you win. And we picked out some bomb-ass prizes too." This list was a mix of regular things, pens, hairbrush, compact, lipstick. And the unusual, bottle opener, fishing lure, a darning egg, when she hit condom, everyone figured it would be one of the younger set, not Great aunt Eliza.

She hooted and waved her hand. "I got one." She pulled it out of a lime green handbag straight out of the seventy's. "What? Never know, I may find a young blind stud. He won't know I'm old."

"Auntie E; where are you going to find a young stud?" Molly still hid her face as she asked.

"I dunno, maybe I'll hop a bus to Bonnaroo." Mouths hung open.

"Bonnaroo. Where in the world?"

"I listen to the radio." JJ played along and threw some beatbox down, G.A.E, as she called herself did a rendition of "Put a ring on it," mixed with a little Slim Shady. When the laughter settled down, Molly promised to take her in June. Sophie recorded it and sent the clip to Noah. He managed to not choke, but Trent and Deacon both snorted beer through their noses.

SOPHIE PULLED INTO the yard to see Noah getting out of his truck. He ran back, wrapped his arms around her and kissed her until she couldn't remember what she was going to ask him. "Twenty-four hours from now, we'll be legal."

She poked him in the chest, "You still have not said a word about where we're going for our honeymoon."

"Yeah, that's why I came back, most of the guys have crashed out so I won't be missed." He helped carry bags and boxes up to the treehouse.

"Set them against the wall." He couldn't see over the top of the collection of bags and boxes sticking out of them as he bent over. "I'm making a sandwich, you want one?"

"No, lord no. Luke was trying to fatten me up like a sacrificial pig." Madge gave him the sniff over and then surprised him when she licked his hand. "Aw. What a good girl."

"Rayna is coming over to feed Mojo and work with him, and take care of Mokie."

"Cool. So, for our honeymoon." He patted the seat next to him. Sophie curled into the crook of his arm. "I'm cheating. I went to Chase to see if I could rent the beach house. I've heard all about it. He recently acquired a place in the Keys. We're flying down on Family Air, taking a boat out and the place is already stocked with anything we could want." He showed her the pictures Chase sent him. "You said once you missed the salt air. I can't bring it here, but before you get super busy, I can sure as hell take you to it."

"It's perfect." She leaned up and kissed his cheek, "Just us and Madge." They sat, content to listen to the night sounds for a while. "Now, off to the trailer with ya."

Noah grumbled but went. In the morning, he yelled up "I love you, see at the altar."

"Love ya, now scat." She put her makeup and brushes in a tote bag, the bag with the gifts, Madge's brush and bows and looked around. "It's really happening Madgey, mama is getting married and he loves me." Her paw batted at Sophie, "Yes baby, mama will always love you, so does the big guy."

Madge spun in circles and then ran for the door and back. Sophie grabbed the bag, her dress bag and the one with all the stray pieces and headed for the door. Clipping Madge's new pink leash to her collar took a second, she kissed Mokie and out the door they went. With everything loaded in, they were on their way.

Her tribe of female friends gathered in the bride's room. "Evonay, can you please run this over to Noah and get his ring," Sophie handed over a card and her ring." "Sure thing sugar." She hot-footed it down the hall and knocked on the door. "I need a groom." He stepped out, jeans and a tuxedo shirt, black and pink brocade vest, his jacket still on a hanger. "She said give you this and this," she handed him the heavy card and ring, "And get yours."

He pulled it off and held it for a second. "I feel naked without it." He reached in his back pocket, "Give this to my love, please."

"You betcha." She scooted back down the hall, handed the bride the ring and the box from Noah. Sophie unrolled the letter from around the box. She started reading, *My Sophie, The history of emeralds go back to the second century BC. They were thought to keep the wearer healthy, invoke fertility, and ease the eyes. They've been worn by Kings and Queens, adorned shields, and used to ransom royalty. I found this, in an abandoned city. Its setting was bent and broken. When I dove to take cover, I landed next to it. For all this time, it sat in a cigarette pack in my footlocker. I know looking on you with your emerald eyes soothes my soul. Wear this as a symbol of my love. Yours always, Noah*

Slowly she opened the box and snapped it shut, "Oh, my...holy cats." She opened the case again and held it out to Charlie. The setting was Persian, intricate, and the stone was a huge teardrop. Gasps came from her entourage when she turned for their inspection.

Walt knocked at the door, "You ready Punkin."

"Yep." They filed out, stopping at the doorway, Frances fussed about making sure the dresses were straight, the flowers perfect and all was ready.

Molly, Shelly, and Melissa led the way, Lara air-kissed her friend's cheek and stepped into the archway. The stunning array of men at the other end took her breath away. Evonay handed over Madge's leash, scrunched her face up, did a fast happy dance and then composed herself for her stroll down the aisle. Sophie crouched in front of Madge and kissed her nose, leaving pink lip prints on her. "Mama loves you. Now, remember, you go to the big guy okay?" Madge's tail about wagged off of her. She stepped into the doorway, looked back at Sophie and slow motioned the first four steps and then ran and jumped at Noah. He caught her, hugged her, and gave her a huge pink "diamond" chew toy. She sat by the officiant, proud as she could be. Her tail went into hyper wag as her person stepped into the opening.

Noah was stunned, she took his breath away, his brothers whispering back and forth, "he's gonna faint," Luke elbowed him, "breathe brother man, breathe."

Sophie and Walt made it to the altar, "Who gives this woman into marriage?"

Walt's rich voice rang out, "She does." He kissed her cheek, shook Noah's hand and took a seat.

"I'm not going to mess around, we all know why we have gathered here, and no one better think twice about objecting." It got a round of chuckles. "Noah, you have your vows?"

"Yes sir, he cleared his throat. "Sweet, sassy, Sophie, You know me better than anyone else in this world and somehow you still manage to love me. You are my best friend and one true love. There is still a part of me today that cannot believe that I'm the one who gets to marry you. In your eyes, I have found my home. In your heart, I have found my love. In your soul, I have found my mate.

With you, I am whole, full, alive. I pledge to listen to your advice, and occasionally take it. I pledge to never keep score...even if I'm totally winning. I pledge to always admire your huge, strong, kind, and determined heart. I pledge that I will love you. I can't promise to love you perfectly, but I vow to love you messily, overwhelmingly, inexorably. I promise to be your navigator, sympathizer, sidekick, best friend, and your husband. Finally, I promise you myself, heart, soul, for eternity."

Women sighed, guys, gave him a look that could be read as 'gee, thanks a lot buddy.'

Sophie thought her face would break from smiling. "Noah, not that long ago, I was a broken mess. You let me be mad, you let me cry, you let me rage, and you were there any time I needed a rock to lean on. With you, I am whole, full, alive. You make me laugh. You are my breath, my every heartbeat. I promise to create a life for us of unexpected and strange adventures. From this day forward, you shall not walk this life alone. My heart will be your shelter and my arms will be your home. I promise I will love you. You said once you didn't think your name was on any woman's to-do list. I'm proving that wrong today. I will be your rock when the dark times come back to say hello, when you are not strong enough to chase them away, I will. I promise to always have your back. I promise to make you dream bigger and will happily help make those dreams become a reality."

Walt knuckled an eye, several women fanned their eyes trying to not cry. "Do you have the rings?" Noah held up her ring. "Sophie, I give you this ring as a promise to love you, to be there in thick and thin, good times and bad. This ring has no expiration date, to show our love will last forever." He slid their promise ring back on her finger.

Her voice was clear and steady, belying the butterflies in her stomach. "Noah, I gave this ring as promise and today I keep that promise. This ring is a circle, with no end, so is my love for you." She put his ring back on his finger.

"By the power vested in me by the US Government, and the state of Wyoming, I pronounce you husband and wife. Now and forever." Madge barked loudly.

During their first dance, Noah whispered to her, "I know something you aren't"

"Really," he nodded, "What would that be?"

"Broken."

"The Japanese fix broken pottery with gold, it shows the beauty in the imperfections. I feel that's where I am. Still broken, but instead of covered in gold, I'm surrounded by your love."

ALSO BY THE AUTHOR

Confessions Of A Rebel Child
    Ship Of Fools
Beastly Beauty (steampunk beauty & the beast)
Me & Evangeline
Bus 47 * book of the year award 2015*
REALM OF NIGHT SERIES
That Bites
Run-In With A Devil
Blood Dance (Fall 2023)
Border Lands-Whitehall
At Last
Forever
Destiny
Broken
Hellfire, Brimstone & Whiskey
Dirty, Messy, Love (Spring/Summer 2022)
Hooked(Spring 2023)

BORDER LANDS
    (B&N Exclusive) Second Chances

HEROES N HEARTS
    Love Is A Battlefield
    Love In Their Stars
    Love By Design
    Assigned To Love
    Ambushed By Love
    Tides of Love
    Hustled By Love (Summer 2022)
    The Gold Standard
    A Little Christmas Magic in Cedar Springs